FOLLOW
THE
FREE WIND

**Center Point
Large Print**

**This Large Print Book carries the
Seal of Approval of N.A.V.H.**

ॐ श्री गणेशाय नमः

LEIGH BRACKETT

FOLLOW
THE
FREE WIND

CENTER POINT PUBLISHING
THORNDIKE, MAINE

This Center Point Large Print edition
is published in the year 2002 by arrangement with
Golden West Literary Agency.

The text of this Large Print edition is unabridged.
In other aspects, this book may vary from the original
edition. Printed in Thailand. Set in 16-point Times
New Roman type by Bill Coskrey.

ISBN 1-58547-174-7

Library of Congress Cataloging-in-Publication Data

Brackett, Leigh.
    Follow the free wind / Leigh Brackett.--Center Point large print ed.
        p. cm.
    ISBN 1-58547-174-7 (lib. bdg. : alk. paper)
        1. Beckwourth, James Pierson, 1798-1866--Fiction. 2. African American pioneers--Fiction.
    3. African American trappers--Fiction. 4. Large type books. I. Title.

PS3503.R154 F65 2002
813'.54--dc21
                                                                                    2001047769

For edmond,
who first introduced me to
the enemy of horses.

AUTHOR'S FOREWORD

There are numerous authorities for the things James Beckwourth did, but none at all, as far as I know, for why he did these things or what he thought and felt while he was doing them. This is true even of Jim's own autobiography, which is most strongly eloquent in what it never says. Therefore, this book is a work of fiction, based on certain incidents in the remarkable life of a very remarkable man.

However, I have not knowingly altered any historical fact. And while Dave Richards, Sam Carson, and a few of the minor characters in the story are products of my imagination, Jim himself, the redoubtable Ashley men, the Bents, Pegleg Smith, Walkara, and most of the Crow and Cheyenne warriors are not.

ONE

THE NOISES CAME from the end of the lane, where it wound out of sight into the mud and mist of the riverfront. Jim stopped where he was and listened. Fighting. Three men at least. Maybe four or five. Mean fighting with a sound of death in it. Drunken men brawled and shouted and sometimes somebody got killed for sure, but that was different. These were sober quiet men, and if they killed it wouldn't be from hot blood or accident.

Jim shifted from one foot to the other, scratching the back of his neck and thinking.

It was late, well after two o'clock of the morning. There weren't many houses around here, only big ramshackle sheds and warehouses, and there were no people to see what he did. He had left Francie less than half an hour ago and he was still feeling high and happy, keyed up for anything.

He didn't think long. A chance like this did not come too often. He went down the lane toward where the sound of fighting was.

He made very little noise, going light-footed on the soft ground. He was young and lightness came easy. He stopped again by the corner of a shed and peered around it.

The fight was right on top of him now. There was a flat space between him and the black gliding water and the men were there, moving in and out among the roiling mists, in the heavy wet river-stink, their feet sucking in the mud. A little light came from the stars, a little more from lower down along the shore where raft and keelboat hung in the slack and the waterfront life of St. Louis went on and on as though sleep was a word nobody had ever heard. Put all together, the light wasn't much. But it was enough to show that there were four men, and that three of them were doing most of the moving. The fourth had his back set against the rotten pilings that were all that was left of an old wharf washed out in some spring flood. The three men wore dark clothing and Jim was sure they all had knives. River rats. They kept dancing and circling around the fourth man, but he had something long and heavy in his hands and he was swinging it murderously, talking all the time in a rattling, hard-edged voice.

"—know what they'd do to you? They'd put skirts on you, make you sit with the women, do squaw's work. Squaws? Why, you ain't even that good. I've seen little Sioux girls hardly out of their cradle boards could fight rings around you." He brought his bludgeon whistling and whacking down and laughed as the men scattered. "Run away, little polecats. You ain't wolves, to pull down big game."

Jim smiled. Here was a man who liked to talk so much he couldn't shut his mouth to save his life. But Jim knew from the talk what he was, though he couldn't see much of him. He was a trapper, and the heavy thing in his hands was a long rifle, clubbed.

All of a sudden the flow of talk stopped short in a grunt of pain. The trapper bent sideways as though a big hand had pulled him and Jim understood why the three men were not in any hurry to get their skulls cracked. They had already cut their man. They were just waiting for him to bleed out so they could finish him easy.

Seeing him waver, they thought perhaps the time had come. They moved.

Jim hunched up his shoulders and went in.

He caught the first man before anybody knew he was there, coming up behind him and swinging a hammer blow behind the ear that put him down grunting and floundering. The knife dropped out of his hand. Jim reached for it, feeling for it with his fingers, not taking his eyes off the other two men. The trapper let go an Indian yell.

There was some quick and vicious French from the two men. One of them came for Jim, sidestepping around the third man who was trying to get up again. Jim got his fingers on the knife. He waited, watching the shape of the man loom over him black and swift like something in a dream, and he was hot and his eyes shone. He caught the dull flicker of steel high over his head, saw it start down, and came up fast under it and inside. His body shocked against another body, squat and broad and powerful, smelling of sweat and dirty wool. An eye glared at him briefly, wide and startled above a thick cheek. Jim's hand drove down with the knife in it and the man fell away from him with a hoarse cry. Jim didn't think he was dead. He didn't care.

He stepped aside and the trapper yelled, "Behind you!"

Jim whirled. The man he had knocked down was on his feet again and coming. There was no time to get out of the way. The man's bullet head took him in the belly and flung him back breathless onto his shoulders, and now the knife went spinning out of Jim's hand. The man fell on top of him.

He was a big man, and heavy. Jim felt mud streaking cold and slick under his collar. He reached up and got a fistful of clothing. He wrenched and kicked as they rolled. His mouth was full of mud, sour, gritty. A thumb gouged at his eye and he squirmed his face deeper into the all-pervading muck, thrashing his legs and clawing with his free hand for the other man's face. He lost track of the third man and the trapper. He did not really care much whether the trapper's life was saved or not. The fight was the main thing. The fight was everything and it filled the world. He was feeling pain now and the immediacy of more pain, fingers clawing around his eyes and then hot wine-and-tobacco-smelling breath puffing at him as the man came snapping like a bulldog after his nose. "Come on," he panted, "you dirty gumbo, I'll kill you." Filled with an ecstasy of hate, Jim arched his body and heaved, kicking powerfully.

The balance shifted. He found an ear and dug his nails in and tore. He bore down with his knees, his elbows, roughing, savaging, mauling the man down deep into the mud, and the man fought back and it was good. After a while Jim realized that the man was not fighting any more. He climbed off him and stood looking around bleary-eyed, his fists balled and swinging.

The other two river rats were gone. The trapper stood with his feet wide apart and his back braced against the piling. He was doing something with the rifle, very deft and quick even in the darkness, and before Jim knew what was happening the long barrel was pointing his way.

"Much obliged to you," the trapper said. "Reckon they could have pulled me down at that."

Jim felt relaxed, every muscle pleasantly stretched and wrung. The sore spots wouldn't really hurt until tomorrow. The trapper had a Tennessee accent. Malice brought out

Jim's best high-toned Virginian. "That's the damndest way of saying thank you I've seen yet," he said, and laughed.

"I've already been trustful once too often tonight," the trapper said. "How did you happen in on this?"

"I happened, that's all. And now I'll be going." He paused. "When you're carrying money, stick to the lighted streets. Good night."

"Just a minute." The long cold barrel gleamed, rock-steady in the starshine. "How do you know I'm carrying money?"

"Even gumboes don't kill for a pair of old moccasins. And if I didn't know already, there's that." He pointed to the rifle.

The trapper grunted. "I guess it was a silly question. Gentleman, eh? You sure don't fight like one. Mostly they're too proud to use their hands. Well, all right." The barrel wavered and sank. "I'll take a chance on you. Got any wherewithal to plug up this hole?"

"Let's see it."

The trapper fumbled with his belt, muttering all the while. "I would have stayed to the lighted streets, right enough, but I ain't used to the town way of thinking. Worse'n Blackfoot country—" The hunting shirt fell open. Jim spread back the buckskin. It was wet and slippery with blood. "My sweetheart kissed me good-bye as pretty as you please and sent me on the shortest way. Hah! And when these three jumped me, I found she'd taken the flint out of my rifle—" He broke off with a gasp and a curse. "What are you doing there?"

"They cut you long," Jim said, "but they didn't cut you deep. You'll live." He started hauling out his shirttail, found it was already out and soaked with mud. Then he re-membered the handkerchief Francie had given him tonight. She had made it out of a piece of the fine white cambric left over from the petticoats of the French lady she sewed for, and she had expected him to be excited about the rolled hems. It was in his pocket and still clean. He laid the folded cloth over the gash in the trapper's side. The man's body felt light and lean to his fingers, with hard ropy muscle over the bones. Out of the tail of his eye he saw the man he had beaten roll over and get to his knees. The trapper stiffened. "Forget him," Jim said. "He's through for tonight." The man crept clumsily away. Jim held the wad of cloth tight while the trapper closed his shirt and cinched his belt over it.

"That'll hold you till you get where you're going," Jim said. "Good night."

"Hold on." The trapper caught his arm. "You ain't going to go and leave me like this. What's to stop them from coming back as soon as you're gone?"

"You've got a flint in your rifle now."

"And I'm too weak to lift it." This was an exaggeration, Jim knew, though the man had lost a lot of blood. "If it was my own money I wouldn't care so much, but it ain't mine, it's the General's. General Ashley. And he can't afford to lose it. So I'd be obliged—"

"Ashley," Jim said.

The calmness that had been in him vanished and the old gnawing, raging hunger was back full force. In 1805 Jim had come joggling in his father's train from Virginia to find a whole new universe spread before his seven-year-old eyes. There were blockhouses, and Indian attacks, and scalpings, and the polyglot swarming streets of a town that was more Spanish and French than American but where in three languages all men talked of something called the West. In 1806, uncomprehending but shaken none the less with a tremendous excitement, he had seen Lewis and Clark come down the river with all St. Louis on the levee to welcome them, and he had learned new words, the names of waters that rang mysterious and splendid in his head—the Missouri, the Yellowstone, the Columbia, the far Pacific.

Since then the words had multiplied and so had the men. Manuel Lisa's brigades of the Missouri Fur Company brought the peltries down the river and Jim watched them come, saw them carouse like grizzly bears, shaking the waterfront, and then set out again, the hard free dirty men fighting the keelboats up the current, up and up and up to where the Shining Mountains stood holding the sky and there was an end to all eastward-flowing waters.

Lisa was dead now and a lot of others with him, but the men and the boats still went and the word was still West. Last year William Ashley, General of the Missouri Militia and Lieutenant Governor of the state, had advertised in the St. Louis papers for a hundred men to go clear to the headwaters of the Missouri and trap there for three years along the beaver streams.

Jim looked at the dim shape of the trapper and hated him.

"—a man waiting for it," the trapper was saying. "It's all my fault this happened, but it generally is. The Old Man's threatened to sell my hide for a penny more than once, and he'd do it, too, if he could find a buyer. So I'd be much obliged if you'd go with me. Besides, I don't like to be beholden to a stranger." He held out his hand. "My name's Richards, Dave Richards, but everybody calls me Rich. I'd be proud to know yours. I'd be proud to buy you a drink, as an earnest, you might say."

His hand in Jim's was small but very strong. A monkey paw, Jim thought, poke and pry and pull and never let anything alone. He smiled to himself. "All right," he said. "I'll come with you."

"Much obliged," said Richards. "Much obliged."

They walked side by side in the mud and dark and the river mist. Richards' moccasins padded softly beside Jim's big stiff-soled boots. Richards talked, about Ashley and his partner Major Henry and beaver and Blackfeet and many rivers. Jim thought of high plains and open sky and wind that had no taint in it, no stink of crowded slave quarters, fever flats, and garbage, all rotting together in the heat.

"I hear," said Jim, the malice leaping again to his tongue, "that Ashley's a bad-fated man, and some of it because he's a fool. He didn't have to stick his head in the trap at the Rickaree towns. I hear he lost fifteen men and all his horses because he wouldn't listen to good advice."

"I won't argue with you," Richards grunted. "I was there, pinned down on a sand bar listening to the shot plunk into the dead horse I was cuddled up to. Finally managed to get back into the water and swim for it—the damned cowards on the keelboats wouldn't come in for us. Sure the General was a fool. Sure Rose told him true about the Injuns and he didn't listen. I reckon you've made your mistakes too."

"I didn't get fifteen men killed by them."

"Did you have fifteen men?"

There was no answer for that. Jim walked, hungry and hating, and there were lights ahead.

"What's he doing now, the General?" Jim asked. "He can't even get past the Rickarees, how's he going to get past the Blackfeet? I hear they've closed the river at the Yellowstone. I hear they pretty near wiped out Henry—"

"Don't you do anything but listen?" asked Richards mildly. "And I'm getting a mite doubtful about that drink."

Jim laughed.

"There's a fleer in your voice I don't just like, friend," said Richards.

Jim laughed again.

"And I'll tell you what the General's going to do now," Richards went on. "He's got a whole new scheme. He ain't going to depend on Indian trade any more. We're going to get the furs ourselves. Henry's men are out there now, working, and we're going to join 'em. And the General's going to leave the big river to them that want it and do his business overland."

The lights were closer, splashing circles of yellow radiance on the ground. They walked on cobbles now and there were human sounds in the air, voices, clatterings, thumpings.

"Nobody's ever done that," Jim said.

"Does that say it can't be done?"

"A lot of people say it can't. A lot of people say Ashley'll lay his bones on the prairie, and every man with him, too."

Richards said slowly, "A lot of people know more'n a jackass can haul downhill in a wagon, and I've noticed they're generally the people who do the sitting and talking, not the doing. And I—"

He stopped short in mid-breath, in mid-stride. The circle of lamplight had taken them in and now they could see each other. Jim looked at Richards, waiting for him to speak. He was a wiry man, as Jim had thought, not very big, and perhaps ten years older than Jim, a hard ten years that had weathered and lined his skin and shrunk it tight over the sharp bones of his face. His eyes were pale, as bleached of color and as bright as the long heartless horizons they were used to looking at.

Abruptly Richards threw back his head and laughed. "I will be damned," he said. "A gentleman! Where'd you learn to talk like that?"

"Listening to my father," Jim said. "He's a gentleman. My mother was a slave, and that makes me a blacksmith. Would you still be proud to buy me that drink?"

"No," said Richards, "but a debt's a debt irregardless." He opened his belt pouch.

"I thought that was the General's money," Jim said.

"I got that where it's safer. This is my own, what's left of it."

"All right, white man," Jim said softly, "how much do you think your life is worth?"

Richards looked up at him. "You mean I can't settle it like that."

"That's right, you can't settle it like that."

"How then?"

Jim shrugged. "Maybe some day I'll tell you."

Richards stood, narrow eyed, silent, thinking. Finally he nodded like a man accepting something he can't help.

"I told you I don't like to be beholden to strangers. What name shall I call you on that day?"

"Beckwourth," Jim said. "James Pierson Beckwourth."

"I'll remember."

"Maybe," Jim said cynically, and went away into the dark.

TWO

I AM A blacksmith, Jim thought, and brought the hammer clanging down on the soft iron. I am not a mountain man. I am a blacksmith, a black smith, and I will never see the headwaters of the Missouri.

Clang, clang, clang on the yielding iron.

The shoe is shaped. Wild horses wear no shoes, the Indian ponies run barefoot. Only the enslaved wear iron shoes, and iron yokes around their necks. I am not called a slave now, but I might as well be.

Take the shoe with the tongs and thrust it down into the water. The steam boils up and the live cherry red turns a dead black.

Pull it out cold and heavy and nail it on, a weight for the free-striding hoof.

"Stand still, brother," Jim said, and gave the restive sorrel a crack under the belly with the hammer. He stood. Jim drove the nails home.

"Out late again last night, Jim?"

Jim looked up. Sam Carson was standing watching him. He had probably been standing for some time and he had a look in his eye that Jim knew well after ten or eleven years of apprenticeship. There was nothing wrong with Sam Carson. He was a fair man by his standards, and his standards were of the best. Jim had always had plenty to eat and a decent place to sleep, and Carson had not habitually worked him over twelve hours in the day, sometimes less. He had been moderate with the harness strap in the early years and Jim's adult back bore no scars such as marked many another. He has treated me well, Jim thought. I ought to be grateful that he's treated me well. But I'm not. Why shouldn't he treat me as well as he treats his horses?

Aloud he said, "I guess so, Mr. Carson."

He continued to hammer on the shoe. The horse quivered nervously with each blow.

"Been out late just about every night, haven't you, Jim?"

The sweat ran on Jim's body under the leather apron. Inside his belly the nerves were tight. He kept his eye on the upturned hoof, the hairy fetlock, the lapped and folded frog. He hammered with even strokes, the sinews of his shoulder moving rhythmically.

"Yes, sir," he said. "I guess I have."

"I don't like it, Jim," Carson said. "Even at your age you can't rabbit all night and work all day. From now on, you get your rabbiting done early."

"Yes, sir."

"Ten o'clock, Jim. You're not in by then, you'll hear some more from me."

"Yes, sir."

He kept his head bent over the shoe. Inside himself now he was hot. Even his fingers burned. The heat swelled in his head and blinded him. But he could feel Carson looking at him, with his sharp shrewd eyes in a broad face that was neither brutal nor kindly but merely businesslike. A broad man all the way down, a successful man and well-respected. And if he calls me, Jim thought, if he questions my tone of voice or the way I look, I'll put this hammer straight through his head.

And this morning, he thought, they started. Twenty-nine men, hunters and trappers, with General Ashley at their head and a long train of horses and pack-mules, going to the Rockies overland.

But you, Jim Beckwourth, you be in by ten o'clock.

He heard Carson turn and walk out past the forge, out of the smithy and into the sweet hay-and-horse-smelling gloom of the livery stable adjoining, where black men and boys worked with pitchfork and currycomb, or polished up the rigs that were for hire, or washed the country mud from the carriages of gentleman farmers come to town.

Jim let the sorrel's hoof drop down with a suddenness that made the horse skip sideways, snorting. He walked to the open door of the smithy and stood in it, breathing as though he had run all the way from Beckwourth's Settlement.

Get through with Francie and be home by ten.

Yes, sir.

He did not see anything at all of the street in front of him, and he was quivering like an aspen tree in a spring wind.

It seemed like an endless time before that day was done.

He washed carefully. He had a good body, of medium build but very strong and quick, with the muscles laid on long and lean. He was not dark, at least no darker than the Spaniards and the swarthy French, certainly no darker than the Indians who shared the streets with them. He dressed in the best he had and went out into the evening.

The lighted windows showed yellow in the blue dusk. The pulse of life was flowing away out of the places of sober business as they closed and darkened, to quicken again in the drinking places, the gambling places, all the resorts of pleasure high and low. Carson lounged in the doorway of the livery stable, underneath the sign that had his name on it in huge letters. He nodded at Jim, not only to say hello but to remind him. Jim made a respectful salute and passed on.

Ten o'clock, Francie, I have to be home.

He walked, and the dusk became full night and the October stars came out.

He was within shouting distance of Francie's place before he understood that he was not going there tonight. He was not in that kind of a mood, and he did not want to talk, especially to Francie. He kept on walking, and after a while he was beside the river. He sat on the levee and watched the slow, thick, massive flowing of it, pouring south to New Orleans and the Gulf, carrying with it the mixed and muddied waters of a hundred rivers, the Yellowstone, the Powder, the Bighorn, the Rosebud, and the Grand. Farther along the levee a party of Negroes set their lines for catfish, laughing and talking among themselves. Their voices reached him mellow and sweet with distance. Somewhere out on the black current of the river a loose snag pounded the water with a rhythmic hammering, up and down. It was a mild night. The frogs and the crickets still sang in the bottoms. Jim sat for a long time. After a while he understood another thing.

He was not going to be home by ten o'clock.

The stars wheeled over him. The Negroes went off with their catch and all human noises died. Mist crawled up out of the low places. The frogs sang and the river flowed, and it was midnight. And then it was even later.

Jim smiled. He knew now that he was not going home at all tonight.

The bitter taste in his mouth and the writhing of his stomach went away. He lay back. Presently he slept, quite peacefully.

When he woke again it was already getting light. He stood up stiff and chilled, shaking off the dew. He was hungry, but he was pretty sure he would get little breakfast this morning. He stood for a moment or two looking out over the dim water with the dawn just glimmering on it cool and gray. He was not frightened, not even greatly upset. He merely wanted a little space to breathe and gather himself. Then he began to walk, heading in a straight line for Carson's.

It was still early when he got there, barely sunup, but the day's business was well under way. He walked in through the front door of the stable and down the long broad aisle between the stalls. The boys who were mucking out and the men who were mending harness or throwing down hay stopped what they were doing and looked at him as he passed and he greeted them pleasantly and went on, feeling what was in their thoughts, the suppressed fear, the suppressed admiration, the suppressed excitement, the not-at-all suppressed relief that none of them was standing in Jim's boots, and the tired certainty that his little gesture of defiance was perfectly useless anyway.

Maybe it is, thought Jim, but I've made it.

He went into the smithy and removed his coat and took down the leather apron. He did not hurry. There was no reason to hurry.

Carson came in and closed the two wide doors behind him. He said, "Don't bother with that, Jim."

Jim hung the apron back on its peg. He faced Carson and waited.

Carson looked at him. Jim stood straight and easy, meeting his eye, and he saw Carson's face flush over with an angry red. But his voice was even when he spoke.

"For special reasons you've had some special privileges around here, Jim, and it hasn't been good for you. I'm going to have to teach you where you belong."

Jim said, "Maybe I'm over old for learning." And he added, "Mr. Carson."

"You'll learn. It's a simple lesson. You do what a white man tells you, and you don't talk back." Carson reached out and took down a harness strap from the wall. "Take off your shirt."

Jim said softly, "You go to hell. Mr. Carson. Sir."

The angry red went out of Carson's face, leaving it pale. His eyes turned cold and hard as two little chips of ice.

"Take off your shirt."

"You lay a hand on me and I'll kill you," Jim said, so softly that for a moment Carson was not sure he had heard right. Then he made a small strangled noise in his throat as though the words he wanted to say were choking him. He stepped forward.

Jim crouched slightly, his shoulders bending. He looked steadily into Carson's eyes.

Carson hesitated, not from fear but because the strap he carried was no longer adequate for what he wanted to do. He dropped it and seized a hammer from the forge. He was a big strong man. He threw the hammer with all his force at Jim's head.

Jim dodged. The hammer went whirling past his ear and cracked into the wall behind him, then fell onto the floor. He turned and picked it up, moving lightly, moving swiftly, and he threw it back at Carson and saw it hit, a glancing blow on the shoulder that nevertheless brought out a bellow of pain. And I might just as well have killed him, Jim thought, for what'll happen if they catch me.

He ran out of the smithy into the still-drowsy, half-deserted street. His boots hit the paving hard and fast and the woods were far away. But it seemed to him that he was lightened as of a great stone, and the morning sky had never looked so bright.

THREE

The BLOCKHOUSE HAD fallen out of repair, but it was still a shelter. Jim sat amid dust and spider webs and the smell of rotting wood and looked out over his father's fields, worked by his father's slaves.

And I would be one of them, Jim thought, but my father is a generous man. More than that he's a proud man, too proud to see his own children sweating in the fields even if we are mongrels.

More than that, he has a sense of humor. And maybe even a sense of shame. He's a contrary man, my father.

Jim sat hungry and waited for the sun to go down.

The broken door creaked below as the wind moved it. Jim remembered a time when it was strong and solid. He remembered the many hours he had spent here—it seemed when he thought about it that in the early years he had lived here almost as much as he had at home—waiting for an attack that often did not come, but just as often did. Then the guns would crack and there would be yellings and screechings outside. The women would hold the children tighter and sit all huddled together, and the powder-smoke would fill the place like fog.

The land was tame now. Men could work it without fear. But only a few years ago half the male population had stood guard while the other half worked. And sometimes no amount of care had been enough. Jim remembered a day when he was nine years old. He had ridden past a neighbor's house on his way to the mill, and he had called out but there had not been any answer. The sun was high and bright, but he could remember yet how strangely the sky had seemed to brood above that unnatural silence. And then he had seen a bit of cloth blown idly in the breeze and he had ridden closer and seen that it was the petticoat of a little girl. She was lying in the grass. She was two years younger than himself, and her name was Sarah. Her throat was cut and she no longer had any hair. He remembered how the big workhorse had shivered and tried to blow the smell of blood from his nostrils. Jim had wanted to vomit. He had wanted to scream and kick the horse into a run. But he could not do any of these things. He could only sit rigid on the broad back, with the sack of corn in front of him, and look and look until he had seen all there was to see, Sarah's seven brothers and sisters, and her mother, and her father, all dead and scalped, the blood still fresh and bright in the sunlight. This he remembered in his dreams, though he would have liked to forget it, but of his flight homeward he remembered nothing, and he never knew what happened to the sack of corn. The men of the settlement had picked up their guns and gone out, and two days later there were eighteen scalp locks drying to pay for Sarah and her family.

Hard days. But now the slaves could work without fear.

They went home from the fields at last and the night came down dark and heavy with a feel of rain. Jim left the blockhouse and made his way across the open land.

After a time he saw the house. It had grown since the first early days, putting forth wings and porches and balconies until now it stood quite grandly in its grove of trees. But it was still the house where Jim had spent most of his queer anomalous childhood, the conscious part of it at any rate, and it still had the power to tug at his emotions. He passed silently through the trees, avoiding the slave quarters and coming at the house from the front. But he was able to see that there was a big gray horse in the stableyard and even at that distance there was no mistaking what horse it was. Jim had shod him too many times. Sam Carson was here ahead of him.

Jim was not surprised. He paused only a moment and then went on to the terrace outside the long windows of the room that was his father's office, study, and sanctum inviolable. He had been inside it only once before, when he was eight years old. He was strictly forbidden to go there, and he was allowed in the "front" of the house only with his mother or one of the other servants, so he was breaking two commandments when he sneaked in to see this room that even his mother couldn't enter. Only Marshall, his father's bodyservant, was trusted in here. He had been awed, disappointed, and bored because there had been nothing in it but furniture, like any other room. He had not been caught.

The inside shutters were closed, but there was a light behind them and a mutter of men's voices. Jim lifted his hand and knocked.

The voices fell silent. Jim waited, knowing there was no need to knock again. In a minute the shutter catch rattled. The panel swung back and a man was looking at him through the glass, seeing Jim's face in the lamplight that came now from the room.

Beckwourth opened the glass door and said, "Come in."

He seemed almost to have been expecting Jim. He turned away, walking back to the table where he had left his glass and a cigar.

"Close it behind you," he said, and Jim closed the door and latched the shutter over it. Carson sat massively in a chair, his face very red and ugly as he looked at Jim.

Jim looked at his father.

He was a handsome man, spare and well-built. In his youth he had fought in the Revolution. Later, being of a restless nature, he had come west to fight the frontier. He was settled now, successful and taking his ease, but there was still no flabbiness about him, either of mind or body.

"You've made a lot of trouble, Jim."

"Yes, sir." He could call his father "sir" without the word tasting bitter on his tongue. And in all these years, Jim thought, I've never called him father and he's never called me son. The whole thing is never mentioned by anybody, and I might have got my name like any other slave, Beckwourth because a man named Beckwourth owned me. But I have his face. Darker. But his. Maybe that's why he set me free, to get rid of me, so he wouldn't have to see himself walking around in a black skin.

Carson started to speak, but Beckwourth silenced him.

"I freed you, Jim. I gave you more education than a lot of white men have. I had you taught a trade. And this is what you do in return. You could hang for it."

"And damn well ought to," Carson muttered.

"Maybe," Jim said. "Hang or no hang, I can't stand still to be whipped."

Carson swore. He rose and stamped up and down rubbing his shoulder, unable to contain his rage. "If it wasn't that I owe a lot to you, Beckwourth, I'd—" He looked at Jim, and then at Beckwourth, and became speechless.

For the first time Beckwourth faced Jim. Very coldly and quietly he said, "I've been at some pains to save your neck this time."

Jim said, and meant it, "I'm grateful to you."

"I will not do it again. Is that understood?"

"Yes, sir."

"I hope so," Beckwourth said. Then he looked into Jim's eyes and his expression changed and he shook his head. "Don't mistake me, Jim."

"I don't." Jim glanced at Carson. "And don't mistake me, either. If I go back to work for him I'll be swinging before the week's out. I didn't come here to beg for that."

Carson, who had been overcome with a sense of his own nobility at his willingness even to discuss taking Jim back, now stopped in mid-gesture to stare at Jim in such astonishment that Jim would have laughed, except that there was nothing funny about any of it.

He saw the study, the polished wood and the warm fire in the grate, the fine carpet, the big desk that held the records of crops and sales and many human lives, and he felt the room close around him like a trap. He saw the men, the white men with all the weight and power of authority behind them, Carson to whom he was still bound as an apprentice, Beckwourth who was his only hope of escape, and he knew that he was at the end of his plunge, the long wild leap that had started somehow on the night he met the trapper, to reach its peak when he threw the hammer at Carson. In the next few minutes he would know whether that leap had carried him to freedom or the gallows.

He heard Carson say harshly, "This one's dangerous. He don't know his place and I don't reckon he ever will."

Jim turned to his father and waited.

Beckwourth said, "What did you come here for?"

"Permission to leave Mr. Carson. Permission to—" It was hot in the room. Jim's mouth was dry. "To go west."

"West?" said Beckwourth.

"With General Ashley. Overland. He'll need a black-smith." Jim took a deep breath and made his voice stay steady. "Give me permission and the loan of a horse. I can catch up with him in two days."

"I'll be damned," said Beckwourth.

The sweat stood on Jim's forehead. He waited, and the silence was a hundred years long.

Carson broke it. "What the hell business has a—"

"Just a minute, Sam," said Beckwourth. He looked at Jim. "What makes you so sure Ashley will take you?"

"He don't have a blacksmith. There wasn't one would go with him." He didn't mention Dave Richards. Now was no time to be questioned about that. The gumboes he had beaten up were, after all, white.

"Suppose he does take you. You know what your chances are of ever coming back."

Jim said slowly, "Not much worse than yours were when you first came to Beckwourth's Settlement." He added, "Sir," but his meaning was plain, and Beckwourth understood it. They faced each other and for a moment neither of them moved, and Jim felt the blood beating in his temples and he wanted to speak, to cry out a name that had never been spoken, to ask a question that had never been put into words. And then Carson, who understood nothing, said scornfully, "The Indians'll cut him up for dogmeat," and the moment was gone, and they were both relieved.

"Ashley too," said Carson. "Damn fool. He'll never see the Rockies."

Beckwourth turned to Carson, jerking his thumb toward Jim. "You want him back, Sam?"

Carson made an emphatic gesture. "Let the Indians have him. Save us all a lot of trouble."

Beckwourth nodded. He did not look at Jim again. He went to the desk and took a sheet of paper and a pen and began to write.

An hour later, with a full meal in him and a borrowed coat on his back, Jim mounted the old brown nag provided for him and rode out of the stableyard. Black clouds boiled and raced across the moon but it had not yet begun to rain. Jim rode out slowly past the house, knowing that this might very well be the last time he would see it.

He saw Beckwourth standing on the terrace.

"Jim!"

He rode over. The lights were out in the study but the moon showed bright for a moment and Jim could see that

Beckwourth stood with his legs braced wide apart and that he held a long dark object in his hand.

"You'll need this," he said, and threw the object to Jim, who caught it. It was a rifle, cold and heavy, beautiful in his grasp.

He started to say thanks, and Beckwourth spoke again, his voice thick and stumbling but with a sound in it that Jim had never heard before.

"You'll need more than that. Your skin won't be any lighter or the men any kinder in the Rockies than they are here."

The moon went behind a cloud. Out of the pitch dark Beckwourth said, "Good luck, Jim." Jim blinked and peered. The terrace was empty. A gust of wind blew the door of the study in and out on its hinges and behind it the room was black and still.

Jim sat for a moment, stupidly, with the rifle weighing in his hands and a shaken feeling inside him. Softly, gently, it began to rain, and Jim laid the rifle across the saddle in front of him and covered it with the skirts of his coat.

The hoofs of the old nag clip-clopped out of the drive and into the deepening mud of the road, pounding steadily, heading west.

FOUR

THEY WALKED TOGETHER across the prairie, Jim Beckwourth and Dave Richards, somewhere west of the Loup Fork of the Platte. It had taken them a little over a year to get this far. Ashley had had his troubles and the Rockies were still far beyond the horizon. They walked in vast openness, in the flat treeless land with the wind blowing clear across it, a November wind that bit freezing into their flesh.

"I still say the General's a bad-fated man," Jim muttered, "and mostly because he don't know what he's doing."

The sky, naked and enormous, flowed with a tremendous millrace of gray cloud. There was a thin skift of snow underfoot. The wind picked it up and tossed it in powdery whirls. Brittle grasses rattled together with a dry sound, and in that sound Jim could hear the rattling of his own bones.

"You wanted to be free," Rich said. "You are. Free to starve, free to get your tail froze off, free to die. It's all of a piece. If you don't like it, go back to your boss-man."

"Way I hear you bitching, you don't like it much yourself."

"I like to bitch. I just don't like to be bitched at." The statement was not meant to be funny. Rich did not stand hardship well. The humor turned sour in him, making his tongue longer and sharper than ever. What was more, he hadn't had to speak for Jim at all as it turned out. Ashley was in such need of a blacksmith he didn't even ask Jim if he was a runaway. So not even that much of Rich's debt had been paid off, and he didn't like it. Sometimes he acted as though Jim had worked some kind of a plot against him just to make him unhappy, and the more he acted that way the more Jim took pleasure in having Rich in his debt.

"You won't get rid of me that easy," Jim said.

"I know," said Rich in a tone of weary disgust. "You're going to prove you're as good a man as I am if it kills both of us."

"Better," said Jim.

Rich looked at him stonily. "General's orders were to spread out. Go bring in a buffalo."

"I might do just that," Jim said.

He walked away from Rich, breasting one of those deceitful slopes that appeared level until you started to climb it. Rich did not look after him. It seemed to Jim that neither one of them was really moving, but after a while he noticed over his shoulder that the small figure in the tattered capote had dwindled by about half. The next time he looked it was gone.

The slope was still ahead of him. So was the wind. The free wind. the prairie wind, bitter cold, bitter hot, the eternally lashing flail of the Lord, summer, winter, spring, and fall. The snow was like sand. It stung his eyeballs. He bent his head, watching his feet plod one after the other. They were wrapped in strips of blanket under the moccasins and the moccasins were leather rags tied together with whangs off the fringe of his hunting shirt. He was running out of fringe.

At the top of the slope there was nothing but another slope going down, and beyond that a slope going up again. No sign of game. There was never a sign of game. The downslope at least was easier. Coming up, Jim had leaned forward with the weight of his rifle. Now he leaned back against it. His eyes were unnaturally bright, the eye sockets deep sunk, the cheeks hollow, the shoulders hunched, the belly tucked up tight under the ribs. For days he and Ashley and Dave Richards and thirty-one others had been marching west on half a pint of flour each a day, mixed with water to make a gummy gruel. The diet did not put fat on a man.

"Does the General mess up one more time—" Jim muttered, reeling down the slope. In the trough there was a boulder and he sat on it. His head was ringing. "One more time and I will quit," he said, "if they have to dig me up to do it."

The ringing in his head was a voice, thin and far off. His father's voice? What are you doing, Jim? it asked, and he answered I am running after Pawnees. That's the mainest thing you do for the General, that and starve.

The voice asked Why? why? why?, trailing off thin like the whine of a ricochet ball.

Why? said Jim. Well, that's a funny thing. The General's a big important man. He's a gentleman, and he knows his position and he knows my place, but he don't know how to plan things very well. Food and horses now, one or the other seems to always give out before he figured, and then he says It's all right boys, the Pawnees have food and horses, we'll buy from them. Only the Pawnees are never there. Seems every year they move from their summering ground to their wintering ground, and the General disremembers when. This time it's food. Last year it was horses and Mose Harris and me walked three hundred miles in ten days to buy more from the Pawnees, and then walked back again.

The boulder was icy. The cold was seeping up into his body, numbing his bowels, reaching for his heart. Jim stood up in sudden panic, shaking his head to drive away the distant voice. Let your mind wander too far and your friends would find you frozen stiff. If they bothered to find you at all. He started to climb the slope ahead.

It was a thousand miles long and he knew he would never make it. He had been close to dying before, when he and Harris walked the three hundred miles back from the deserted Pawnee village without food, through a country bare of game. He thought this time he was closer to it, perhaps because this time they had come farther and there was no going back. Winter was closing in and their only hope was to find help ahead. Meanwhile, the migrating Pawnees they were trying so desperately to catch up with had swept the country like a big broom, eating as they went, and leaving nothing for those who came after them.

Jim dragged on, one step after another, and it occurred to him to wonder why.

Well, a man didn't want to die. But that wasn't the only choice. The camp was hidden in a dip of the prairie but he knew it was there, with the warmth of a fire and the huddled companionship of other human beings. There was no reason he couldn't go back to it and sit down and wait and let somebody else find game if they could. Plenty of the others were doing it.

Except that, as he had just said to Rich, he had something to prove. Jim's father was right, Jim's skin was no lighter and the men no kinder than they had been at home, and it wasn't enough to do just as well as the others, damn them, he had to do better. And why couldn't I have been all white, Jim thought, so I could quit if I wanted to?

Well, he answered himself, you aren't. And anyway maybe Rich is right and you bitch too much. Here you are right now with General Ashley and a whole passel of white men depending on you to save them because you're one of the best hunters in the outfit and they know it and they have to admit it. The General was a fool to start west in November and you were a fool to come with him, but where else would you be? Like Rich says, back with the boss-man. So think of the hungry white men, with their lives riding on your back.

Jim grinned, and then he lost his footing on the icy grass. He went the rest of the way on his hands and knees.

On the other side of the crest the land sloped away to a little stream wandering on its way to the Platte. In the stream bed there was a wide place where the current had kept ice from forming.

On the open water there were two dark objects.

Jim lay on the frozen ground with just his head showing over the rise. He squinted hard at the two dark objects on the water. Rocks? Shadows? The grainy snow stung his eyes. He blinked and peered again.

The two dark objects were still there. They moved on the water. They were not rocks or shadows. They were teal ducks.

Jim's mouth watered. His heart banged so hard he could hear it thump on the ground. He raised the rifle and it was like lifting a great tree, or a mountain. He squeezed the trigger.

The noise and the recoil nearly stunned him. He saw one of the ducks get up and fly away with a desperate churning of stubby wings. He didn't see the other one and he thought he had missed, and then he saw a dark blob floating on the water. The current was moving it, sliding it away. Jim ran down the slope. He splashed into black shallow water, the thin ice at its edges crackling under his moccasins. Instantly his feet seemed to freeze solid and he wanted to cry with the shock but the bird was slipping away from him and he chased it and caught it and stood with it dripping in his hands, the outer feathers oily cold, the inner body warm. He had shot the head away as clean as though he had cut it off with a knife.

He got out of the water and stomped up and down holding the duck.

There were four other men in his mess. Richards, Mose Harris, Tom Fitzpatrick, and a whiny young greenhorn. They were all hungry, just as hungry as he was. Camp law said he had to take this duck back and share it with them. Camp law said it was as much as a man's life was worth to hold out food or water on his comrades.

Jim looked at the duck, picturing it divided into five equal portions. The more he looked the smaller the duck got, until it seemed no bigger than a hummingbird.

His feet were freezing. He had to have a fire now, and fast, before he did anything else. There was an elbow in the stream a little farther on, with a thick scrub growing in the little bay where the cut bank sheltered it. Jim stumbled in among the bushes and hunkered down with the wind whistling above his head. In the lee of the bank it seemed almost warm. He made a fire. When he had it going well he spread his footgear to dry and then crouched over the welcome heat, looking at the duck. He looked at the duck for a long time. Then he stood up and looked out over the bank. The prairie was as barren and empty as though man had never been invented.

Jim whipped out his knife.

All the time the duck was roasting Jim kept looking nervously over the cutbank, afraid that Rich or Fitz or another of the wandering hunters might see the smoke. He was far too hungry and afraid to wait until the bird was properly done. He ate it half scorched and half raw, tearing and gulping like a famished dog, and when he was through he thought for a dreadful moment that he was going to heave it up again. He remembered that when the Kansaws had found him and Mose Harris almost dead from starvation after that long walk, they had fed them nothing for several days but little mouthfuls of gruel. But his stomach decided to accept the unaccustomed luxury of meat. He sat a few minutes longer over the fire, glorying in the sensation of being warm and full. Then he scattered the embers among the feathers and the gnawed bones and stood up, ready to face the world.

Remember the hungry white men, he thought, and grinned again. He set off along the edge of the stream.

It was dusk when he approached the camp, weak from hunger all over again, and tired out. He came from the west. The clouds had broken in that quarter and there was a pale lemon-yellow sunset at his back. Everywhere else the sky, the low air, and the snow-dusted ground were shades of the same cold blue. The horse herd was close by, a sorry-looking lot with their rumps all hunched into the wind, but at least they could fill their bellies with the frosty grass. In the camp itself, which the General liked to run in military style, the loads—excepting of course the ones containing powder—were neatly stacked into breastworks. The fires looked bright and cheerful but the forms of the men were dejected, sagging lumps around them. Jim could distinguish his own group, with Fitzpatrick's scarlet blanket between the faded capotes of Rich and Mose

Harris. The greenhorn was warming the dreary pannikins of flour gruel, and it appeared to be the same at every fire. The hunters had found nothing.

Jim shouted.

The whole camp stirred but Fitz was the first one to his feet, red blanket brilliant in the sunset, and Jim saw but did not believe the snap of the rifle to his shoulder. It was almost too late when he dropped. The ball passed so close that the wind of it tweaked his hatbrim. Jim was astounded. He had never been shot at before. The astonishment passed into fright, and the fright into a shaking rage. He hugged the ground among little scattered rocks and grass clumps that would have been no shelter at all by day, but he was below the light now and he and the grass together were part of the shadow. He flung up his own rifle. If it had not been for the bad angle and the breastwork he would have killed Fitz on the spot. Instead he had to content himself with shouting furiously, "What the hell's the matter with you?"

He knew what the matter was, what it had to be, but he had to ask anyway.

Very distinctly Fitzpatrick said, "You dirty black son of a bitch."

And Rich said, "We found your fire, Jim."

"Oh." All of a sudden Jim's voice was quiet and sweet, almost singing. "You found my fire. All right. I admit it. This dirty black son of a bitch killed a duck and ate it, every little bit, all by himself."

A wolf snarl that was half a groan came from the camp.

"One little teal duck," said Jim. "How far would it go among thirty-two men? How far would it go among five?"

Ashley said sternly, "That's no excuse, Jim. Put down

your rifle, stand up, and come in."

"Just a minute, General. I want to tell you all what more this dirty black son of a bitch did after he ate that duck. He had strength enough to go on hunting, when the rest of you had to come draggling your tails back to camp because you were too weak to stand up any longer. He shot a fine big fat buck and two fat does, enough to feed the whole lot of you, including *you,* General. And wouldn't you have felt silly, Fitz, if you'd blown my head off?"

He stood up, letting his rifle trail. "Now you tell me if I was wrong to eat that duck. And then some of you can build up the fires while the rest of us go and bring in those deer."

Twenty-odd men charged out at Jim and tried to pound him on the back all at the same time. Fitz stood apart, re-loading. So did Rich and the General.

"That's a dangerous game to play, Jim," the General said. "Suppose you hadn't found any deer?"

Fitz shot the ramrod home with a vicious thump.

Rich said, "He has the devil's own luck, this one."

"When it's a case of have-to," Jim said, "a man makes his own luck." He looked straight at the General, the fine-looking dignified man who was a gentleman and almost governor of a state, who knew the exact tone in which to address his inferiors. "Your stick and mine float the same way, General. And this child ain't fixing to go under."

He saw Ashley's face start to redden and he laughed and turned away, leading a string of eager trotting men out across the prairie. The General returned to his fire and sat down.

Fitz said, "Your friend is fixing for trouble." Rich was

doubled up laughing, and Fitz looked at him. "What's pleasing you so?"

"The General's face," Rich gasped.

Fitz grunted. Maybe he was wanting to laugh too. It was hard to tell about Fitz, who could be poker-faced as any Indian when he wanted to.

"Well," said Rich, "you're not over fond of Jim, I know, but are you too proud to eat his deer?"

"No," said Fitz, and now he grinned.

"Neither am I," said Rich. They followed after Jim.

General Ashley sat by the fire, hanging on hard to his temper. His first impulse was to have Jim whipped, but this was not the time and he knew it. So he controlled himself. But it was not easy. Jim's taunt was worse than insolent. It was true.

All the failures, the losses and disasters of the past few years for which he was in some measure personally responsible, rose up to mock him. Bad judgment, bad planning, inexperience—he had never intended to lead this expedition in person, that was supposed to be Major Henry's job, just as it had always been. Henry was one of Manuel Lisa's veterans, in the trade since 1807, and he knew the wilds. Ashley did not, and did not pretend to. Politics was his real love, and he enjoyed all the things that went with it, the social affairs, the fine houses and handsome women, the conversation of important men. The fur trade was to him merely the means of acquiring enough money to support his ambitions.

It hadn't worked out that way. He reflected bitterly that somehow all his business ventures had come to nothing, and this fling at the fur trade was no exception. Instead of making him wealthy it had plunged him so far into debt that unless he succeeded in this, his last hope and chance, his only way out was bankruptcy, and of course that meant the end of his career.

A case of have-to, that damned insolent bastard had said. Your stick and mine float the same way, and *this* child ain't fixing to go under.

Ashley's face grew hot, and hotter still.

All his troubles had started when Henry lost that keelboat, sunk in the Missouri with ten thousand dollars' worth of merchandise aboard. It wasn't Henry's fault, it was the same old treacherous river at work, but Ashley had had to borrow more money to replace that which was lost, and then take the new keelboat upriver himself after Henry, who had continued on to the Yellowstone. Ashley had not made it past the Arikara towns.

The memories leaped sharp and clear into his mind, memories he hated. Edward Rose, the interpreter, another dark bastard, black, white, and red, had warned him that the Indians were hatching treachery. The Arikara Little Soldier had warned him too. But the other chiefs had been full of assurances and persuasion, begging him to stay and trade, and Henry had sent word that he was in urgent need of horses, asking him to buy all he could. So he stayed and traded for horses, and in the night the Arikaras attacked the men who had been left ashore with the herd, killing all the horses and fifteen of the men including two who died later. Even so, he could have brought off all or most of his men safely except that his boatmen mutinied and refused to approach the shore. So he had had no choice but to drop back down the river, doing his best to save those who managed to get off the shore alive.

Or had he?

He could smell the powder and hear the rattling of shots, the howling and screaming, the sounds of death. He could see the faces of his boat crew, indomitable with the determination that comes to cowardly men in the avoidance of danger. And the moment came back to him clearly, the moment when he could have stopped the mutiny with one well-aimed pistol ball—and did not. Why?

And why had he been so stupid, after all the warnings, as to leave forty men ashore in a hopelessly exposed position with the river at their backs and the fortified towns in front?

Why indeed? So that a mulatto blacksmith could look him in the eye and mock him?

Ashley shivered between his anger and the cold wind at his back. Since that unlucky night everything had gone wrong. Colonel Leavenworth, sent to punish the Arikaras, had only succeeded in convincing them that the white men were afraid to fight. This word spread through all the Missouri tribes, and even the Mandan began shooting at trappers. The river was closed. North on the Yellowstone the implacable Blackfeet forced Henry to abandon his fort and move south through the Rockies. His men opened up virgin country, incalculably rich in beaver, but Henry himself wearied of the struggle and quit—probably, Ashley thought, because he believed the whole project to be an irretrievable failure. And he was awfully close to being right. The whole of Ashley's revolutionary concept of the white trapper, as opposed to the old system of trading forts where you tried to persuade the Indians to bring in furs for barter, depended on his ability to supply his men in the field. So far he had failed to do that. If he failed this time he was through. The men in the field would have to quit, the furs so far collected would be lost for lack of transport, and he would have to draggle home—if he managed to survive at all—to face his creditors.

A case of have-to, and a man makes his own luck. The luck he had made so far had not been very good. He knew it. And he hated Jim Beckwourth for reminding him of it.

It was not until he was in the act of filling his starving belly with the hot meat of Jim's deer that he realized he hated Jim so much that he was actually thinking of him as a fellow man, a competitor. And this was beyond his power to forgive.

FIVE

THE PLAIN WAS black with buffalo.

Rich put his hand on Jim's knee. "Wait," he whispered. "Wait for the signal."

The sun was brilliant in a blue sky. The herd threw up the dry snow like dust and it glittered in the air, streaming out where the wind blew it. There was a warm wild smell in the coldness. The pony snuffed it and quivered. Jim settled himself on the pad saddle, his own thigh muscles twitching with eagerness. He watched the herd, a plunging shaggy mass that bellowed and snorted steam. Then he looked where the Pawnees were strung out in a great ragged circle, waiting, and he wondered how long they were going to wait, now that the buffalo had started to move.

"Give the pony his head," Rich was saying. "He knows his job." It was Old Raven's buffalo horse, and Jim was sure he did know his job. He hitched the bridle rope under his belt where it wouldn't trail and devoted both hands to his rifle. Amid the Pawnee circle he could see Fitz and Jim Clyman and some others who had been invited to join the surround. Only he himself and a few of the white men carried guns. The others, including Rich, preferred the bow and arrow.

Two Axe, the chief, was so far away that Jim did not see the signal when he gave it. But suddenly the Indians began to rush in upon the herd from all sides, yelling, and the beginning stampede became a mill as the leaders turned. Rich let go a shrill screeching and kicked his pony.

It jumped away like a rabbit with Jim's pony after it, stretching out into a flat run. Almost before he knew it Jim was on the edge of the herd and it changed from a single mass into individual animals, into massive heads and forequarters, into sharp curving horns that could disembowel a horse, and heavy hoofs that could trample it under, rider and all. Rich fled around the edges of the herd, notching arrows and shooting as accurately and as fast as the Indians. Jim lost track of him. He found himself ranged up alongside a young cow and he fired, aiming behind the shoulder. The cow dropped. Jim began to reload, letting the pony run, and now he understood why the experienced hunters preferred the bow. Jim was better than most at loading the long rifle on horseback, but even so a bowman could knock down half a dozen buffalo while he was getting ready for his next one. He would know better next time. The wind hammered at him cold and strong. The snow dust flew, the world was thunderous with hoofbeats, the faces of the Pawnees he rode with were as wild and as natural as the faces of the buffalo. Jim filled his lungs and yelled with sheer exultance.

Buffalo were dropping everywhere. There was blood on the snow, and a great bellowing. The rifle was part of Jim, an extension of hand and eye. He looked at the buffalo and made them come. He did not feel like a butcher. He did not feel like a sportsman, either. He had seen the gentry riding out to hunt, but this was nothing like that. This was food and shelter, survival, life. This was triumph over the bleak, cruel, beautiful land that had tried so hard to put him under.

Those providential deer had not lasted long. Neither had the relatively open weather. Presently the Pawnee Trace was under two feet of snow and the horses were dying. The men ate them as they fell and stayed alive, barely. But they watched the rapidly shrinking herd with alarm and Mose Harris muttered over the fire of nights that if they didn't catch up with the Pawnees pretty quick they would see some hard doin's. Freezing, starving, and exhausted as he was, Jim would shake the snow off his hatbrim and figure that the doin's he had right now were hard enough to suit him.

They caught up finally with the Pawnees, only to find that they were in about as bad case as the white men, having been through the same weather. They were about to cross the Platte and head south to the Arkansas where they wintered, and they had nothing in the line of food or horses to spare. But their cousins the Skidi, the Pawnee Loups, they said, had a permanent town at the Forks of the Platte where they wintered, and it might be that Tirawa had smiled more brightly upon them. So the General marched on westward, praying. And then, incredible as a vision of paradise, there were the big earth lodges, warm and dry, and steaming pots of food, and nothing to do but eat and sleep, hunt, and bargain for buffalo robes and new moccasins. The General wrote up his journal, conferred with the Skidi chiefs, and pondered. As of today, the twenty-second of December, they had been in the village for two weeks.

Jim Beckwourth, on Old Raven's buffalo horse, fired and reloaded until his arm was tired from pushing the ramrod home. The frenzy cooled. The survivors of the herd streamed away across the plain. Rich came up beside Jim. He was grinning, his long hair flying, his eyes wild and bright. "We made 'em come," he said. "Wagh! We made 'em come!" He and Jim rode with the braves, yelping their triumph.

These tribal hunts had officers to see that every family got its fair share, so that even if a man was sick or unlucky or away somewhere his lodge would not be empty of food. Jim and Rich had done well for their host, Old Raven, who was past his best days as a provider. Jim liked Raven, and Raven's quiet wife, who set enormous dinners before them but did not eat of them herself. They had been unlucky in that they had only one daughter to provide them with a son-in-law. Of their three sons, two had died in battle and the third was living where custom required him to, with his wife's family.

Raven talked a great deal. Jim couldn't understand a word he said but Rich jabbered Pawnee pretty well and he acted as interpreter. The son-in-law was a lean, hard man verging on middle age, a respectable warrior and a good hunter, but a reserved and sour-looking individual made more forbidding by the Pawnee scalp lock, stiffened with grease and pigment to resemble a horn. Rich said that Pawnee meant horned and was a name that other tribes had given them. Their own name for themselves was Cha-hiksahiks, Men of Men. By the third day of their stay in Raven's lodge, the son-in-law had gotten used to them and amazed Jim by turning as merry as his own children. Jim had always thought of Indians as remote and stony in their habits, and here they were as full of laughter and liveliness as anybody. The young ones, as numerous as puppies, tumbled and scuffled about the big round room, their bright eyes shining in the light of the central fire that burned all day and all night. Mother took loving care of them, and so did Big Sister, except when she was making wide shy glances at the two strangers. Big Sister was pretty enough, too, once you got used to her red facepaint and the red parting that divided her two black glossy braids.

That night, over the smoking hump ribs, there seemed to be an unusual amount of talk from Old Raven, seconded by grunts from the son-in-law. Jim saw that Rich was smiling to himself and he asked why.

"Well," said Rich, "we was some today, way we made the butter come, and Old Raven's hinting around that his granddaughter is ready to take a husband."

"H'm," said Jim, gnawing a rib. "What's her father say?"

"He thinks they could use another man around the lodge."

"Which one?"

Rich looked at him. "Feeling tempted?"

Jim didn't answer immediately. The lodge was big and comfortable, dug partly into the ground and finished solidly with timbers and thick sod that turned the weather, hot or cold, rain or snow. A better house than many a one that stood in St. Louis. There were things in it to please the eye, beautiful shields and quivers, and bow cases bright with color. There were furs and buffalo robes for the comfort of the body, and there was food, and all these things were hard-won and uncertain, but they were between you and nature, not between you and other men.

"These people don't bow and scrape," Jim said. "They don't suck up to each other, not even to the chiefs."

"I reckon," said Rich dryly, "that if any Indian went to set himself up for one of these kings or emperors, the others'd give him reasons why he ought to change his mind. They'll follow a good chief in war, or they'll listen to one in council, but they won't put up with a bad chief, and no warrior will take any foolishness from anyone. Proud as eagles and independent as hogs on ice. Like you, Jim, only there ain't anybody to say they shouldn't. Kind of like it here, don't you?"

"I've seen worse."

He looked at Big Sister, with her long braids down her back like two black horsetails, and he thought of Francie. He thought of her quite often, and with a certain amount of regret. She was a handsome girl and loving enough, but she had never understood his hankering to go follow a free wind that blew somewhere beyond the horizon. To her there was only one possible future, marriage, a neat little house, nice respectable children, hard work, and a thrifty old age. She had often, and furiously, demanded to know what was wrong with this and Jim honestly couldn't tell her except that it made him feel like being buried alive.

Big Sister probably wanted exactly the same things. Women seemed to, for some reason. They liked everything small and tidy and pulled in where they could manage it. But Big Sister was an Indian and so what spelled respectability to her was a long way off from Francie's Sunday-go-to-meeting starch and picket fences. Jim thought it might work out just fine.

"—about an Indian wife," Rich was saying. "They don't mouth and tromp all over a man. They keep your lodge warm and your moccasins dry, they cook your food and tan your leather and make your clothes, and if you go off and leave 'em for a year or two, why they're right there waiting and smiling when you come back. Fact is, a man just near-about can't do without one."

"Why don't you have one, then?" asked Jim, smiling.

"I did," said Rich, quite unexpectedly. He shook his head, his eyes faraway and tender. "Never had to lodgepole her but once. She was some. She was a Crow woman. Blackfeet killed her, up on the Rosebud." He remained sunk in reverie, chewing absently on his hump ribs. Slowly his gaze focused again, on Big Sister. "Tell you what, Jim. You go find your own wife. I don't know what I've been doing so long without one."

"Suppose the General decides to move on. You'll hardly have time to kiss the bride."

"Move on?" said Rich, and snorted. "The General ain't going to tackle the mountains this time of year."

"That's what I hear," Jim said.

"Hear! Hear!" Rich snorted. "You listen to everything you hear you'll never know where you are. Every camp's full of—"

He broke off as Tom Fitzpatrick came stooping in through the entry tunnel. Old Raven motioned him to the visitor's place of honor on the right side of the fire. Fitz squatted down crosslegged and let his red blanket fall. Jim envied him, with his restless eyes and his Indian ways, and it pricked his pride that Fitz was two or three years younger than he and had already done so much more. He had been clear up to where the Missouri headed, and he had been through the northern passes and the inner valleys of the mountains, with Jed Smith and Clyman and Sublette and some others, looking for a way to make the General's crackbrain scheme come true. It was Fitz coming back down the Sweetwater and the North Platte with news of the South Pass and a route to it that had started Ashley and his expedition out of Fort Atkinson in the lunatic month of November. Someday, Jim thought, people will say my name the way they say his, when they talk about men who know the mountains.

In the meantime, Jim sat silent while Fitz talked.

Fitz scooped up a lump of fat out of the pot with his thumb and two fingers. Everybody sat decorously quiet while he ate it. Then Old Raven said something and Fitz answered him, and Raven and his son-in-law put their hands over their mouths in the gesture of surprise.

Rich sat up straight and said, "What the hell—"

"What's wrong?" Jim said.

"We're moving on," Fitz told him. "When?"

"First daylight."

Rich stared at Fitz as though he were waiting for him to laugh and admit it was all a joke.

"The Pawnees told him to wait till spring. I heard 'em.

Two Axe told him there wasn't any wood on the North Fork betwixt here and the mountains. I heard *you* tell him that, Fitz. So did Jim Clyman, and you ought to know you've both been that way." Clyman had got lost from the party and had to walk all the way back to Atkinson from the Sweetwater by himself. "How's the General expect us to live without fire? How's he expect the horses to live without even cottonwood bark to eat? Summer, now, when there's grass and buffalo chips without three feet of snow on top of 'em—"

Fitz said, "He's going up the South Fork."

"Oh," said Rich. "He is. And what's he know about the South Fork?"

"Nothing," Fitz said, "except Two Axe says there's some wood on it. So pack your possibles and get your horses in." He rose and added, "Merry Christmas." He went out.

"There goes your wedding," Jim said.

Rich shook his head. "The man's clean out of his mind, that's what he is. He nearly put us all under getting us here, and now he ain't content to stay where there's food and shelter, he's got to go on where he don't know where he's going, and in December—!"

"Almost January."

"Clean out of his mind," Rich muttered.

"Clean out of money," Jim said. This was no secret to anybody, here or at home. "I'm just a blacksmith yet, but you're a trapper, Rich. Suppose he waits here till the weather breaks. Suppose he isn't on the ground. What happens?"

"We miss the spring hunt."

"And he's paid thirty-three men for a nice long walk. All

those beaver are still sitting there snug with their coats on their backs, and it's a long time till fall."

"Reckon you're right," said Rich bitterly. "Reckon his fortune is worth more to him than our necks."

"Sure it is," Jim said. "Wouldn't it be if it was yours?"

"I'd cut all your throats for a pack of beaver plews. All right, I'll show him. I'll go with him to the goddam Rockies in January, and I won't go under, just to spite him." He began to shove his belongings into his war bag, grumbling.

Jim laughed. He pulled on his capote and went outside to bring in the horses. The air was still and at first it did not feel cold, but in a few minutes Jim was shivering. Beyond the clustered smokes of the village the west was dark and empty, the jumping-off place of the world.

SIX

THE WEATHER WAS steady, the men well rested, the horses fat. Ashley wrote in his journal that he anticipated a quick and easy passage to the mountains, and that happy frame of mind endured for two full days. On the morning of the third Dave Richards rose grumbling and shivering and sniffing the air.

Mose Harris, the large man with the powder-burned face and the longest, strongest legs west of the Mississippi, stood beside Rich wrapped in a shaggy buffalo robe and looking much like a bull with a hat on.

"Your nose ain't as good as mine," Rich said. "Nobody's is. But anyway, tell me what you smell."

Mose grunted. "Snow."

"Wagh!" Rich turned to Jim. "Don't know when she'll hit. Maybe half a day yet, I'd guess, but when she does she'll rip. So don't draggle off too far behind."

"Tell that to my horses," Jim said sourly. He went to load up, shivering with the raw cold and aware himself now of the snow smell in the air. He put the pack saddles on the four led animals assigned to him, getting madder by the minute. The General loved military neatness and discipline in his camps. Each man had his duties, and one of them was to be personally responsible for a certain number of pack horses and their loads. Jim couldn't quarrel with the arrangement except for one thing. Among the four horses assigned to him was the sorriest worn-down nag of the whole lot, the one that would have been left behind if the General had bought twenty-four fresh horses from the Pawnees instead of twenty-three. For two days, at the tail end of the procession, Jim had had to hold his pace to the flagging steps of the weakest and on both days he had ended up half a mile behind the party. That was with good weather and easy footing. If things got really bad, Jim was going to have some problems.

He took extra pains with his loads. He checked harness and gear and examined each separate hoof. He took so long about it that the rest of the party was mounted and ready to go before he was. The General looked at Fitz, who came over and spoke to Jim.

"Trouble?"

"Not yet," Jim said. "I'm just making sure that when this critter gives out nobody can say it's my fault."

"You'll have to make do," Fitz said. "Twenty-three is all

the horses the Pawnees could spare, and we've got barely enough to carry the loads as it is."

He rode away back to the General without waiting for an answer. Jim glowered after him. Rich was nearby and had made it a point to listen. He said, "You spoilin' for fight, Jim?"

"No." Jim swung into the saddle. "But I won't run if it's brought to me."

"You can generally run halfway to meet it. Figure the General give you that broke-down horse on purpose, don't you?"

"What do you think?"

"Well, I got to admit the General don't much like you. But you ain't been at much pains to make him."

"I've shod his horses," Jim said. "I've found him game when nobody else could. I do my full share. What's he got to complain about?"

"Well," said Rich, and stopped.

"Go on, tell me."

Rich scowled. "You go looking for it," he said querulously. "I swear you do."

"I do, huh? Go on, then. Tell me why the General don't like me."

"Same reason Fitz and some of the others don't, and you know why."

"Because," Jim said, "I ain't been at much pains to make them like me."

Rich looked at him. He shook his head and rode on. Jim followed, pulling his reluctant pack animals into motion. The Ashley party moved on west along the South Fork of the Platte.

There were buffalo moving west along the river too, shouldering massively against the wind. But the horses were naked where the buffalo were clothed and they didn't like to face the wind. They kept trying to turn and drift with it. As the day wore on and the insistent cold worked closer to the bone, the weaker animals began to lag. Jim's crowbait was the weakest and lagged the most, and at the nooning he was so far behind that everybody was finished eating and ready to move on again by the time he caught up.

The General was mounted on his long-legged bay. He looked fine and soldierly. He was forty-six years old, but he was always in the lead, always tireless, sturdy, and brave, heartening his men to endure as cheerfully as he did the messes he got them into, and his men stayed with him because he was brave and wouldn't let anything stop him. The General looked down at Jim and said, "You know the rule against straggling."

"Yes, sir," said Jim. "I do." The whole company was looking on and listening.

"Then remember it. We can't afford to lose horses now. If you can't manage yours—"

"Oh, I can manage them," Jim said, talking his best Virginian because it annoyed the General so. "Don't worry, General. I can manage just about anything."

The General's face reddened. Jim looked him hard in the eye, and he got redder, and his mouth opened, but before he could say anything Rich spoke up, pointing to the sky.

"Them clouds look more troublesome all the time, General."

Ashley grunted angrily, but he glanced at the sky and muttered something about finding a sheltered place to camp. He gave the signal to move out. Jim looked at Rich and said, "I'd just as soon had it out."

"There's a big blow coming," Rich said. "Your temper can wait. What did you have to rile him for?"

"Because he riles me."

"You don't have to make it worse. You could pull in your horns a little bit."

"Why should I?" Jim demanded.

Rich sighed. "Well, I know better'n to answer that." He caught up his string and rode off.

Jim dug some half-frozen dried meat out of his possible sack and gnawed it in the saddle, plodding at the tail of the party and looking hatefully at the backs of the men ahead. He was angry. He knew Rich was partly right and that made him angrier, because it made him unsure. He didn't want any difference between him and the others and maybe just because of that he was making the difference, getting sore where another man wouldn't and then being afraid to back down. It was true the Skidi couldn't spare another horse. They were not a horse-rich people and they had had their own losses. And it might be only chance that he had wound up with this footsore wreck.

He didn't think so. And there wasn't any doubt at all that the General was riding him. Pull in my horns a little bit, he thought, and wondered how Rich would act if the moccasin was on the other foot. He thought he knew. He chewed the hard cold meat and brooded, angry because he was angry, tired of being angry about the same old subject, bored with it, and wanting vaguely to kill somebody. He thought of Francie and hoped she had found somebody better suited to her than he was. Somebody who knew his place. Francie knew hers and took pride in it, and she had been used to lecturing him severely about his attitude. "Why do you want to make a lot of trouble?" she would ask him. "You can't change the world, but you can live good in it, or you can live bad. I am what I am, and I'm going to be the best there is of it." Maybe, Jim thought, that was the root of the difference between them. Francie knew what she was and he did not. He only knew what he wasn't.

The old horse pulled back harder on the lead rope and the gap between Jim and the rear of the party became imperceptibly wider.

There was no time when it positively began to snow. The sky thickened, turning slowly from gray to white. The figures of the men and horses ahead, the low sand hills that bordered the river, a band of buffalo on the opposite bank, and finally the river itself became more blurred and indistinct, smudges of charcoal on a white sheet, gradually vanishing. The air was filled with little fine whirling flakes, and before he knew it Jim was all alone.

For a while he could follow the tracks of the party, but then they began to sift in and disappear, and he had no way of telling how far behind them he was, or even whether he was still behind them. He kept the wind in his face, but even that was not a sure guide because the ground currents could eddy around a lot between the sand hills. The fine thick snow seemed to blot up all sound as well as sight. Deaf, blind, lost, he moved in a white cloud and the world was gone.

Panic might have taken him then, but he was madder than he was scared. He laid on with the whip, working the horses into a staggering run. After a while he saw what he thought were tracks not yet quite filled, but before he could be sure of it the old horse missed his footing and went down.

Jim's mount was pulled back onto his haunches. There were flounderings and heavings as the other pack animals fought to keep from falling. Jim hung on, talking to them until they quieted. Then he set about trying to get the old nag on his feet again. It was obvious after a few minutes that he was not going to get up with the weight of the pack on him. Jim struggled with the wet, half-frozen lashings, and all the time the little snowflakes whirled into his eyes and his nostrils and his mouth and ears like a swarm of cold white midges. The pack came loose. He raised the horse's head and heaved, lifting the animal's forequarters. The horse got up. They stood panting and shaking and glaring at each other. When he got his breath, Jim began putting the load back on.

He was about half finished when he heard shouts somewhere in the wind and the white smother. They sounded like his name. He shouted back. A couple of blurred shapes appeared, lumbering and monstrous. They resolved themselves into Rich and Mose Harris, pawing snow out of their eyes and cursing him.

"Thought we'd never find you," Rich said.

"Am I lost?" Jim asked.

Rich groaned. "Hark at him, Mose. That's thanks for you. Is he lost? Why damn you, Jim, we're probably all of us lost now. They're making camp in the sand hills a half mile or more from here, and I doubt well ever find our way back to it."

Mose said, "Why don't you shoot that old horse and put

him out of his misery?"

"General gave him to me," Jim said, tightening the lashings. "General said not to lose him. I don't aim to."

Mose said absently, "General's in a tower of rage."

"Too bad about him," Jim said.

"Ain't nothing to the tower he'll be in when we get back," Rich said. "If we get back. His orders were for everybody to stay in camp." He clapped his arms around him and his voice rose to a petulant snarl. "You figuring to spend the night here, Jim?"

"Don't hurry me," Jim said. "I hate to be hurried." He could hear the old horse breathing in a kind of wind-broken roar. He lightened the load as much as he dared, distributing some sacks of powder and lead among the other horses. Then he mounted.

"Lead on."

They moved slowly, their heads bent, their eyes seeing only whiteness until it became indistinguishable from blackness and total dark.

The old horse fell again.

"He's played out," Mose said. "Shoot him."

Jim shook his head. This time he cut the lashings of the pack saddle. The load fell free and when he got the horse on his feet again he left it on the ground. Barebacked, the horse was able to walk.

They moved on. Their ears heard silence and the tiny hiss and tap of snowflakes around their hatbrims, and beyond that the vast dull voiceless roar of wind rolling between earth and sky with nothing to stop it. White men on white horses, they moved like ghosts.

In their effort to stay away from the river and the treacherous ice, indistinguishable now from solid ground, they went too far the other way and floundered among the outlying humps of the sand hills. Rich and Mose Harris wrangled briefly over whose great pathfinding was responsible. Jim laughed.

"Beats me why you came at all. I could have found my way."

"I wasn't worried about you," Rich said. "I was thinking of them horses and all the dried meat and ammunition they're toting."

"I was worried about Rich," Mose said, "is why I came. All right, Jim, find it."

"Find what?"

"Your way."

"Ha," said Rich. "That shut him up in a hurry."

"Give me time," Jim said. He did not have any idea where they were, or where the camp might be, or whether they had come half a mile or ten miles or fifty yards. He only knew he had something to settle with the General, and he was bound to find him somehow. They wallowed back to more level ground. The snow was piling, getting deeper. The old horse would not be able to go much farther, even carrying nothing more than his own weight.

Jim undid the rawhide cover of his rifle and fired it into the air. They stood still, straining their ears.

Nothing.

They moved on.

"Wait," said Rich. "Whoa." There was a place where the wind curved out over the top of an unseen ridge, making a space of dead air where only a light sifting of snow dropped from the driven mass of it overhead. Rich climbed out of the saddle, stiff as a wooden man, and creaked to his knees. He took off his mittens and paddled with bare fingers in the snow. Suddenly he yipped.

"Here she is, boys, here's the trail." His fingers scrabbled out the cupped tracks. "We're all right now. Broad as a turnpike road and all we got to do is follow it." He jumped up, grinning. "Just you leave things to Dave Richards, boys, and you'll live long. Never been a trail yet I couldn't find or follow."

"I mind one," Mose Harris said. "Fact is, I mind a couple. Fact is, Rich, you're a notable old liar."

"That's no lie," Rich retorted, pointing to the track. "What do you say, Jim Beckwourth? We're even now, ain't we?"

"Why?" asked Jim.

"Why? Why, because I just saved your life, is why."

"Well, now," Jim said, "I didn't know I was about to lose it."

Rich stared at him. "If it hadn't been for me—"

"Us," said Mose.

"—comin' to find you, you wouldn't never have—"

"Thought it was the horses you were after."

"Well, of all the low-down ungrateful—! I never said no such thing. I'll leave it to Mose if I did, and anyway, I still say—"

Jim broke out laughing. So did Mose. "You did me a service," said Jim, "you and Mose together. So just to show you I'm a gentleman at heart I'll cancel half the debt."

Rich cried out as one in agony. "Half the debt! *Half* the debt! Did you hear that, Mose? I swear I never knew such a—"

Jim and Mose looked at each other and nodded. They

rode on together. "That long tongue will be the death of him yet," Mose said. He shook his head and sighed. "Someday he'll tramp on it and pull it out by the roots." Behind them Rich swore and grumbled, outraged.

The wind caught them again, beat and howled at them, drowned them in snow, but now they could hardly lose their way. The track was buried, but it led between high banks and Jim thought it was one of the paths the buffalo had worn through long ages, coming down to the river.

It widened into an irregular bowl that offered some shelter from the wind, and suddenly the horses were walking among little low mounds that erupted human curses when trodden upon, and they were in camp. The horse herd appeared dimly, a mass of patient misery close-huddled for warmth, tails to the wind. There was shouting back and forth, the burden of it being that here was Harris and Richards and Beckwourth, they made it. There were cries of congratulation. Some of the men even crawled out of their warm robes to pound them on the back and help them unsaddle.

Tom Fitzpatrick came up, his scarlet blanket all frosted white. "I'm glad you made it," he said, and grinned. "But maybe you won't be. General wants to see you—all three."

SEVEN

THE GENERAL WAS hunched under a low shelter improvised from a blanket stretched between two heaps of piled-up goods. Rich and Mose Harris had to squat down Indian-fashion in order to face him. The wind screamed and the snow eddied down and from time to time the General reached up and punched the blanket to knock the snow off it. Fitz hunkered down nearby. Some of the men, smelling trouble, drifted up to listen.

"The order was to stay in camp," the General said. "Why did you disobey it?"

Mose grunted and occupied himself in wrapping his buffalo robe more tightly around him. Rich had a faraway look in his eye.

"We didn't rightly intend to," Rich said. "But when I went to unsaddle my horse the critter just hopped away from me, and kept on hopping, and Mose tried to help me catch him, and before we knew it, General, we were clean out of camp—"

"And you decided to go looking for Jim," said the General, not bothering to take issue with Rich about his hopping horse.

"He was a long ways behind," Rich said, in a different tone.

"Jim," said the General, looking around. "Jim! Fitz, where is that black son of a bitch?"

"I don't know," said Fitz. "I told him—"

"He's right here," Jim said. He materialized out of the dancing snow veils, holding something in his hand. Rich saw the look in Jim's eye. He glanced at Mose, who had seen it too. They waited.

The General said, "Jim, you were warned about straggling. Now here you are risking not only four valuable horses, but the lives of two men who had to come and look for you—"

Jim tossed the thing he held in his hand into the snow at

the General's feet. It was a headstall with a coiled rope attached.

"You gave me a horse you knew couldn't keep up," Jim said, "and then you began to ride me about straggling. Well, there's your horse back. You told me to bring him in, and I did, and if he isn't dead by morning you can do what you want with him." He looked at Rich and Mose. "As for them," he added, straightfaced, "they were wandering around lost when I found them."

A subdued rumble of laughter went around the circle of watching men. The General leaned forward. He picked up the rope and headstall and threw them aside. He stood up, quite slowly and deliberately.

"Jim," he said, "I have had all the insolence from you that I choose to take. I—"

Jim cut him short. "Don't insolent me, General. I'm not your child, your slave, or your servant. And only my friends call me Jim. My name is Beckwourth."

The General's eyes got slaty. He started to speak, and again Jim stopped him.

"You can save the rest of your breath. I'm through. I won't work with a man that tries to punish me because I won't lick his boots. This isn't St. Louis, General. I don't have to."

He turned away. He was hot and shaking.

"Just one minute," Ashley said. "That's fine big talk, but where do you expect to go?"

"Back to the Forks," Jim said, "as soon as the weather clears."

"You'll walk it."

Jim shrugged. "I'll walk it."

There was another small rumbling around the circle and this time it was not laughter. The circle had grown. Rich sighed and stood up.

"I reckon I got to go with Beckwourth, General."

"Well," said Ashley, surprised and upset. "I didn't know you loved him that much."

"I don't," Rich said. "Fact is, I don't even like him much."

"Then why?" Ashley was genuinely amazed.

Rich said, "Because he's right."

Mose Harris stood up, shaking the snow in a great cloud off his buffalo robe. He stood beside Rich.

The General looked at him. "You too, Harris?"

Mose nodded. "Fair's fair, General, and there ain't a man here don't know it."

There was a mutter of assent from the circle, and a voice spoke out of the group, saying, "It ain't right not to give him a horse. Might as well shoot a man as not give him a horse."

"Do we get horses?" Rich asked. "Or do we walk?"

"What the hell," said another voice suddenly above the screaming wind, "let's all walk. That Pawnee town was mighty warm and dry. I don't know why I'm settin' here hungry in a blizzard when I could be lyin' by a fire eatin' fat cow."

The response to this was so great that for the first time Ashley became truly alarmed. He looked around at the men. Only the faces of those nearest him were recognizable, the others blurred by the snow that was falling ever thicker. Fitz remained squatting, his scarlet blanket over his head. He watched the General.

Ashley spoke quietly, but his voice carried above the wind, or perhaps beneath it, because every man heard.

"Anyone who wishes to turn back will be given a horse and provisions. As for myself, I shall go on, even if I must do so alone."

He meant it, and they knew he meant it. He looked at them for a moment longer and then returned to his shelter, managing somehow to do even that with dignity. There was no more talking, and the circle broke up. The snow poured down heavier and it was getting dark. Jim walked away. Rich said behind him, "Our mess is over here. I think."

They dug in the snow like dogs. The greenhorn kid was already buried, with just a blowhole open. Mose Harris appeared and began to dig beside them.

Rich asked, "Where's Fitz?"

"Stopped behind to talk to the General," Mose said. Rich grunted. He and Jim spread the buffalo robes and crawled into them. In cold camps like this the men customarily slept in pairs for warmth. Mose bedded himself down and cursed Fitz for keeping him waiting. Jim lay quiet. He felt strangely peaceful, much as he had when he made up his mind not to obey Carson's curfew.

"Rich," he said. "Mose."

"What?"

"I'm obliged to you. But you don't have to go with me."

"That's the bad of it," Rich said bitterly. "We do. We got right up in meetin' and said we'd do it and now we got to do it."

"Fire and fat cow," Mose said thoughtfully. "Don't sound half bad."

Rich made a derisive sound. "Fire and fat cow! Think of

the beaver streams, with nary a trap ever laid into 'em. Think of the beaver plews, bale on bale of 'em. Think of the money. Fire and fat cow! Hell's full of fire and fat cow." He rolled over with his back to Jim, trying automatically to take the top covering with him as he rolled. "Trouble, Jim. That's what you are. Trouble."

Jim said, "But you said I was right." He locked his fingers on the robe and hung on. Rich gave up and stopped pulling.

"You are," he said. "It's still trouble."

"Meaning none of the rest of you ever had it," Jim said, "and if I wasn't here you wouldn't have it now. That's almost enough to make me change my mind about going."

"What is?" asked Fitz's voice out of the thick dark. Jim heard him scramble in beside Mose, amid bitter complaints that he was bringing the blizzard into bed with him.

"Forget it," Jim said curtly.

"I was hoping you would change your mind," Fitz said. He was an Irishman born and he could be charming as a spring day when he wanted to. He was being charming now. Jim smiled.

"Why?"

"If you go, Richards and Harris go with you—and you heard the men. As many as half of them, maybe more, might go too. You know how everybody felt about this move anyway, and now hitting weather like this—"

"Fire and fat cow," said Mose dreamily.

"That's right. Weakens me when I think about it," Fitz said. "But think about it the other way. Think what's waiting for us. Jim, you haven't seen that country, but I have. Great mountains, fat valleys, and enough beaver in those streams to make us all rich. It'd be a pity to throw it all away now."

"If I'm all that important," Jim said with quiet wickedness, "why wasn't the General a little more polite?"

Rich groaned. "You've given him a sense of power, Fitz. Now the devil only knows what he'll do."

Some of the charm had gone out of Fitz's voice when he answered. "It's the fire and fat cow that's pulling the men, not Jim, or you either. It's just the idea of anybody turning back. It could split the party."

Jim chuckled. "That makes me feel real good."

"Listen, Jim," Fitz said. "The Old Man was wrong. You won your point. He won't ride you again. Now why can't you—"

"He'll have to do better than that," Jim said.

"What?"

"Watch his goddam tongue. If he calls me that name again I'll kill him."

"Then you will stay."

"I didn't say so, did I? I was all fixed to go, I can't change my mind without thinking about it. I'll let you know."

He could hear Fitz clap his jaws shut on something he was just about to say. Rich groaned again.

"Jim—"

"What?"

"Nothin'. Nothin' at all."

Jim smiled. He settled his hat so that the brim stopped the snow from trickling down his neck and drifted sweetly off to sleep.

The blizzard blew itself out during the night of the

twenty-seventh. The morning of the twenty-eighth was clear and windless. The men emerged from their holes into an arctic cold that seemed almost warm because the air was still. Four of the horses had died, including Jim's old pack-horse. The snow was very deep.

"Don't look to me," Rich grumbled, up to his chest in a drift, "like nobody's going noplace."

But the General was brisk and cheerful. In the predawn dark the men dug out the packs and got the horses loaded, and the General went first on his tall bay to start breaking open the trail through the sand hills and down to the river. The winter sun came up and turned the world to a glitter of purest white, very beautiful under the clean blue sky, and very painful to the eyes. They fought and floundered in relays, sometimes riding, sometimes walking where the drifts were too deep for horses, trampling, digging with their hands to make a path.

"We won't get far this way," Rich said. His breath steamed. He threw snow around like an angry terrier. "Either forward or back. Made up your mind yet?"

"No," said Jim.

"You're a liar. It was made up long ago. You wouldn't tell Fitz just so's he'd sweat a while and make the General sweat too."

"When was it made up?" Jim demanded.

"Soon's the General humbled down and asked you."

"When was that?"

"When he sent Fitz. Don't play simple with me, Jim. I know you."

Jim blew two plumes of steam out of his nostrils like a horse, and did not answer. He threw snow aside in showers, feeling the blood run warm in him. It was good after the long cramped wait to move again. All of a sudden he broke through a wall of drift and the river valley lay ahead. Something moved in the blinding dazzle. He cupped his hands over his eyes and then he shouted.

"Buffalo!"

The herds were still moving, the great powerful shaggy bands treading pathways in the snow where the weak might follow, baring the grass so the weak might feed behind them.

Jim mounted and rode his horse plunging to the buffalo trail. The others came after, shouting as they went.

They stood together in the broad path and the horses tore hungrily at the cold grass.

The General looked at the men. "There was talk," he said, "that some of you wanted to turn back." His gaze centered on Rich and Mose.

They looked at Jim. Jim looked at the General. He seemed to be waiting for something.

Reluctantly, coldly, the General turned to Jim. He said one word, not as though he liked saying it but as though a soldier must do many things he does not like and do them efficiently.

He said, "Beckwourth?"

Jim smiled, settling himself in the saddle. "I guess I just got to see the Rockies, General," he said. "That's what I came for."

Ashley looked away from him, at the other men. "Anyone else?"

There was some harrumphing and shuffling, but Rich said loudly, "This child's for beaver!" Mose echoed him. It seemed that since the ringleaders weren't going, nobody else quite wanted to take the limelight. The General nodded and reined his horse around sharply, making him prance. Some of the men lifted a shrill wild yell and the whole cavalcade started off, heading west in the wake of the buffalo.

On the twentieth of January they reached a small island in the South Platte. It was grown to sweet cottonwoods, the second life-saving oasis of fuel and fodder since they left the Forks. At the western edge of the island Fitzpatrick lifted his arm and pointed to a line of distant peaks that rose white and shimmering into the clear sky.

Jim Beckwourth got his first look at the Rocky Mountains.

EIGHT

THE SECOND LOOK was closer, and the mountains were twice as grand. But instead of being unreal and mysterious like the mountains in a dream they resolved themselves into a solid wall of rock and ice, cruel, threatening, and deadly.

They camped at the foot of the Front Range for most of the month of February. It was a good camp. There was shelter from the wind, plenty of fuel, plenty of sweet bark, and even grass for the horses. The men would have been willing to stay there until spring, but each day the General went out with Fitz or Mose Harris or Jim Clyman to hunt for a way over the barrier range. Each night he came back exhausted and half frozen, looking grimmer and more obstinate every time.

Rich watched the General one particular evening as he stomped by in the dusk. Ashley had had Fitz with him to-day. Rich and Jim and Mose were sitting by the fire while the greenhorn broiled the elk steaks they had shot that day.

"I don't like the look of him," Rich said. "I don't like the look of him at all."

"Reckon," said Mose, "he's about to do it again." They all turned as Fitz came up to the fire and hunched over it, shivering. "How about it, Fitz? Is he?"

"Is he what?" Fitz grabbed one of the half-raw steaks and began to wolf it down. "Wagh! Hungry work."

"Fixing to go over the mountains," Rich said, "whether or no. I been with the General a long time and I know the signs. Whenever his jaw sticks out like that he's about to do an evil of some kind."

Jim looked away from the fire. They were on the shadow side of the mountains and the shadow was a clear pure blue, very pale on the snow fields, shading deeper and deeper into the folds and clefts. The high peaks caught the sun and blazed, so that the top of the range seemed to be splashed with hot gold.

"Ask the General," Fitz said. "I don't know what's in his mind."

"Modesty don't become you, Fitz," Rich said. "You're the proud kind, high-headed and haughty. You're the General's right hand, leastwise when Diah Smith ain't around, and if you don't know you ought to. Is he going over the mountains?"

"He's going," Jim said, although nobody had asked him.

"How do you know?" Fitz asked.

"Same reason he left Atkinson. Same reason he left the Forks. He's got to."

The hot gold darkened to red and the peaks were like spearheads after a battle.

Rich sighed. "Have you found a pass, Fitz? Or do we have to chop one out with our hands?"

Fitz said, "Beckwourth knows everything. Ask him."

"I don't have to be extra smart to see from here that the passes are full of snow. He'll go just the same, you watch. And pretty quick."

Jim turned again to the fire. He ate, and slept, and in his dreams he was no bigger than a little fly climbing, climbing, up a dark wall that ended in the stars. The air was black and windy and it was terribly cold. In his dream he knew that he could never reach the top.

Two days later, on the twenty-sixth, Ashley led his men out of camp and up the knees of the mountains.

And it was not too different from Jim's dream, except that the toiling was done by daylight and the air was bright. The shine of the snow fields pierced the eyes like javelins. But the cold was as he had dreamed it. In the summer he thought these mountains would have been fairly easy to cross, for the pass was not awfully high nor awfully steep. But now it was choked with the packed snows of a long winter, and the approaches to it were treacherous with wind-polished ice and crusted stretches that appeared solid and then broke beneath the foot, crumbling into gullies that could swallow up a man or a horse. They crawled. In places they took the packs off the horses and carried them on their own backs and then went back to guide and support the animals one by one. Darkness caught them and they huddled in their robes to shiver out the night, and then crept on again in the rainbow dawn, so heartbreakingly, bone-freezingly beautiful. It took them three days to cross, and every minute of that time while they all danced precariously on the thin edge of death the General was there, leading them step by step, a man unafraid of mountains or cold or the devil himself. Jim shook his head. You had to admire the man. Like him or not, you had to. At times like this you were proud to be one of his men. At times like this you would follow him to hell, even though he would not speak to you along the way.

They came down out of the pass not knowing what they would find. They were far south of the country Fitz and Clyman had been through last summer and no white man had ever crossed the Front Range here before. But the General's luck was in.

Between the mighty ranges that marched behind and before, the ground was easy, the south slopes bare of snow, and game was thick. They moved west and north. Somewhere in this direction, beyond the Divide, was the valley of a river the Indians called the Siskadee and the Spanish called the Green, and it was along this river and its tributaries that the General expected to find his men. They kept on this course until their way was blocked by a range that refused to be bulled out by the General, though he killed some horses and wore out his men trying to get through the passes. Now they went north along the base of these mountains, and again the General's luck was in.

The country rolled magnificently in ridge and valley, splendid to look at and rich in game. The men could gorge themselves on buffalo and antelope and mountain sheep.

And most beautiful of all to the eyes of the trappers were the very many little streams that came down cold and pure from the snow fields, their banks fringed with willows.

"Beaver," Rich said, and grinned a greedy grin. "Break out the traps, Jim. You got a lot of learnin' to do before I turn you loose."

The General moved slowly while the men worked, and Jim began to learn what it was like to be up to beaver.

He waded in icy water, working always upstream, moving on numbed insensible feet that had still to feel for holes and snags and hold steady in slick mud. Rich taught him to look for the runs and slides and how to find the most carefully hidden lodges. He taught him how deep to set the trap and how to anchor it to the long float-pole, and when to use a float-stick attached to the trap so that it could be found in deep water without having to dive for it. He taught him the use of the "medicine" stick, the bait-stick set above the trap to draw the beaver by the strong musky scent of a substance Rich carried in a little horn bottle. But he would not tell Jim the secret of the concoction, except that it was based on the musk glands of the beaver. Jim found out that every trapper had his own recipe for "medicine" and that none of them would tell what it was, not to their wives, their children, or their dearest friends. He thought they were being a little childish about this, but pretty soon he was carrying his own little antelope-horn bottle and being as mysterious as the next about what was in it. And after he had, from sheer ignorance, fouled up two or three sets of traps, he learned to keep his own scent off the trap, out of the "medicine," and off the banks of the stream.

"Beaver ain't like other four-footed critters," Rich told

him. "The Indians think they're medicine people, pretty much like us except they live in the water, and I wouldn't want to say they're wrong. Look at the lodges they build, as good as the Pawnee, and look at the way they live in 'em, not all helter-skelter like, the way most animals do, but all ordered and nice with the Old Man beaver having the say and the young ones saluting him polite-like with their paws and listening to what he tells them. Their tribe law says everybody's got to do his share. If there's a lazy young beaver that won't work, why they throw him out of the village. And look how they build their dams. I've seen milldams at home weren't half so good."

So had Jim. It didn't really seem possible that a mere animal could plan and build such a construction and then keep it in perfect repair. If the sharp hoofs of a passing deer disturbed the dam you would see the fresh clay brought up from the bottom and plastered on, patted and smoothed by busy little paws. But this was not the most of the marvel. The way they arranged their spillways and canals to keep the water level just where they wanted it regardless of flood or dry season was something Jim figured no animal could do unless it had some pretty special powers.

"But they can't really talk?" he asked Rich. "Not the way we do?"

"I dunno," Rich said. "But I can tell you this much. Once you let one beaver get up to trap, you might as well pack up and move on. I can't just say how the word gets around, but it does. You'll find no beaver in your traps, and that ain't all. Every trap'll be sprung, and maybe hauled out and buried."

"How do they spring 'em?"

"With a stick," Rich said, "with a stick. How else would they do it?"

Jim learned a lot and he learned fast, partly because he had a good teacher and was willing to listen to him, but also because he had a natural talent for these things and understood them instinctively. Some of the greenhorns were hopeless from the first. The old trappers could tell them something a hundred times and they couldn't grasp it. Their muscles didn't function right, their eyes could not be trained to see, and if they remembered one thing they forgot a dozen more. These men were soon relegated to holding the horses and doing the bulk of the skinning and curing. Jim looked at them with pity, and his own pride was great.

He was beginning to think that life in the mountains was a pretty fine thing, and he couldn't understand why Rich began to get uneasy and nervous, always peering about and sniffing the wind and working his shoulder blades up and down as though he had an itch between them.

He was unwise enough to josh Rich about it.

"That's 'cause you're still a greenhorn," Rich snapped. "You don't know no more'n a baby. When things go best is the time to worry, and when you don't see any Indian sign at all is the time to be scared."

Jim shut up, but privately he thought Rich was up to his old trick of enjoying himself being miserable. They reached the main branch of the North Fork of the Platte, and went on to claw their way over the Divide and then on northward through a great basin where the waters drained neither to west nor east. There was no sign of the Siskadee, but nothing happened except the familiar things of running into bad weather and out of grass for the horses. Jim was prepared to laugh at Rich's old-womanly gloom.

They camped near a huge rough butte, to rest and let the horses graze on the first grass they had found for some days. Jim was off watch and sleeping peacefully in the deep night. A sudden scatter of shots and yells brought him up standing. There was a wild shrill crying out in the darkness, *Ough! Ough! Ough!* like the laughter of wolves, and under it a rush of hoofbeats, and it was all over and done in a space of minutes. Men were springing up out of their robes. The horse guards were still shooting a little and shouting a lot. Rich came up.

"There's the best part of our horses gone. Still feel like laughing?"

Jim shook his head. He was really not thinking about the horses yet. He was excited, the blood stinging in his veins and something strange going on in his middle, something that was partly fear and partly a queer eagerness. This was the first time he had heard the sound of an enemy.

Rich said, "Where's your rifle?"

It was still in Jim's bed, under the buffalo robe where it would keep warm and dry for instant use. Rich swore in anger and despair.

"Your hair'll be drying in somebody's lodge before summer. I'm ashamed to know you."

He stamped away. Jim picked up his rifle and went to see what he could do.

There wasn't much. Fitz and the General rode off after the raiders as soon as it was light enough to track, but the rest of them became beasts of burden alongside the few remaining horses, carrying on their own backs the loads of the stolen animals. The General returned that night with three that had been left behind by the Indians, but he and Fitz had not caught up to the main party, which was moving fast over familiar terrain.

"Crows," said Fitz, pointing east, and the old hands nodded.

"Slickest horse thieves on the Plains," Mose said, honestly admiring them in spite of his sore back. But then Mose liked walking better than most.

"What were they doing way up here?" Jim asked.

"Raiding," Rich said. "Young men after Shoshoni horses. The Snakes and the Crows are friendly, but—" He shrugged. "Young men got to make their fortune somehow."

"But not with our horses."

"Ours, anybody's. Horses are where you find 'em, to an Indian."

"Crows," said Jim, savoring the name.

"It's more rightly Sparrowhawk," Rich said. "Absaroka is their own word."

"You're such an expert," Fitz said, "you can be one of the party. We're going after them hard tomorrow."

"Thanks. You'll never catch 'em, but I'll go. Take Jim too—he needs to learn."

Jim rode out with eight other men at the first light. He rode for five days. It was hard but exhilarating work, and he learned several things, chiefest of which was that Indians had the power to make themselves and their stolen horses disappear like the morning mist when the wind blows.

"Absaroka," Jim said. The word had a magic sound. "Someday I'm going to find out who stole those horses, and I'm going to make every mother's son of 'em wish they hadn't."

Rich laughed.

They rejoined the party and moved on over rolling prairie, high and cold, and now the General's luck was out, out and gone. Men and horses labored under their heavy loads, and the men cursed the beaver skins they had piled up to ride on their backs. It came on to snow and it was all they could do to travel six or seven miles a day. There was no game. And still there was no sign of the river.

"We ain't going to make it," Rich moaned. "Come all this long hard way and we ain't going to make it."

"We'll make it," Jim said, and nodded toward the General. "Look at his jaw, sticking out undershot as a bulldog."

"He can't do anything about it if we die on him."

"Oh, yes he can. He can kick us on our feet again and make us go." Jim managed a frozen, lopsided smile. "The son of a bitch, he's *some!*"

But finally even Jim began to wonder. The miles got longer, the camps colder and the bellies emptier. The pack on Jim's back weighed like the whole main chain of the Rockies. He began to hate the men for whom he helped to carry all this mass of lead and powder and merchandise. He had never seen them but he knew some of their names—Smith, Sublette, Provot, Bridger—and now he began to put faces to the names. They were fiend-faces, bleared and hideous. They wanted to kill him. He told Rich about this and they both laughed, but the laughter was a little edgy.

There came a day of raw wind and drifting snow, when the clouds lay gray and leaden on the mountains and the sun was only a memory, and the men could not go any farther without food. The General made camp and sent his hunters out. And it was as it had been before on the low prairie along the Platte, with Jim and Rich and the others staggering away in the last stages of starvation to search for food. It seemed to Jim that in this life it was always either fat cow or poor bull, and sometimes not even that, but never a happy medium.

Rich snarled wordlessly and went off. The men spread out, as they always did, going singly in order to cover as much ground as possible. Jim walked alone. The land was a gray blur, merging into cloud, into nothingness and nowhere. If you kept on you could climb right out of the world. You could catch a big gray dragon and ride him and make the clouds boil. You could kick the mountaintops and make them boom like thunder, and shake the big rockslides down. You could—

But you couldn't because you couldn't climb that high. You couldn't even climb the ridge in front of you and that wasn't much higher than the fences you used to shinny over when you were ten.

But you had to climb it.

Why?

Because you're curious. You're curious like a cat. You have to kill yourself like a damn fool cat just to see what's on the other side.

Climb.

And now you can't think anything, not even foolishness. There's nothing but breathing and that hurts and makes you cough, and your legs have to go and they don't want to.

Climb.

The top of the ridge and gray space beyond. Cloud

above, pale grass below frosted over with snow. Dark belts of cottonwood, box elder, and willow, and a big wide gray-green river running, running fast. And buffalo, many buffalo. Fat buffalo, grazing.

Grazing in the valley of the Siskadee.

YELLOW GRASS

NINE

I T WAS 1826 and the summer rendezvous was in full whoop and holler.

Jim Beckwourth lifted a coal out of the fire with a pair of green willow twigs and held it to his pipe bowl. He blew smoke luxuriously, letting his audience wait. There were three French-Canadians around the fire, one of the several Iroquois who had deserted last year from the Hudson Bay Company, a couple of loose-jointed cotton-haired farm boys who had been in the mountains no longer than it took to cross them, and Dave Richards, in front of whose lodge the fire burned. When he was ready, Jim went on.

"That night we camped beside the river. When everybody was sleeping the General came to me and said, 'Jim, I have come to depend on you. I don't want the others to know how desperate bad off we are, but I am at my wits' end. I have all these supplies for my brave trappers in the mountains, but the Indians have stolen my horses and my men can't go any farther. Jim, what am I to do?' " Jim paused. "Boys, it would have made your hearts break to the General right then."

Rich made a choking sound. Jim ignored him. One of the French-Canadians was a youngster about sixteen. His name was Baptiste and he watched Jim with worshipful shiny black eyes the way Jim had wanted to be watched ever since he left St. Louis. The farm boys, who had themselves just finished crossing the country with General Ashley on his second—and, it appeared now, his last—trip, were not worshipful but annoyed. From Jim's account it seemed that their journey, undertaken in the spring when the weather was good and grass and game were plentiful, had been no more than an unusually long stroll in the country. Jim gestured widely at an imaginary Siskadee.

" 'General,' I told him, 'there is your answer.' And I pointed to the river. 'Let the river carry your burdens,' I said. The General, he shook his head. 'That's a fine idea, Jim,' he said, 'but how?' And I told him, 'General, there's a plenty of buffalo about. We can make a bullboat and float the supplies downriver to some place of rendezvous, and meanwhile some of us can be busy trapping and looking for your other men.' The General wrung my hand. 'Jim,' he said, 'Jim, my friend, I think you have hit it.' "

"Fact is," said Rich, "hadn't Jim here been along to tell him how, I reckon General Ashley couldn't hardly have got himself out of St. Louis."

"Oh," said Jim largely, "I wouldn't say that. Anyway, it turned out that piece of advice I gave him about the bullboat was a bad one."

Rich sat up straight, astonished. "But he did build the bullboats, he did float the stuff down to Henry's Fork and cache it, and then he went on down Green River clear beyond the Tewinty just to see what he could see."

One of the farm boys said, sneering, "Mose Harris was with you that time, and I never heard *him* say——"

"Boy," said Jim, "didn't I just tell you Mose was sleeping, along with the others? How's he going to know what I said to the General?"

A tall young man came catfooted out of the shadows. "Evenin'," he said, squatting down by the fire. He was hardly more than a boy himself, but there was nothing childish about the broad strong jaw and the quiet blue eyes. His name was Jim Bridger, and he had been in the mountains breaking new trails and seeing wonders while Jim Beckwourth was still hammering out horseshoes in Carson's forge. Bridger was another one like Fitz and Clyman for whom Jim had an enormous and envious respect.

"Boy," said Bridger, fixing the cotton-haired youth with a cold stare, "you got a lot to learn about manners." He turned to Rich. "And you ain't setting him much of an example. Where I was raised, one man didn't tread on another man's story."

"But——" said Rich.

Bridger said, straight-faced, "Why don't you wait your turn polite-like, and then you can tell us how *you* tried to warn the General about Grey Eyes at the Rickaree towns, and how *you* went in alone to parley with Bear, and how *you* took fifty men off the shore singlehanded after the fight started though there weren't no more than forty there to begin with as I ever heard."

The two older French-Canadians laughed. So did the farm boys. Baptiste just stared, and the Iroquois thought his own thoughts, whatever they were, behind a mask of fine weathered bronze. His name was Joseph. He was a Christian and spoke good English, but not often. Rich looked aggrievedly at Bridger.

"If you wasn't twice as big as me I might take it that you called me a liar and get mad." He waved at Jim. "Go on, go on."

"Yes," said the boy Baptiste. His English was broken and barbarous. "Go on, please. How was the advice bad?"

Jim glanced at Bridger, then solemnly shook his head. "Why," said Jim, "it almost got the General killed twice."

Rich's eyes opened wide, but he did not speak.

"How was that?" asked Bridger.

"Well," said Jim, "first time was when we were hunting buffalo for the hides. General's a fine shot, mind you. He'd just killed his animal when a bull somebody else had wounded started to charge him. His gun was empty and there he was with this great shaggy beast rushing down on him, snorting fire and fury—"

Baptiste was leaning so far forward now his elbows were almost in the coals. "What 'appen then?"

Jim said with quiet modesty, "Fortunately I turned and saw this in time. I dropped that bull with one shot, so close to the General that the bull's nose was almost touching his boots."

Baptiste exhaled a long shivering breath. He looked at Jim's rifle leaning against a tree. Rich shut his eyes. In a grave voice Bridger asked, "When was the second time?"

"After we built the first boat. The General stepped into it to test it, and the little rawhide line snapped. The boat went drifting away with the General in it, right into the Green River Suck."

"Suck?" said Rich under his breath. "Suck? We weren't

nowheres near the Suck!"

Bridger kicked him.

"The General was thrown into the water," Jim said, "and I knew he couldn't swim. There was only one thing to do. I plunged in—"

Rich sat stonily listening, while Jim described his terrible battle with the waters of the Suck while saving Ashley's life. Rich's expression changed gradually. Admiration crept in, much against his will. When Jim finished Rich shook his head. He looked at Bridger and muttered, "I got to admit it. He's going to be the greatest liar west of the Mississippi."

"Likely," Bridger agreed, "but there's them as'll give him a hard run."

"Meaning me?"

Bridger didn't answer that directly. He called out, "Harris! Mose Harris!"

Harris joined them. He had been back to St. Louis and then out again with the pack train of a hundred or more mules and horses that had come into Cache Valley two days ago. The General had led the train with Diah Smith and Bill Sublette. Diah had been his partner since last year's rendezvous, and now there were still greater changes afoot.

"Any news?" asked Rich.

"I guess it's all settled," Mose said, glancing toward a distant lodge. "The Old Man's been in there jawing with Bill and Diah for hours, and I seen Dave Jackson there too. Last time I looked in they were shaking hands all round."

Bridger shook his head. "First Major Henry and now the General. All these changes—it makes a man feel old."

Mose stifled a grin and turned to Rich. "That squaw of yours got something on the fire for a hungry man?"

Rich hollered out in Shoshoni and a minute later his wife Grass came with food from the cook-fire. She was a tall, strong, handsome woman, clean and a good housekeeper. Rich had taken her last winter, after a successful fall hunt. Now he always had good moccasins and fine-tanned skins for his clothing. His best shirt, which he was wearing now in honor of the rendezvous, was embroidered with dyed porcupine quills. Jim watched Grass as she moved around serving the men. In private she was smiling and cheerful with Rich, always there when he wanted her, content to recede into the background when he did not. Rich was more contented himself these days, a little less wasp-tongued and carping. Maybe I need a wife, Jim thought. Maybe that would take the restlessness out of me.

The men were talking about Ashley selling out to Smith, Jackson, and Sublette.

"Two years ago," Rich was saying irritably, as though the whole thing was a personal affront, "I could'a seen the sense of it if he'd give it away. But now we've got the Rocky Mountain Fur Company going like a house afire. Last year the General hauled enough prime beaver back to St. Louis to pay off all his debts and some left over. This year's catch'll make him rich. Why's he want to sell out now?"

"You just said it," Jim told him. "He's rich. Why would he want to stay? He's no mountain man, never pretended to be. He did what he had to do and he got what he wanted." The General and me, Jim thought, we both did what we had to do, and he got what he wanted. Will I? Because I haven't yet. What I want isn't as easy to get as money.

"He's got no more reason to stay."

"He just got married again, too," Mose said. "A right pretty woman. Why would he want to squat out here, staring at your ugly faces?" He grinned at them around the fire. "Anyway, talk has it he'll stay in the business this much—he's going to supply the new company."

One of the old French-Canadians made a rude gesture and said something in his own tongue.

Jim said, "What was that?"

The boy Baptiste translated. "He says, 'Now the prices will go up more.' "

"How's he know?" Rich demanded.

"Long time he traps. The Northwest Company, the HBC. He leave the HBC because never can he get out of debt. Last year at General Ashley's rendezvous he get good exchange for his furs. This year, not quite so good. Next year—" He finished with a shrug.

It was true that the prices of powder and lead, traps, tobacco, cloth, coffee, flour, and spirits had risen. The old man added a few more words. Baptiste smiled.

"He says if he had the brains of a donkey he would be in that part of the fur trade where the money is, selling traps in exchange for furs instead of furs for traps."

"Well," said Mose, "however it goes I reckon I'm bound to stay here. Been walking up and down the country so much my legs are stretched too long for the settlements. Why, do you know when I was in St. Louis this last time the General asked me to come to his house and danged if every time I started for it I didn't find myself clear out on the other side of town 'fore I knew it? Only way I could hold myself down that short was to git right down on my marrow bones and crawl, and even then I overshot her three times." He selected another piece of roast meat and settled himself comfortably. "Boys, did I ever tell you about how I found the Putrefied Forest? I was going along one day somewheres between the White Clay River and——"

Jim had heard Mose's story many times, about the putrefied trees all turned to stone, with a putrefied wind blowing through them and putrefied rabbits under them and putrefied birds in the branches singing putrefied songs. It was a good story. It was even partly true, at least about the trees. But he was suddenly not in the mood for any more stories, including his own. He got up, rising easily from the ground in one smooth movement.

"Where you going?" asked Rich, behind Mose's back.

"Got a few more plews in my possibles. Reckon I'll see if there's any medicine water left in the General's kegs."

He went into the lodge. He shared it with Rich and Grass, and such of Grass's relatives as happened to be visiting. Actually he rarely slept there except in bad weather, preferring to roll up in his blankets under the trees. There were eight Indians inside now, all from the large band of Snakes camped in the valley, Grass's people come in for the rendezvous.

Jim's winter outfit was wrapped and piled neatly, new traps to replace those lost, or broken, or stolen by Indians, enough powder and lead to last him until next rendezvous, a small hoard of luxuries like coffee and tobacco to last until they ran out. He had held back a few skins from the trading. He took them now and went out again, picking up his rifle not because he was likely to need it, but because he had got into the mountain habit of never leaving it farther away from him than he could leave his right hand. Men who did not learn this habit tended not to live long.

Cache Valley, on the western flank of the Wasatches above the Great Salt Lake, was one of those garden spots provided by the Almighty so that man in the wilderness might not totally lose hope. It was sixty miles long and anywhere from ten to twenty miles wide, so there was plenty of room in it. It had water and grass, fuel, and shelter from the winds, so that it was a good place to camp both winter and summer. The trappers had wintered here, sitting out the long bitter days between the fall and spring hunts, when the streams were frozen and the passes blocked with snow.

Now the willows were thick and rustling with summer. Everywhere in the dark there were fires, and nowhere in the dark was there any quiet. Ashley's liquor barrels had been thoroughly broached. The valley rang with laughter, with roars and whoops and howlings. A bunch of men stood around two others who were wrestling on the ground, laying bets and yelling them on. The wrestling match might stay friendly or it might not. There had been half a dozen fights so far in the two days that had needed to be broken up before somebody got killed. No matter who else might be drunk, violent, or careless, Diah Smith was always there to handle things, and the odd part of it was that he could handle them. Diah didn't do or say the things the other men did. He was never separated very far from his Bible. He talked like a preacher, and in some way he looked like one, too, in spite of his size and strength and the ugly scar he had across his head and face where a grizzly had torn his scalp off and Jim Clyman had stitched it on again, with the loose ear slightly askew. Perhaps it was his eyes. He always seemed to be looking somewhere far off, beyond the mountains, beyond anything you could see, and thinking of things that were private and important. But the men respected him. Nobody laughed at Diah's piety and nobody made fun of him when he disapproved of brawling and profanity. He was a man, and they knew it. He was a great man, and they knew it. They allowed him the right to his peculiarities.

Jim passed by the lodge where Diah Smith and Ashley and Sublette were concluding their arrangements. It was a time of breaking up, a time of change. Jim walked on. He wanted to think, but when he felt the edges of his thoughts they were painful and he pushed them away. A Cajun who had come a long way up the rivers from his native cane-brakes was playing *Sault Crapaud* on an old concertina. Two burly trappers whirled and pranced with their arms around each other until one of them tripped and they both went crashing into the fire, shooting up a fountain of sparks and ashes. Their comrades rolled on the ground howling with laughter while the two drunken men smoked and floundered. Beyond them a group of men were absorbed in playing the Indian hand game. They had their stakes piled on a blanket, things they had worked a year to buy. They did not look around even when the scorching drunks began to yell.

The packs of furs, mostly beaver, that would go back to St. Louis with the General were stacked together in a clearing. The stack was still growing even though the first rush of trade was over. A few parties were late coming in, and there were the free trappers and the Indians. Word of the 1825 rendezvous had spread though the mountains. The

Rocky Mountain Fur Company hoped to lure much of the free trade away from the distant forts, and now that the Platte route was a practical reality it looked to Jim as though they were likely to succeed. This rendezvous was many times bigger than the last. It was not going to make their fort-bound competitors happy.

He had to stand in line at the keg. Pretty soon he realized Rich was behind him.

"Thought you'd sworn off," Jim said.

"That was this morning." Rich shook out a prime otter skin, smoothing the sleek fur. "Foolish-time only comes once a year and a man ought to enjoy it. Besides, I want to be around when the trouble starts."

"What trouble?"

"The trouble you're fixing to make."

"Me?"

The line moved up.

"You. Oh, I ain't going to try and stop it, I just want to watch."

Jim told him where to go.

Rich grinned. "I know the look in your eye. You're feeling mean, and all you need is some of that chain lightning to kind of loose you up and let you go. I just want to see the fur fly."

The line moved again.

Jim made his trade for a double measure. The clerk gave it to him. He poured it down and handed the dipper back. Instantly his insides were on fire and his ears rang. He walked away. Rich calmly paid down his otter skin, calmly drank, and followed him.

Jim ignored him. He walked.

Rich walked after him.

Jim started through a little grove of trees. It was shadowy here and fairly private. He heard Rich padding behind him. He turned and made three long strides back and caught him.

"Maybe you're right. Maybe I do feel mean," he said. "And if you don't leave me alone it'll be your fur that's flying."

Rich made no move to push his hand away. He might have been unaware of it. He shook his head slowly from side to side, looking at Jim. "You're the contrariest cuss. You're not happy. What's it take to make you happy? You were howling because you couldn't be a man in St. Louis. You wanted to go west. Well, you're west. You're a man. What more do you want?"

Jim couldn't say what more he wanted. He dropped Rich and walked on.

Behind him Rich said, "If you figure everybody ought to like you whether or no, you're going to be a long time unhappy. All white men don't like all other white men. Ain't no man alive that everybody likes."

"I don't give a damn who likes me or doesn't like me."

"I'll tell you something else," Rich said. "A son-of-a-bitch is a son-of-a-bitch no matter if he's black, white, red, or green."

Jim stopped and turned around. "Meaning I am one?"

"Meaning you got what you came for. You're free as the wind. Be glad of it, and stop looking for trouble."

The whisky burned in Jim. Rich's face wavered, dim in the shadows of the grove.

Rich said, "You think no mutton-eared lout of a kid has ever spoke out of turn before?"

Jim thought he had forgotten the kid with the sneering voice. He had not.

"And anyway," Rich said, "those were some godawful big lies."

Jim hit him. Only it didn't connect. Rich had doubled up and jumped forward like a buck deer with his head down. He butted Jim square in the wind and Jim sat down, his mouth opening and closing and nothing coming through it, in or out.

"I taught you to trap and track and fight Indians," Rich said conversationally, "and I taught you to load a rifle on the run and to shoot a bow straighter'n most Indians, but it's only a fool teaches every trick he knows." He leaned against a tree, waiting.

Jim managed to suck in a ragged gasp of air. He got up on his knees, still gasping. Rich watched him. Finally he stood up. He stopped gasping and looked at Rich.

"Good-bye, Rich," he said.

"Ah," said Rich. "That's what you've been studying up to do these last few days. Why?"

"I don't want anyone around me that knows me that good."

"You ain't too hard to figure. Mostly."

"You taught me real good, Rich. Everything you said. I figure you and me are even."

"Maybe I don't."

"I'm saying it. I'll say something else, too. I can't abide a man that gives me good advice." He grinned. "I'm sorry I hit at you—and missed."

He walked on out of the grove. The heat was run out of him and he felt cold. He still felt as mean as ever but he no longer had any vague urge to do something about it. He had torn it up with Rich, that was done and he didn't have to think about it any more. Up to now he had needed Rich to teach him, and he could say that Rich owed him that much and it sounded all right. But from now on it would be different. From now on it would be hanging on, and he was damned if he would hang on to any man.

He hoped desperately that Rich in his shrewd prying mind hadn't figured out what was really prodding him.

It was a sore and shameful thing. It was a way for a child to feel and not a man. It enraged him. But he could not deny it.

He was cutting loose from the only friend he had. He wasn't sure he would ever have another.

The night wind blew fresh and clean across the stars. Free as the wind, Rich had said. Well, that was true. Even white men were not as free as this in the cities and towns. That was something. Jim stood still in a dark place listening to the wind. The man-noises and the fires were remote and small. He felt his body, a whole and hardy island enclosing him from the world-sea, complete in itself, deep with strength. There were wells in that island he had only barely drawn on, sufficient for his needs. There were worse things than being alone. You could live with that. You could be alone and still be proud.

He was saying good-bye to Rich because he chose to, but good-bye might be said for him any time by a Blackfoot arrow or a falling horse. Friends died like other men. Even wives and children did not belong to you. In the end the only thing you could depend on, the only sure strength you had, was yourself, because that was the only thing that truly belonged to you as long as you lived.

But the self that belonged to you had to be free while it lived, or it was nothing. And he was free.

The wind blew and the stars burned bright in the clean sky. He sat down to watch them, his back against a rock that still gave off the day's warmth into the summer night. After a while he slept.

He was roused up sharply into a cool mountain dawn. A string of mules and horses went pounding past him, running hard. He jumped to his feet. Horses were stampeding through the camp. Beyond the willows he could see parts of the huge herd belonging to the Snakes, broken into bunches and running wildly. There was a bedlam of voices, a ragged crackling of shots, and from the Snake lodges a screaming and wailing of women.

One word rose clear out of the confusion, repeated over and over. The word was "Blackfeet!"

TEN

J IM RAN TOWARD the shots and the shouting.

Everywhere men were picking themselves up, shaking the heavy sleep out of their eyes, grabbing rifles, cursing the loose horses that bolted and trampled among them. This was an old Blackfoot trick, to throw the enemy off balance by stampeding his herd. It meant that this was no sneak raid by a handful of hungry young men after horses. This was a war party, a large one meaning real business. They were far south and west of the Blackfoot country, but there was more than enough plunder here to lure them across the northern passes. Jim wondered if there was any place out here that was really safe from the Blackfeet. Probably not this side of the Rio Bravo.

The long mountain rifles began to crack, sharp and loud against the banging of the fusees. Jim found himself among the Snake lodges. Men, women, children, and dogs ran about. Picketed horses kicked and plunged. Balls from the Blackfoot smoothbores tore holes in lodge covers or plowed up dirt. Warriors were running with guns, with bows and quivers. Coming out between the lodges, Jim saw the Blackfeet. There were many of them, a hundred and fifty, two hundred, coming in a long ragged line. Puffs of smoke went up as they fired their fusees. They were painted for war, riding their best horses, the rich men in beautiful feather bonnets and fine war shirts, the poorer ones stripped to clout and moccasins, their personal war medicines bound in their hair or tied around their necks. Bright-painted shields caught the light. From time to time men would dash out from the line and race in close to the Snake camp, yelling and waving fresh scalps. Jim saw five of these, and three of them had belonged to women. Some small party had been out early digging roots or gathering wood, and the Blackfeet had caught them. Jim saw to his priming and fired.

One of the scalp-wavers doubled over his horse and rode back to the line. The attack swept in with a scream and a thunder of hoofs, leaving a wall of dust behind it. But the Snakes were enraged by the sight of the scalps. Among the lodges the families of the slain slashed themselves and bled and cried for vengeance. The warriors harangued each other and sang their war songs. They stood their ground. Those who owned guns fired them, and when the Blackfeet came within arrowshot the air suddenly flickered with arrows thick as minnows in a stream. The Blackfeet began using their bows from horseback. Men of the Snake warrior societies mounted and rode out toward the enemy, weaving and bending in the saddle as their horses ran. The line broke up. There were swirls of individual fighting. A Blackfoot warrior rushed in and struck a lodge cover at the edge of the village, counting coup, and was killed as he rode away.

The trappers' rifles, with far greater range and accuracy then the trade guns the Indians used, were beginning to make things hot and uncomfortable among the Blackfeet. It became obvious to the leaders that this first charge was not going to carry the encampment. While Jim watched and fired, the Blackfoot war party dissolved and flowed away and was not. There were three Snakes dead on the field and some wounded. The Blackfeet carried their dead and wounded with them so it was hard to tell their losses, but the only scalp the Snakes had to show for the battle was the one belonging to the man who had counted coup on the lodge cover.

Jim headed back toward Rich's tipi. The Snake warriors were now doing the things they had had no time to do before, painting themselves and tying on their medicines, singing their ritual songs. Those who owned medicine bundles opened them and prayed. The picketed horses were being saddled. These were the best, the long-winded fast-running buffalo horses, the war mounts, kept close to prevent them from being run off or easily stolen. Here and there a man painted his horse with symbols according to his dreams. In the trapper camp the men were making ready for war in their own way, cleaning rifles, eating, chasing horses, getting a tonic dram at the whisky barrel, laughing and cursing with a huge noise that shook the willows. Jim ran. The air was still cool on his face but the sun had a sting to it. He felt alive, sharp and tingling with life to his finger-ends, body and senses all tuned to perfect pitch. He was ravenously hungry.

He could hear Grass wailing long before he reached the lodge. Rich was outside where their own two best horses were picketed, saddling up.

"Some of her kin?" Jim asked.

"No, she's just being neighborly. Go on in, there's some cold meat in the pot."

Jim ducked inside. In the semi-darkness Grass was sitting with her hair over her face, howling. She paid no attention to Jim. One strong shaft of light fell through the smoke hole. Jim found meat and wolfed it down, then replenished his ammunition and picked up bow case and quiver. They were very handsome ones that he had paid one of Grass's many aunts to make for him. He went back outside and began to work with wiping stick and patches, cleaning his rifle.

"Saddle up for me, will you?" he asked Rich.

Rich grumbled but he started saddling Jim's roan. It was a Snake horse, big-barreled and slender-footed, and its Shoshoni name meant simply Roan Horse. Roan Horse had heard the firing and smelled the powder smoke on the wind. He knew what was up and he was dancing with eagerness. Rich's black-and-white paint was standing quieter with the saddle on him, but his one marled eye rolled wickedly. Jim looked at Rich as he worked. He was remembering last night, and he smiled.

Rich said crossly, "What're you grinning about?"

"You're my friend," Jim said. "I love you."

He was free of Rich, free of all man and womankind, so now he could say that and mean it. He felt that he had stumbled upon a great secret. You had to be free of all dependency before you could truly be any man's friend or any woman's lover. He wanted to explain this to Rich, and then he realized that of course Rich knew it. For the first time he felt complete equality with Rich, an equality that had nothing to do with race or even with experience. For the first time he felt easy with him.

Rich banged Roan Horse in the ribs to make him blow out the air he was holding, and pulled the cinch strap tight. "Last night you loved me so much you wanted to knock my teeth out."

"That's me," Jim said. "Contrary."

Rich swore. "Here on I'll stick to making enemies. They're easier to get along with." He looked out under Roan Horse's jaw. "Here comes Sits Alone."

Sits Alone was chief of this particular band of Snakes. He was quite old now, but he had been a great warrior in his time. Four of his principal men including his son Rainbow were with him. They rode into the center of the trappers' camp. Bill Sublette met them. Jim and Rich, along with most of the other men, drifted in closer to see what happened. Jim saw the General standing well in the background, leaning against a tree with his arms folded. This was no longer any business of his and he seemed content to let Sublette handle things. Jackson and the tall, somber Smith stood by.

Sits Alone talked. He told what the Blackfeet had done. He said that the long guns of the trappers had spoken well, but that it was one thing for a man to shoot a gun from cover and another thing entirely to engage the enemy in person. He said he had heard that the white men were brave warriors. He said that he would like now to see this proven.

Sublette answered properly in Shoshoni, and then shouted to the trappers in English.

"He wants to see if we can fight Blackfeet!"

The fierce clamor that went up seemed to satisfy the old man, who nodded and rode away. But the trappers did not need the Snakes to urge them on. The Blackfeet were mean Indians. They hated all white men, except the British traders north of the border. They hated all other Indians. They were constantly at war. On top of that they were brave, far-ranging, and damnation clever. There wasn't a man there, except the greenhorns, who had not been hunted for his life by the Blackfeet. There wasn't a man who had not lost a friend to them.

A long thin bearded man leaped high in the air, howling. "This child is for h'ar!" There was a rush for the horses. Jim could hear Sublette yelling out names, picking men to stay behind and guard the camp. Rich ducked aside behind a tipi which would cover him from Sublette's sight as he ran. "I don't dast let him call my name," he said. "And if he does call it, I don't dast to hear it. You back me up, Jim."

"Sure. But why are you so hell-fired up to fight Indians this morning?"

"It's Grass," said Rich sadly. "I'd as soon stay here, where it's comfortable. I don't hanker for a long ride and maybe an arrow through my guts this early in the morning.

But if I don't go I'll never hear the end of it from Grass."

"You're a poor put-upon soul," said Jim, grinning. He loosed Roan Horse's picket rope and mounted. He yelled *Hi-yah!* and Roan Horse leaped away running between the trees, out onto the open plain. Rich's paint was close behind him.

A quarter of a mile away the Blackfeet stood and watched them.

Jim looked over his shoulder. The mounted trappers were bursting out of the dappled green-gold shade into sunlight, brown men with long browned rifles glinting and long hair flying. American, Frenchman, Spaniard, breed, going to lift hair if they could catch it. They came out white from the settlements, but this was not white man's country, and pretty soon it was hard to tell them from the red men they lived and died among. Out of the Snake camp came more than a hundred braves, stripped for war, their bodies a clean copper splashed with red and yellow, black and white. Shield and quiver flashed back color in the sun. Feathers blew in the wind. Jim fired and then lifted the empty rifle over his head and shook it high, screaming like an eagle. Roan Horse stretched himself and flew, biting the wind. There was a drum roll of pounding hoofs, and the guns began to talk.

The Blackfeet fired back. Balls went whistling past Jim's ears. And now from among the Blackfeet a single brave came riding. He wore a fine war shirt and his gray horse had splendid trappings. At first he rode alone toward the Snakes and the trappers. Then four or five young men followed him, their naked bodies weaving back and forth in the saddle to give as little target as possible. The leading brave did not look back to see if anyone was with him. He was obviously a famous warrior, and this was how a man got glory in war, and why other men who wanted glory followed him. He came straight toward Jim.

The Blackfoot carried a round bull hide shield on his left arm and he had both bow and war club, but he was not using the bow. He did not wish to kill Jim at long range. The highest war honor was not the mere killing of an enemy but the act of striking his body or taking his weapons from him, because there was more danger in this. The war club was headed with stone, skin-covered, short-hafted, and deadly. Jim looked at it, feeling the powerful thrust of Roan Horse under him bearing him swiftly into combat. The gray Blackfoot horse raced toward him. Red symbols were painted on its hips and shoulders, red feathers fluttered from its knotted tail. The face of the rider became quite plain, the curved nose, the straight mouth and broad chin, dark bronze, with two deep lines cut from the nostrils to the corners of the mouth. Jim had never fought like this before. He was used to the horse raid and the sniping attack, used to shooting at half-seen targets beyond the campfire or across a narrow valley or in a clump of trees and being shot at in return, but you never saw your enemy close up until after he was dead, and maybe not even then. He flinched somehow from looking at the man's eyes, but when he did he saw that they were impersonal as the eyes of a butcher, measuring him for death. Jim's belly muscles pulled in tight. He watched the course of the oncoming gray. The horse was racing and yet it seemed to come on very slowly. Jim saw the foam flying from where the war bridle was knotted around its lower jaw. On Jim's head and shoulders the sun burned hot, but inside he was strangely cold. In his right hand he held his rifle delicately, balancing it.

The Blackfoot would go past him on the left, striking at him over the protection of the shield, or under it. All Jim had to counter with was his rifle and he wished to be very careful with it. He did not want it damaged if he could possibly help it. He had run buffalo on Roan Horse many times and he knew what he could do. At the last moment he checked and turned him squarely in front of the gray. The gray was a good horse, too. He squatted down and then jumped sideways like a cat. The flat pad saddle had neither horn nor cantle, but the Blackfoot stayed on it. He even managed to swing the club as Jim shot past him on the right, but he did not hit anything but air. The long barrel of the rifle, held sights-on like a spear, caught him in the navel and bore him back over the gray's rump. He fell hard onto the ground. Jim was out of the saddle and on him. He rammed his heel hard in the man's throat and reached for the club. He found it a very useful weapon.

There was no time to lift the scalp. The five young men were almost on top of him. Jim stuck the club in his belt and jumped for the saddle. Rich and Bridger came pounding up. Bridger fired and one of the young men went pitching to the ground, his arms flung wildly in the air. His pony ran away, the long war bridle unreeling behind from where it was folded under the warrior's belt. When it came to the final knot the pony stopped and stood shivering, anchored to the corpse but too well trained to drag it.

The others fired their fusees. Rich's paint horse went down but Rich himself fell free. He got onto one knee and took very careful aim. Jim was busy unslinging his bow.

He heard Rich's rifle crack and saw one of the warriors fall forward over his pony's neck. The pony ran away with the wounded man hanging to him. Bridger had dismounted and was reloading behind the shelter of his horse. Jim sent his arrows flying. He shot one man through the thigh but it didn't seem to discourage him. The three rode erratically, making poor targets, firing off their own arrows as they wished. They were using their bows now. Jim lay flat on Roan Horse as much as he could, making him jump back and forth.

The gray horse had backed off from his dead master, but not far. He was a good horse and well trained. His eyes rolled wildly. He stamped and shook froth from his jaw. Rich caught the trailing bridle and cut it free. The horse watched him. Rich tried to mount, Indian-fashion, from the right, but the gray laid his ears back and danced away. Jim shoved Roan Horse in against the gray to hold him and Rich sprang up agile as a monkey. Bridger fired from the ground. One of the Indian ponies fell. The unhorsed rider picked himself up and ran toward one of his comrades. Jim shot at him. The man stumbled but did not fall and the mounted man took him up behind. The pony galloped off carrying double. The man with the arrow in his thigh loosed off one more arrow and followed them. Jim let out a startled yell and squirmed his head around to see the back of his shoulder, where the buckskin shirt had been slit open as neatly as with a knife blade. Blood was already running down his arm.

Rich came up beside him, swearing at the gray horse in four Indian languages. He looked at Jim's shoulder. "Ain't much," he said. He handed Jim his rifle. "Load her for me.

I want to keep both hands on this critter yet awhile."

He fought it out with the gray horse while Jim rammed home powder and ball, wiping his left hand dry on his shirt from time to time. Bridger had mounted again. Half a dozen Snakes came up and jumped off their horses by the dead Blackfoot. They struck the body, counting coup, and then stripped it. They looked at Jim with great respect. "You will make a big song tonight," said one of them, fastening the scalp to his belt.

The Snakes rode away again. Bridger grinned at Jim. "You're an honor man now."

Jim looked down at the body. This had been a famous man, a great warrior. He had come to kill and plunder, to add to his long list of honors by doing to Jim what Jim had done to him instead. White men in the settlements prayed for a long life and a peaceful death, but an Indian prayed to die young, in battle. Jim felt that other, eastern world fading far behind him, with its fat tame cattle and tame green fields and the little rivers yoked with milldams. The plain spread around him shimmering in the sun, and on all sides were the mountains, high and hard and shining, making no difference between man, hawk, bear, or beaver, playing no favorites, taking no sides. The dry air smelled of crushed grasses, sun heat and blood and the sweat of horses. Some of the blood was his. It seemed right. The plain was covered with swirling knots of battle. There was a howling and a harsh screaming, men speaking with the voices of wolves and eagles. Jim took the captured war club out of his belt. He stood up in his stirrups and yelled, and Roan Horse, who loved war as much as he loved to run buffalo, neighed and ran.

ELEVEN

J IM LOST TRACK of Rich and Bridger. The fighting was broken and confused, hand-to-hand with friend and foe all mixed together and no clear lines drawn. But after a while something happened. The Blackfeet began to pull out. Pretty soon they were running, whipping their horses. The Snakes chased them fiercely. The trappers followed more leisurely, glad of a chance to smoke and clean their guns. Jim fell in with them and presently he found Rich again, still fighting the gray horse.

"I've lived with Indians so long I thought I smelled like one," Rich said, "but I reckon I don't. Or else there's a difference between tribes."

The gray horse crowhopped and swung his head around to bite at Rich's moccasined foot, temptingly barred in the narrow stirrup. Rich kicked him in the nose and grinned. "Ain't he a caution?"

"He's some," Jim said. He looked ahead at the flying Blackfeet. "They're in more of a hurry than they were this morning."

"Sun was on our side today. Their medicine was weak. Some of the young men went ahead of the war bundle, or else somebody did something to spoil the leader's personal medicine, rode on the wrong side of him or killed his spirit animal."

"You believe that?"

"They believe it." There was a fresh scalp at Jim's belt now and Rich looked at it. "Making quite a name for yourself today."

"They came looking for trouble," Jim said. "I'm just trying to see that they get it." He would have been content to quit now. He was dirty and hungry and tired and even Roan Horse was beginning to play out. But the Snakes were furies. This day their medicine was strong. It wasn't often that they had Blackfeet running from them. Generally it was the other way round, and there were many Snake scalps hanging from the lodgepoles beyond the Marias. They had a lot of vengeance coming.

All of a sudden Rich said, "Now watch."

The Blackfeet had been making for Bear Lake. Now Jim saw that there was a deep hollow at the edge of the lake, thickly grown with willows. The Blackfeet vanished into it. Almost immediately puffs of white smoke and the sound of shots came from among the trees. One Snake fell, and was picked up and borne away by comrades. Two or three others and some horses were wounded. The Snakes turned around and rode away. Rich grinned.

"Those Blackfeet," he said, "they're some."

The retreating Snakes merged with the trappers. Sublette was shouting, telling his men to spread out and pour rifle fire into the willows from long range, out of reach of the fusees. Jim and Rich picked a spot and dismounted. Bridger joined them. He looked at the willows, his head first on one side and then on the other.

"What do you think, Rich?"

"Waste of powder and lead. They're down inside that hollow like a breastwork, and the trees cover 'em."

"Bill knows that too," said Bridger. "I reckon he's just wanting to look good for our friends. Well, I don't mind wasting a little powder. Might even get lucky and hit something."

They fired one by one into the willows. The sun was hot and there was no shade. The blood on Jim's arm had caked hard and the gash on his shoulder pulled and stung.

He looked up to see Rainbow and three others coming toward them.

Their horses were all rimed with sweat. Rainbow's fine white war shirt with the brilliant quillwork on it was stained and dulled. On the bare bodies of the other men the painted designs had run together, mingled with dust and blood. They stopped, and Rainbow looked down at Jim.

"A Snake has been killed," he said. "Steps-from-the-water is dead."

Jim did not know Steps-from-the-water but he must have been the man the Blackfeet shot when they took to the willows.

"We wish to have revenge," said Rainbow.

In fairly good Shoshoni Jim said, "Many scalps have already been taken." He pointed over the plain. "Look, the Blackfeet could not carry all their dead. The Snakes have fought like men today. Their women will dance tonight."

"The women of Steps-from-the-water's lodge will not dance. They will gash themselves and go about crying continually unless there is Blackfoot hair to dry their eyes."

Other Snakes had died today, but apparently they had been paid for. Jim contemplated the willows, the deep protected hollow beside the lake. Rich and Bridger stood by, politely silent.

"You're a war chief, Rainbow. You have so many honors it takes a day to tell them. Why do you come to me?"

"You have a name now. Formerly you do not have a

name, but now you are named Bloody Arm. You struck the first coup. Your medicine is good, that is why."

Rainbow was a handsome man, tall and well-made. He wore a little stuffed hawk tied in his forelock, his personal war medicine. Sitting on his red horse he looked as though Sun had made him out of the red rock and then set him free. He watched Jim with dark, proud eyes. He did not speak again.

After a moment Jim said, "Thanks. I'll come."

He nodded to Rich and Bridger and mounted. He rode off with Rainbow and the three braves. He felt hot and flushed with pride. Part of his mind stood aside and laughed, and he couldn't blame it. He was prancing out on a fool's errand with a bunch of savages and he was more than likely to get himself killed, all because he wanted to show off. You could put it that way, he knew, and you might be right. But you could put it another way, too. "Formerly you did not have a name," Rainbow had said, "but now you are named." Better than any white man Jim understood the importance of a name. Formerly, he thought, I did not really have a name, even though I claimed one, even though I am my father's son. Formerly I had an earmark, a stamp of ownership. Now I am named, with a name I earned.

He rode tall beside Rainbow in the sun and forgot that he was tired.

"How shall we do this?" he asked.

Rainbow said, "We will ride over behind that little rise of land where they can't see us. Small Belly will stay there and hold the horses. There's a fold in the land where the water runs down in the spring. It comes close to the hollow where our enemies are. If we crawl carefully like snakes they won't notice us."

"Maybe," thought Jim cynically. But when they were over the rise that hid them from the Blackfeet he handed Roan Horse's rein to Small Belly and slid down flat after Rainbow.

The fold in the land, of which the little rise was the head, was simply a natural drainage channel that carried the runoff of melting snow and spring rain to the lake. It was dry now, grown up with tall grass. Jim hugged the bottom, his forward horizon filled by the soles of Rainbow's moccasins and the muscular working humps of his buttocks. It was excessively hot down there below the wind and the rifle had to be watched constantly to keep it from clinking against the rocks that hid treacherously in the grass. In the outside world the rifles cracked steadily. Jim hoped the Blackfeet would be too busy watching the visible enemy to pay attention to anything else.

A very long time later, Rainbow stopped and Jim saw the waters of the lake beyond him. They lay still. Close by Jim could hear the Blackfeet talking. His mouth was dry. His heart pounded against the ground, shaking him.

Rainbow squirmed carefully around until he was crouched against the slope of the bank. Jim followed suit. Somewhere among the willows horses stamped and whickered. They sounded very close. The top of the bank ended in a fringe of grass against the sky. He could not see what was beyond it.

After a moment he realized that Rainbow was waiting for him to move. My medicine is good, he thought, that is why. He hoped Rainbow was right.

Slowly, very slowly, he inched himself up the bank until his face was thrust among the grasses at the top and he could see.

He could see the rim of the hollow perhaps ten feet away. He could not see down into the hollow because he was a little below the rim, but he could see the willows now as separate trees with spaces between them. Rifle balls went whistling and thunking among them, showering down leaves but not doing any other damage. The Blackfeet were laying low.

Suddenly, for no reason at all, Jim felt easy and confident. My medicine is good, he thought. I know it.

He nodded to Rainbow and went with a smooth rush over the top of the bank and toward the hollow.

The rim ceased to be a sharp line and became the rounded top of a slope that dropped down like the side of a big bowl. Inside the bowl there were men and horses. Some of the men were wounded. Some were tired and sat or lay about. Most of them were ranged around the curve of the bowl that was nearest the enemy, protected by the bank but watchful, waiting for attack. Jim was somewhat behind these and they did not immediately see him. He was almost at the rim when the man closest to him let out a startled "Huh!" and sprang up firing his fusee. The ball went high and Jim shot without shouldering the rifle. The man doubled up and fell forward over the top of the bank. There was much noise now in the hollow. Jim dropped flat, grabbing for the dead man's outflung arm. He pulled with all his might. Blackfeet came bounding up the side of the hollow toward him. There was a sudden burst of firing from behind him, one gun quite close, two farther back, and a yelling of Snake war cries. The Blackfeet took cover again, startled for the moment into thinking that they had been flanked by a large party. Rainbow came beside Jim and caught the other arm. Together they dragged the dead Blackfoot toward the channel.

Enraged by the sight, the Blackfeet began another charge. The two young Snakes had reloaded. They appeared, yelling, and fired. This time the Blackfeet did not stop. Jim and Rainbow felt the ditch open behind them. They fell into it, still hanging doggedly to the body. Balls and arrows whistled over them too close for comfort. Jim dropped his rifle from his free hand and pulled out his knife, ready for close fighting. But it did not come. The trappers finally had some targets to shoot at. There was a heavy burst of rifle fire and the Blackfeet vanished again into the shelter of the willows.

In what seemed a deafening silence, Jim and Rainbow hauled the body into the ditch.

The young Snakes began stripping the dead Blackfoot. Jim rammed powder and ball into his rifle as fast as he could on the grounds that somebody ought to have a loaded weapon. The Snakes had all dropped theirs. From far away he heard a wild clamor of shouting, Rainbow's tribesmen yelling triumph and insult at the enemy. Rainbow kneeled between the Blackfoot's shoulders. The man's two thick black braids lay spread in the grass. At the back of his head just below the crown there was a third braid, a thin one carefully tied and decorated with beads. This was the scalp lock. Rainbow grasped it and pulled it straight out with his left hand. His right hand held the knife.

Moving away from the body, Rainbow said, "Steps-from-the-water's women will dance tonight. His mother's tears will dry quickly."

They began the long crawl back to where Small Belly waited with the horses. The Blackfeet did not come out again to challenge the long rifles.

With Rainbow and the others Jim rode back to where he had left Rich and Bridger. He did not know whether the trappers were watching him with admiration or not. He was too proud to look. Rainbow saluted him and went on with the others to join the Snakes. They sang victory songs as they rode.

Rich said sourly, "What are you going to do next?"

Jim grinned and shook his head. "Not a damn thing." Roan Horse had run all the fire out of himself. Jim patted the sweaty neck. "We're through."

"I think," said Bridger, "just about everybody is through."

The men had been fighting since daybreak. They were thirsty, tired, hungry, and now the fight had turned into a stalemate, they were rapidly getting bored. An attack on the hollow would cost far more lives than either the trappers or the Snakes were interested in giving. They had won a victory, a big one, and there did not seem to be any more reason to hang around in the dust and sun, wasting powder. The trappers went back to camp, and the Snakes came with them.

Later in the afternoon a party rode back out to Bear Lake and Jim went with them, curious to see what had happened. The Blackfeet were gone. They had taken their wounded with them, and such few of their dead as they had been able to carry. They had a long hard trail ahead of them, north and east over the mountain passes and along the valleys and across the rivers, home. They would bury their dead along the way, Indian-fashion, in the wind-shaken branches of trees, and some of the wounded would inevitably join them. By the time they reached their villages on the Marias it would be time for the fall buffalo hunt and the move to winter quarters, and the passes would soon be blocked with snow. There would not be any more big Blackfoot war parties in the mountains until next summer.

That night the dancing began. It went on for three days, and for three days Jim was drunk, not on liquor but on excitement and a curiously satisfying kind of glory. In the Snake camp the drums pounded and the women danced the scalp dance, danced victory and revenge all night long until they fell out exhausted and slept a while and then rose to dance again. Grass was among them. The trappers joined the celebration wholeheartedly. It was their victory too, and in some ways they were wilder than their red brothers. But Jim sat with the Snakes, among the honor men, the coup-strikers, and not among the lesser ranks of these but among the highest, beside the leaders and the famous men.

Sitting here, he could see the world the way they saw it, painted strong in the colors of earth and sky, with the patterns for living and dying laid out clearly, simple patterns with no barriers in them that a man could not climb over if he wanted to. If a man lacked courage, if he was foolish or lazy or dishonest or if he broke certain tribal laws, he was going to be in trouble. Otherwise, there was nothing to stop him from being a chief, if he could earn the position. Even a captive, a person from another tribe, could do this. It was a cruel, harsh life in many ways and he knew what Francie would think about it, but it called to him as it had called before in the Pawnee town, only now the call was louder. He let the pounding drums hypnotize him. He feasted with the men and pretended he was one of them. But he knew that he was not, and he went back to Rich's lodge to sleep.

Sometime late on the third day he woke up to find the lodge full of strange Indians. There were six of them, sitting in a solemn semicircle staring at him. Grass had taken time enough off from her dancing to cook some food and she was serving it, looking pretty much the worse for wear. Rich had been in the trader's barrel and been in it deep. He had the half-merry, half-malicious look that he always got at a certain stage of drunkenness.

"My friends the Crows," he said. "They wanted to see the mighty warrior Bloody Arm who counted so many coups on the Blackfeet." He smiled at the Indians, cursing them at the same time in the friendliest tones. "Worse than that, they had to hear the story. Over. And over. Bloody Arm Beckwourth, I have had a bellyful of you."

Jim sat up and saluted the Crows, who continued to stare at him. "How did they find out about it?"

"Cut the Blackfoot trail on their way here. Found some dead ones they'd left behind. Crow and Blackfoot—" he made a slitting motion across his throat. "Crows are horse-rich, Blackfeet are horse-poor, and Crow range is right next to Blackfoot range, south. Bad combination. So they were happy. They were real happy when they saw the battlefield. Then they got talking to some of the Snakes that speak Crow, and nothing would do but they had to see you."

Jim didn't want to show it but he was secretly pleased.

"Man could do a sensible thing," Rich grumbled.

"Something important, something that really mattered, and these nit-heads wouldn't pay it any mind at all. But a man does a thing like you crawling down that ditch and hauling a Blackfoot out of the timber, and they think that's some." He looked at Jim, his head on one side, mocking and bright-eyed as a fox. "Hell, you're no better than they are. You think it's some, too."

"What if I do?" asked Jim quietly.

"Nothing. Not a damn thing. Only it sure is a pity."

"What is?"

"You weren't born red instead of black-and-white. Well, go ahead, Bloody Arm. They're waiting."

It was not lodge etiquette to start a fight in the presence of guests, so Jim only said, "Go ahead with what?"

"Sing your victory song. Trot out all your honors. Tell how you got 'em. They've heard the story twenty times from me but they want to hear it from you. Go ahead."

"You know I don't talk Crow."

"I do, so talk anything you want. Only make it good. Do it like an Indian. They won't think you're boasting."

Jim gave Rich a black hard look, irritated by his needling. But the Crows were waiting, watching respectfully. Jim stiffened his back. In English, augmented by what he knew of the sign language which was not much, he began his story.

It did sound boastful. It sounded in fact a little ridiculous. English was the wrong language. Jim got madder and madder at Rich, who was translating, keeping his face as grave as though he was an official interpreter at a treaty council. He's laughing at me, Jim thought. He switched to Shoshoni, which apparently the Crows understood no better than they did English, and which Jim did not speak nearly as well, but the words fitted the deeds much better. He began to enjoy himself. All right, he thought, looking at Rich. Go ahead and laugh. I like to boast. I like to feel big. And anyway I did these things.

He made the story good, Indian-style, but he was careful not to add anything that had not really happened. Lying about a coup was something no Indian ever did unless he wanted to die on his next warpath. It brought the worst kind of bad luck, and anyway, everybody knew it was a lie. He finished.

Rich repeated Jim's closing words. He sat silent for a moment, looking at the Crows with his bright foxy look as though he was thinking about something. Then he smiled and talked some more. The Crows clapped their hands over their mouths and their eyes widened in astonishment. They stared at Jim harder than ever, while one of them talked excitedly with Rich.

Jim asked, "What are you telling them?"

Rich turned to him a look curiously blended of malice and affection. "You're not happy friend. I'm making you a present." He laughed. He was a very drunken man. "Come on, let's get back to the dancing." He rose and went toward the entrance. The drums were going again. Grass had already slipped away. Jim went with Rich and the Crows back to the Snake camp. After a while he lost track of Rich, but for a long time the Crows stood watching him.

That was the end of the rendezvous. The trading was done. It was time for the parties to move out again on their way to the fall trapping grounds, time for the pack train to head homeward along the Platte with its rich lading of furs.

Ashley made a speech. He said good-bye to the mountains, and to the men who had helped him conquer them. Now that he was leaving them to return to his real life, free of debt and with money in the bank, he felt a warm sense of love, even of gratitude, toward both the mountains and the men. And he was touched almost to tears by the response he got. Whatever his faults and whatever his failings, he had managed to earn the respect of this hard-nosed, hard-handed bunch of individualists. He did not understand them entirely. They had a wildness in them that he did not have, and did not want, but in a way he envied them. To have led them was an honor.

Even Beckwourth, he thought, the bastard. I can't forgive him. But I have to admit he has all the courage he needs to back up his gall. If I were in his shoes, I wonder—

But I'm not, he thought, thank God.

He shook Jim's hand along with the rest of them and wished him well, and rode out of Cache Valley for the last time.

The trappers' brigades formed up. Grass took down the lodge and packed it. She would stay with her own people and wait for Rich to join her when the fall hunt was over. For the first time Jim and Rich were going with different parties, in different directions.

"See you at rendezvous," Rich said, and Jim nodded. He said, "Keep your head down and your powder dry." Rich had the gray horse pretty well trained now. Jim watched him ride off, and then went over to his own group. It included Bridger, and Jim was surprised when Bridger motioned to him to fall in beside him. He did so, and the party passed out of the valley and headed east, toward the Green.

It was perhaps ten days later that Jim and Bridger went out to hunt some fresh meat for the pot. They separated to work both sides of a ridge. Jim rode for an hour or two, seeing no sign of game, and had about concluded to cross the ridge when he saw Indians coming toward him. There were six of them. They all had their weapons slung and the leader's hand was raised in the sign of peace. Jim recognized the six Crows who had been in Rich's lodge.

They rode up to him and stood around him in a ring. The leader spoke to him, but Jim shook his head and signaled that he did not understand. He felt deeply uneasy. The Crow nation was friendly. Beyond the inevitable lifting of horses by the young men, the trappers had no trouble with them and Jim did not expect any now, nor did he intend to start any. But he thought it was strange that the same six should turn up like this, almost as though they had followed him. With a twinge of panic, he wondered suddenly what crazy thing Rich had said to them that day.

The leader spoke again. Jim shook his head some more, smiling. He turned Roan Horse around, gesturing for the Crows to come with him back to camp. But all of a sudden there were two fusees stuck in his flanks and another man was holding his bridle. They all seemed very respectful. He wondered if they really would pull those triggers. But when they put out their hands to take his weapons he decided not to find out. He surrendered.

Five minutes later he was riding away from the camp, away from Bridger, away from the white man's world. His six captors rode tight around him. The leader swept an arm northeast and said one word, a word that Jim recognized.

"Absaroka!"

TWELVE

IT WAS STILL the golden time between summer and the first snow when Jim Beckwourth came to Absaroka.

His captors had traveled fast, bringing him by ways he did not know and that he thought probably no white man knew, through the passes of the Wind River range and down into the great basin where the Big Horn headed, and on until a tremendous peak hung over the land like a shining cloud and Jim knew he was looking at the southeastern buttresses of the Big Horn mountains. Rich had trapped this country, roaming over a good part of it with his Crow wife and her people, and Jim had got a grasp on the geography from listening to his stories. They crossed a bitter, muddy river that Jim knew must be the Powder and turned north, with the snow peaks of the mountain rampart on their left hands and the sage desert on their right. They crossed a second muddy stream, and after a while one of the six Crows left them and rode ahead.

At a certain place the men stopped and gave him back his weapons, the rifle unloaded but otherwise all intact. They rode on again, a little faster now.

Rich had told him how it was in this place, but even so Jim was caught by surprise. The change was so abrupt, almost as though God had drawn a line with a stick and said, "Here shall be the end of the desert and the beginning of Eden." Sage and sand vanished, the bitter yellow streams were gone. Bright water rushed down cold and pure from the snow fields. There was grass, and timber, berries and wild fruits, and every kind of game. It was in this rich green land under the splendid wall of mountains that Jim first saw the lodges of the Crows.

At a solemn pace now, singing, the five braves brought him into the village.

The man who had ridden ahead had brought important news, that was obvious. Heralds were going among the lodges, crying out some message to the farthest reaches of the camp and already there were throngs of people waiting, with more coming every minute. The people seemed intensely excited and many of the women wept. Jim sat erect and proud, but inside he was shaking. He remembered Rich's face, the sly mischievous drunken way he looked when he talked to the Crows. "You're not happy," he had said. "I'm making you a present." For the ten-thousandth time Jim wished that he had got Rich down and beaten out of him what he said to the Crows, instead of tamely forgetting about it. If, that is, Rich could have remembered what he said after he sobered up.

They made him get down off his horse and enter one of the lodges, a large one that he guessed must belong to the chief. The crowd, especially the women, would have followed him but they were held back. Inside the lodge there were forty men seated, all the principal men of the village, Jim thought. He was conducted to an empty place on the left hand of a tall and handsome man of middle years who wore his hair rolled up into an elaborately decorated rawhide cylinder, which he carried in the fold of his robe. The other men wore their hair unbraided and falling loose over their shoulders, after the Crow fashion, and Jim knew that he was in the presence of Long Hair, chief of the Main Band, whose hair was ten miraculous feet long, and his personal medicine.

Long Hair motioned him to sit, and Jim sat. The forty eagle faces watched him with forty pairs of piercing eyes. He felt the sweat coming out on his forehead and was horrified lest someone should notice it and think it was a sign of fear. It was.

Long Hair said something, and a young man repeated the words in Shoshoni.

" 'I see you,' he is saying. 'Already I am well,' he is saying."

Jim understood that this was a welcome, and relaxed a little. "Why," he asked in Shoshoni, "have I been brought before Long Hair like a prisoner? When did I offend the Absaroka?"

The interpreter exchanged some talk with Long Hair and said, " 'We were afraid,' he is saying. 'You had lived so long in the lodges of the white man you might have forgotten you were a Crow. You might not have wished to return to your people,' he is saying."

Jim sat perfectly still, his mind racing. You're not happy, Rich had said, I'm making you a present. Pity you weren't born red instead of black-and-white.

Jim Beckwourth, the Crow?

Holding his voice steady, Jim asked, "You heard of this from my friend in the trappers' camp?"

"Yes."

"How much did he tell you?"

"Talks-all-the-time has told how as a little one still riding the travois, you were captured by the Cheyennes in the great battle more than twenty summers ago, when our men were killed and many of our women and children taken captive. Talks-all-the-time has told how the Cheyennes sold you to white men on the Big River and how ever since you have lived in their villages and learned their wisdom."

Talks-all-the-time had done well, Jim thought, and was not surprised that Rich had never told him his Crow name.

"It is true," Jim said cautiously, "I've been with the white man a long time." Would they really believe this story? On nothing more than Rich's word?

Long Hair was speaking through the interpreter. "But when you fought against the Blackfeet you fought like a Crow. You struck a first coup. You were wounded in battle. You killed three men. You took a weapon. You charged the enemy in a strong place and dragged him out. While the white men stood back you did this. Turn your back you did not. Run away you did not. Because of you the Snake women danced strongly. You fought like a Crow. Our hearts were made big when we heard of this. That's why we took you and brought you here. Now we ask you to smoke."

Long Hair lit the pipe and passed it, and Jim smoked. He had time to think while the pipe went round the circle. He could deny what Rich had told them but now he was sure that they would not believe him. They would think that he was denying his Crow blood because he was ashamed of it, and they might even get angry enough to kill him.

I'm making you a present, Rich had said. A present of a people who would accept him wholly and without question as one of their own.

Why shouldn't he take it?

Long Hair raised his hand and spoke, and the door flaps were thrown open. Jim saw a line of women outside. They surged forward, and the interpreter beckoned to Jim.

"Stand in the light where they can see you clearly."

Jim asked, "Who are these?"

"The Crow mothers who lost their sons that time. Perhaps one of them is yours."

Jim looked at the women, the long line of them hoping for a miracle, and his heart failed him. The men he could deceive because he wasn't cheating them of anything—he would simply be one brave among other braves, on his own feet, stand or fall. But this was too cruel. He started to protest, to tell the truth, but the interpreter was already speaking for the first woman. " 'If this is my son, he has a small scar on his left side beneath the rib.' Take off your shirt and let her see." Jim looked again at the women. It was too late, it had been too late when the news first came into the village. Their hopes had been roused and their disappointment would not be any the less now even if he was able to convince them that the whole thing was a fraud. He took off his shirt.

The woman examined his side, shook her head sadly, and passed on. One by one the others followed, looking for this or that mark they remembered or simply trying to see in the man the shadow of the lost child. One by one they passed. And then there came one who said, "If this is my son he has a little mole on his left eyelid."

Jim broke out in sweat. He wanted desperately to run, but inexorably the woman's work-hardened, gentle fingers touched his eyelid and pulled it down and he knew what she was going to find there. It wasn't really much of a coincidence. Many people have moles and there are only a certain number of areas on a human being, so that give enough people some of them are bound to be roughly duplicated.

And at a distance of more than twenty years, how could even a mother say whether or not the match was exact?

Especially a mother who wants with all her heart to believe that it is.

In a sort of daze Jim heard the cry go up and felt her arms flung around him, and then everybody was shouting together, and Jim thought, Oh Lord, what have I got myself into? He looked down into the face of his new-found "mother," a broad honest squaw face with tears running down over the cheekbones, and he remembered his own mother and how small and pinched she had looked when the fever took her, and how he had cried because she was his only real friend in all that big house. He felt mean to be standing here lying to this Indian woman. And then he saw how happy she was, and it occurred to him that he hadn't ever made any single soul that happy before in his whole life. She looked like a good woman. What the hell, he thought, let's be happy together, and he put his arms around her and held her tight, and her hot tears went trickling down his chest.

There was a terrible lot of talking going on and he couldn't understand any of it, but presently the whole population seemed to be carrying them along through the village, with a few running ahead. The interpreter had stayed close. He said to Jim in Shoshoni, "They are going ahead to tell Big Bowl to make ready his lodge to receive his son."

Jim asked, "What is my mother's name?"

"Captures-white-horses."

"But isn't that a man's name?"

"She was named by her uncle," the interpreter said, "for one of his own deeds. It is a custom."

"I have a lot to learn," Jim said. He looked at the young man and smiled. "Stay by me."

"Gladly." The young man smiled back. He had good features and fine intelligent eyes, but Jim noticed that he was poorly dressed, his shirt, leggings, and moccasins without ornament and his blanket very old and worn. "My name," he said, "is Young Bear."

The crowd swept on, bearing Jim and Captures-white-horses with it, and presently Jim found himself inside a good-sized and well-furnished tipi packed to the walls with people all trying to get hold of him at once, women crying and embracing him, men embracing him and making speeches, and one lean, middle-aged man in particular, whom Jim took to be Big Bowl, alternately weeping and addressing the crowd in what managed to be a strangely dignified and affecting way, between holding Jim's arms and looking at him as his own father never had, with pride and love. Again Jim felt shabby and mean to be deceiving these people, but he thought, They're better off with me than with no son at all.

With Young Bear's help he got his immediate family sorted out, chiefly four pretty and still unmarried young sisters. The lost child, it seemed, had been the only son, though there were other "sons" who were actually nephews. There was a welter of uncles and aunts and clan connections among whom Jim got hopelessly lost, but there would be time for them later. Big Bowl invited everyone to a feast on the following night and the relatives began to thin out. Young Bear said tactfully, "You will not need me for a while." He left, and in a little while Jim was alone with his family.

It was a strange experience.

He had had his mother for almost ten years, and he had loved her, but perversely, because he was unattainable, he had loved his father more. It was an unsatisfactory love and completely wasted. He had two sisters, but they were older than he and he hardly remembered them as children. They had been sent away early to begin their careers, and were now very proper lady's maids, who hadn't had much to say to him on the rare occasions when he'd looked them up. Now he sat in this skin tent under the Big Horns and felt himself regarded for the first time as a true son and a true brother.

He understood that these people could not possibly know him or love him as himself and that he was only being given what belonged to their lost Antelope of unknown fate. But it was a good feeling even so. It was easy to let the true past slip away, to pretend and half believe that he really was the Antelope come home.

It was a strange present that Dave Richards had given him. Happily, contentedly, Jim began his life as an Indian.

The white man's world receded, but it did not disappear. It could not. It was already too much a part of the Indian's world. Jim still needed powder and shot, whatever else he might have done without, and so did all the Absaroka, and there was only one way to get it. When he was not taking the war road, winning his spurs in the Crow chivalry, Jim trapped beaver in company with Young Bear and such of the other men as could be talked into it. They had traps but buffalo robes were valuable too and they preferred hunting. They had a place to trade.

"After the first white men left the old fort it was very bad for us," Young Bear said, referring to Henry. "But others came, and now there is a new fort and we have all we need."

Back in the days when he was a white trapper, or a partly white trapper, and not an Indian, Jim had heard about an outfit called the American Fur Company that was supposed to be almighty big and powerful, with a lot of eastern money behind it, and he had also heard about a man named McKenzie, who first fought the company and then joined it, and was not loved by a lot of the trappers because it was rumored that he was too friendly with the Blackfeet. Actually, Jim found out, it was simply that McKenzie was a Canadian, so the Blackfeet hated him one notch less than they hated the American Henry, and McKenzie had a lot more men to hold the fort than Henry had had. So there was again a trading post at the mouth of the Yellowstone, and it was there that the Antelope went in time with his people.

The Antelope had been "home" for more than a year now. Every vestige of the white man's world was gone. Dressed and painted as a Crow among Crows, he stood with Young Bear at Fort Union and watched the bargaining. The man in charge of the fort was named James Kipp, a leathery veteran of the trade, and he did not cheat the Indians, but he did not shower them with generosity, either. When it came Jim's turn to barter his furs he let Kipp go on for a moment and then said quietly in English, "These are prime plews, and if you want 'em you'll have to pay for 'em. Five dollars St. Louis, three dollars mountain. Or I take them back."

Kipp stared at him with his mouth hanging open. "What the hell?" he said. "Who the hell . . . ?"

Jim told him.

"You don't say," said Kipp. He looked from Jim to the assembled Crows, who were watching the dialogue, tremendously impressed. Kipp drummed his fingers for a moment, thinking. "Mr. Beckwourth," he said, "I think we might make an even better arrangement. Come inside."

When Jim rode away from Fort Union he was on the company's payroll as a resident trader among the Crow, and in addition to the liberal return Kipp had made him on his furs he had four pack horses loaded with trade goods advanced by the company. The Absaroka looked upon him with a new respect. The Antelope, the Bloody Arm, was not only a great warrior but he spoke to the white men on their own ground, in their own tongue, and the white men listened, and put wealth in his hands. Truly the Antelope was *batse-tse,* a great man, a chief.

Jim knew what Rich would say. "You ain't content with just being an Indian, you got show 'em you're a little smarter than what they are. You ain't never content to be just as good as anything, you always got to be a little bit better." Maybe. But in this case he had the advantage and he might as well use it. He could make himself look ten feet tall to the Crows, and help them while he was doing it.

The Ashley men had gone over the mountains. They were far away, and the land was so wide and the rivers so many that it only crossed Jim's mind once that some day the Ashley men might come up hard against the giant company that had taken over the whole Missouri.

It didn't seem worth worrying about, even when he realized that if it ever happened he would be caught squarely in the middle.

THIRTEEN

I T WAS HIGH summer, the time of yellow grass. The Crow counted four seasons, Green Grass, Yellow Grass, Leaf Falling, and Snow Falling, and the yellow grass time was the best of all. The land was open then under the hot winds, the rivers were fordable, the buffalo were fat and the ponies sturdy. Ambitious men went raiding all the year round, in rain and snow and bitter cold, but the yellow grass time was the bright season of the war road.

Jim looked over at Young Bear and smiled. They rode in a cloud of dust kicked up by the hoofs of fifty-odd horses which had lately belonged to the Cheyennes. They rode bareback. Horse raiders always went on foot, making it a point of honor to provide themselves with mounts for the journey home, so it was impossible to carry a saddle. They had ridden two nights and a day from the Cheyenne camp without stopping except to change mounts. After that they had driven the herd more slowly, but by then everybody was suffering from the inevitable wounds of the successful horse raid. Every once in a while Jim or Young Bear or one of the eight other warriors would get down stiffly and walk a while.

But if their backsides were blistered, their hearts were high. Young Bear and two others had won honors, cutting out picketed horses from the enemy camp. Jim had picked out a bunch, probably belonging to a single individual, that looked above average for loose stock, and run them off. By way of an added gift of fortune, they had encountered three members of a Cheyenne raiding party butchering a buffalo and killed them all. Most important, nobody had been hurt. Jim carried the pipe this time, which meant that all the responsibility was his, and the success would add very nicely to the Antelope's honors and prestige.

The Antelope had done well. Jim was not more brave than most of the Crow warriors. Nobody could be. But he was not bound by their rigid traditions and habits of thought. By a simple application of the white man's methods of fighting he gained great success on the war road. He struck the coups required to make him a chief, which meant that he had earned his spurs as a war captain. In addition to this, because of his association with Kipp, he was able to get his people better returns for their furs than they had ever had.

These things were his own doing, but part of his success was in the lucky accident of his "family." It was large, and to an Indian relatives were power. The worst thing a Crow could be was an orphan without relations. That had been Young Bear's curse, and because of it he remained poor and undistinguished until—after they had become firm friends anyway in the course of Jim's education—Young Bear proposed that he and Jim become blood brothers. Jim was happy to agree, and by this simple but solemn ritual of adoption he gained a brother, Big Bowl a second son, and Young Bear a family, as firmly as though born into it. Now Young Bear was a distinguished warrior, owning many horses, and was one more in the powerful clique that Jim could call on to back him when he needed it.

There was one other thing as important as family in gaining influence, and that was generosity. Big Bowl had always had a name for it, and Jim added to that name as well as his own by the wealth he gained in these horse raids. A plains Indian counted his fortune in horses. With them he hunted his meat, moved his family, carried his sick, and transported his house with all its furniture and supplies. Most of what he purchased was paid for in horses—the bride price, the services of a doctor, special ceremonies, powerful medicines for the war road. Horses were gifts and largess to be distributed with an open hand, and they were as good for bribing as the white man's gold. Without horses a man was destitute, and tribal memory was still strong of how it had been before the coming of the horse not so very long ago, when the Plains people went afoot with their meager belongings, starving and afraid. Jim was thoroughly indoctrinated in this point of view. He was as proud of his fifty Cheyenne horses and satisfied as though he had turned a fortune in the St. Louis fur market. The notion of stealing never entered into it. This was not theft but war, unending and unregretted, by which a man won honor as well as spoils.

"If I ever get back to the white man's world," Jim thought, "I'm going to have to watch myself."

He thought of Sam Carson and all the horses he had shod for him, and he laughed. The sun was hot, the wind was clean, he was happy, and the horizon stretched forever. If he ever got back to the white man's world he would have worse things to worry about than horse stealing.

He had no intention of going back.

Suddenly Young Bear called to him. "Look! Muskrat is coming."

Muskrat had been sent ahead to scout. They were well within Crow territory, but that was no guarantee of safety—a thing returning war parties often forgot, and sometimes to their sorrow. Muskrat was now racing back toward them, whipping his horse. He pulled up in a wild spurting of dust.

"I have seen some persons," he cried. "Over there persons are riding." He pointed to a rise of land ahead. He was sixteen and this was his first time out as a warrior. He was enjoying it. "They have mules with them."

"White men?"

Muskrat nodded. "They're very good mules," he said gravely. He was Jim's brother-in-law, and the laws of etiquette required them to be respectful and decorous in their behavior toward each other. Muskrat never quite broke the tabu. Jim scowled at him. "White men are our friends," he said, and Muskrat grinned.

"We'll see what the Antelope says when he looks at these persons."

Jim signed to the others. Four of them remained to hold the herd. The other three rode with Jim, Young Bear, and Muskrat over the ridge.

The two white men rode at the head of a little string of mules. Two of the mules appeared to be loaded with supplies. The rest carried nothing but little wooden kegs.

"Now," said Muskrat, "what does the Antelope say?"

"The Antelope says that Muskrat is right. Those are truly very good mules."

Jim kicked his pony into a run.

The white men stopped. They had rifles laid across their saddlebows, but they held up their right hands in the gesture of peace. Jim answered it. He spoke to the men in Crow.

"Where are the white men going?"

The younger of the two, who was apparently the leader, shook his head and began to talk in the sign language. He had blue eyes and a gingery beard and a big wide smile showing broken teeth. The older man sat stolidly, but Jim noticed that he watched Muskrat and the others with a sharp, untrustful eye, and his hand was never far from his rifle.

The ginger-bearded man said that he was glad to meet with his Crow brothers. He was coming to trade with them, and now that they had met they could all go on together to the camp, and there would be gifts for his Crow brothers.

Jim made the sign for Follow and the sign for Camp. In Crow he said quietly to Young Bear, "Get behind the old one and see that he doesn't use that gun." The white men turned their attention to getting the mules started again and the young one said, "There you are, Joe. Plain sailing from here on."

The old one grunted and started to whack the mules, cursing them. He stopped as Young Bear's gun was jammed firmly into his back. At the same moment Jim covered Ginger Beard, who said in a shrill startled voice, "What the hell—?"

In English Jim said, "You're no brother of mine, and the Crow don't need your kind of trade." Muskrat and the others were busy cutting the mules loose. They slashed the pack ropes and let the kegs drop. One of them split and the raw smell of alcohol rose from the sun-hot earth. "What are you doing?" Ginger Beard shouted in a voice of rage and grief. "That's mine, that's my property—" Muskrat and Swift Crane were using the kegs for target practice now while the others drove the mules away, and the liquor fumes enveloped them like a cloud. Ginger Beard looked at Jim. "Who are you?" He was almost weeping with anger.

"The Crow call me the Antelope." To Muskrat he said, "Fire their guns."

Muskrat did, handing them back empty.

"You're a damned thief," Ginger Beard said to Jim.

The old man opened his mouth for the first time. "Ask him what his real name is. Ask him if it's Beckwourth."

"Ask me yourself," Jim said.

"You robbed a friend of mine up on Tongue River last year."

"If he was trading whisky, I did."

"This is free country," Ginger Beard said. "You don't have any right—"

"You're lucky I don't kill you," Jim said. "You're not traders, you're thieves. And you don't even give a man an honest drunk for his belongings."

The old man said, quietly, "You take a lot on yourself, Beckwourth. Considering you ain't even an Indian."

Jim smiled at him. "You'd be surprised how much of an Indian I am. I haven't taken any white scalps yet but there's always a first time."

He looked hard at the old man, who glanced briefly at Young Bear and the others, and shrugged. "Might's well get going, Pete," he said to Ginger Beard. Ginger Beard glared at Jim. His cheeks were redder than his beard and his neck had swelled inside his dirty flannel collar. "I ain't going to forget this," he said.

"I hope not," Jim told him. "And you can spread the word around. Whisky traders won't make any profit off the

Crow." He motioned with his rifle barrel. "And don't stop till you're across the Platte."

He watched the men ride away. The spilled whisky soaked into the dust. It was full strength in the cask, but by the time it reached the customer it would be diluted with water four or five to one and spiked with gunpowder and red pepper to give it strength again.

"Those were very good horses, too," said Muskrat wistfully as they disappeared.

"If you see them again, take them," Jim said. Setting a man afoot in this country was the next best thing to killing him.

They added the mules to their herd and went on.

That night they were close to the village but they did not go there. Instead they camped by a shallow creek, where they killed a buffalo. They bathed themselves and dressed in their war clothes, which they had carried with them on the outtrail, and tied on their medicines. With blood and charcoal they made paint for their faces and for the war shirts of the coup strikers, black paint, the color of victory. When it was morning the scouts put on their wolf skins and ran ahead. The Antelope and his warriors mounted and rode after them, driving the captured herd.

They came out on a crest of land above a wide green river valley. Jim saw the yellow-banded lodges scattered on the plain, with the morning smokes rising blue-gray into the sky. The scouts in their wolf-skin badges ran zigzag toward the camp, turning their heads from side to side and howling. People began to burst out of the lodges and gather in the open spaces. Jim fired off his rifle. Gunshots cracked all around him and the warriors began to yell. The horse

herd moved with a lilting thunder. Drums in the village began to beat. Women came singing, carrying scalp sticks.
The Antelope rode with the hawk-tail plume blowing from
his scalp lock, driving the horses in a circle around the
camp.

When this was done there was paint for the face of a
warrior's wife and the bridle of a white mare to put in her
hands.

Later still there was the feast and the striking of the
pipeman's lodge and the horse dance. Jim and Young Bear,
Muskrat and the other men of the raiding party danced,
each one with his blanket around a girl. Nomneditchee was
small, too small for her name, which meant The-one-who-
strikes-three and had belonged to an uncle who once struck
three coups in a single battle. She had beautiful dark eyes
and her hands were slender, and she did not look like a
coup-striker. Jim called her Cherry, because she had been
carrying a skin bag full of the red fruit when he first met
her. She was a purchased wife and proud of it. It meant that
a man had loved her enough to pay the bride price, and it
also meant that her reputation was unblemished. Jim would
not have to worry about the wife-stealing raids that the
rival warrior societies sometimes made on each other,
when they forcibly reclaimed former sweethearts. Cherry
was light-footed, lithe, and graceful in the circle of Jim's
robe, smiling, her eyes shining as she looked up at him.

After a while Jim happened to glance over Cherry's head
as they danced, and he saw Dave Richards standing among
the spectators watching him.

FOURTEEN

THEY SAT IN Jim's lodge, talking.

On the woman's side Cherry worked quietly with brilliant-colored porcupine quills, embroidering a dress of white buckskin. Jim held the boy in his lap. He was almost two years old now, a wild sturdy baby full of energy and laughter and occasional roaring rages. "When he's behaving himself," Jim said, "he's mine, Little Jim. When he's hell-raisin' he's the Black Panther, and all hers." He shook the boy between his hands and Little Jim kicked him, gurgling with pleasure. "He'll make a warrior."

"Grass has given me two," Rich said. "Both girls."

Jim felt a pleasant superiority.

"Happy here?" Rich asked. "Nothin' to rile you?"

Jim shook his head. He looked around the lodge, at Cherry and the boy. "Nothing to rile me."

"Fixing to stay?"

"Till they wrap me in my best blanket and lay me on the four-pole platform."

"Well, then," Rich said, with a sigh. "I guess it worked out good after all. I kind of worried about it a time or two. I was awful drunk that day, and the way you were prancing around like a turkey cock—" He spread his hands wide. "The idea just came to me. Afterward I didn't hardly think they'd believed me."

"They believed you," Jim said. "Talks-all-the-time speaks with a straight tongue."

"Hell of a name, ain't it?" Rich said. "Never could understand why they called me that."

"Why didn't you tell me, Rich? When those boys grabbed me I didn't know what was happening."

Rich scratched his chin, trying to remember. "Seems like I didn't feel so good for a day or two. Then we were all packing our traps to go. And like I said, I didn't really think they'd believe me."

"You knew damn well they believed you. Runs-fast and Yellow Shield were there and they're good friends of mine now. Belong to the same warrior society, the Big Dogs. They told me what they said to you."

"That's right," Rich said. "You speak the language now. Be damned, I didn't think of that. Well, I tell you, Jim. I was maybe a little sore at you anyway, and on top of that it suddenly come to me that I'd got the boys all fired up now, and if you was to call me a liar and maybe make a fight about it, we might both be in a lot of trouble. I thought it was safer to let it kind of sneak up on you."

Jim grunted. "But you did worry about it a time or two."

"Sure did."

"It's been five-six years. You could have dropped around to see."

"I been pretty busy. I was out to California with Diah Smith. Never thought I'd live to see you or anybody else again. If it wasn't them Diggers skulking like a pack of dirty coyotes, looking to kill us all for our blankets, it was the desert trying to fry us like so many chunks of bacon. Dry! Jim, I ain't never been so dry in my whole born life. When that desert got through with me I looked like a piece of an old lodge cover that's been smoked and seasoned till it cracks. And then the Spaniards threw us all in jail. But it's rich country, Jim. Rich and pretty. And they got horses. They got so many horses you wouldn't believe it. A man's going somewhere, he'll ride till his horse gets tuckered and then he'll just pick another one like you'd pick an apple in an orchard and go on, and it don't matter who the horse belongs to. They got so many they don't care. A Crow would just plain go crazy at the sight." Rich shook his head. "Pity we couldn't bring some back with us. We sure didn't bring nothin' else. Not even most of us, after the desert and the Indians was finished. Poor Diah. He figured to trap, but all he did was open up a new trail. But that was enough for him."

Little Jim became restive and ran to Cherry. Jim accepted the offer of Rich's tobacco pouch and filled his pipe. "Diah's medicine is bad," he said. "He made a spring hunt through the Big Horn country some time back. I didn't see him, but I heard he lost thirty horses and some hundreds of traps, washed down a flooded creek. Fine man, though, in spite of it. Maybe his luck'll change."

"No," said Rich. "Diah's gone under, down on the Cimarron. Comanche."

"Too bad," said Jim, and meant it. They were silent for a while.

"Rich—"

"Yeah?"

"I'm glad to see you."

"Thanks."

"You're always welcome in my lodge."

"Thanks."

"Now you know that, I'll ask you why you came."

"To see how things stood. I been hearing stories about

you, Jim."

Jim settled lazily against the willow backrest. He smiled. "What kind of stories?"

" 'Bout you turning renegade. Robbing white men, running off their stock."

"Depends on the white men," Jim said, "and depends on what you call robbing. Last winter we picked up a little bunch of free trappers, four of 'em, three-quarters starved and more than that froze. We fed 'em, gave 'em fresh horses and supplies, and sent 'em on their way happy. It didn't cost 'em so much as a muskrat skin."

"What about the two I met on the way here?"

"Ginger-bearded fellow and an old man with a mean eye?"

"That's right. It's a wonder you ain't lightning-struck, the way they were cussing you. Said you'd stolen their mules and their trade goods."

"Did they tell you what their trade goods were?"

Rich said, "No."

"Whisky. And nothing but whisky. You know what happens. They clean out a whole village for a few dollars' worth of rotgut, and all the Indians get out of it is sick. Then they've got nothing left to trade for the things they need, and it's a damned hard winter ahead."

"Agreed," Rich said. "But did you have to take their belongings? You could just have run 'em off."

"And they could just have found themselves another village. No. I've seen what's happened to some of the nations that live closer to the white man. I won't have it happen to my Crow as long as I can help it."

"Whisky's in the trade," Rich said sadly. "You can't keep

it out. All the government and all the laws can't keep it out. Indians'll go where it is, and if one man sells it the others have got to."

"When it comes to that I'll sell it myself. Then at least I can see they ain't robbed."

Rich smoked a while. Cherry put Little Jim to bed. Jim thought briefly how beautiful she was bending over the child, with the firelight touching the clean lines of her cheek and temple, shining on her hair. Poor Francie, he thought, how angry you would be! And how thankful I am that I didn't marry you and sell my life for a picket fence.

"That old man with the mean eye," Rich said. "He said you threatened to scalp him."

"I guess I did," Jim said, and grinned. "I only half meant it."

"Don't take it so light," Rich snapped. "These men go back to the settlements. They talk. You're laying up trouble for yourself, Jim, when you go back."

"Told you. I'm not going back."

Rich said quietly, "You'll go back. Someday. You can only be an Indian so long, unless you're born to it."

Jim spoke so angrily that Cherry looked over at him, startled. "Can't you let anything alone, Rich? Do you have to be always poking and tearing and trying to break things up?"

"It's my curse," Rich said, and added reflectively, "maybe that's why I don't seem to be able to hang onto my friends for any very long stretch of time. Seems like there's something in the sound of truth that's painful to the ear."

"Truth!" said Jim. "Spite is more what it is. You just naturally can't let anything or anybody rest quiet."

"This ain't no country for resting quiet. If that's what you wanted you should have stayed in St. Louis." Rich had a maddening way of sliding by the point as fast and slick as a diving otter. "You heard about the Rocky Mountain Fur Company?"

"I heard." Smith, Jackson, and Sublette had sold out to a new group of partners that included Fitzpatrick and Bridger and Sublette's brother Milton.

"Ain't no better men on the mountain," Rich said, "but they're powerful deep in debt." He paused. "You're working for McKenzie, holding all the Crow trade for Fort Union."

"That's right."

"Then you don't need to go to the settlements for trouble. You got it right here."

Jim sat, hanging on hard to his patience. His years among the Crow had trained him to the decorum of the council and the self-control that was expected of a man. He was angry that he had lost it, even for a moment. It seemed to be a concession to Rich's statement that the truth hurt. For some reason he became acutely conscious of himself as he sat there, cross-legged, wearing breechclout and leggins and bare above the waist except for a scarlet blanket draped over his shoulders. For the first time since he came to Absaroka he felt foolish to be dressed like an Indian, as though he were a grown man caught playing a child's game. There was a terrible moment when Cherry and the boy, the lodge, and the life that went with them seemed to slip away from him, becoming insubstantial as a dream.

At that moment, quite literally, he could have killed Rich.

But Rich was talking. "—knock-down, drag-out fight. We got the British pushing us from Oregon, we got the Blackfeet that won't have us in the north and the Spaniards that won't have us in the south, and I don't know which is worse to tangle with. And most of all we got the company. There's McKenzie squatting on the Missouri, and Chouteau in St. Louis, and they ain't just squatting. Every time you turn around now you trip over one of their brigades— the mountain's crawling with 'em. And I hear McKenzie sent Jake Berger up the Marias to talk peace with the Blackfeet. They want this whole country to themselves, Jim, and they ain't going to get it. Not without a big lot of trouble." He looked at Jim. "Most of that trouble's going to come right here in Absaroka."

"If you wanted the Crow trade, you should have stayed with it," Jim said, "instead of going over the mountains. When Henry left the Yellowstone, that was the end of it."

"Fitz don't think so."

"Fitz be damned," said Jim. "I'd hate to have trouble with Bridger, and you're welcome to trap anywhere on Crow range, any time. But the RMF ain't welcome here and they might as well know it."

Rich sighed. "That's what I thought you'd say. I don't know what it is about you, Jim. Maybe you was born under the wrong star, or maybe it's natural cussedness, maybe it's both. But somehow or another you always seem to stand right where you're bound to make an enemy out of any man that walks by."

"Out of you, too?"

"It might be."

Again they were silent for a while.

"You're a free trapper," Jim said at length. "You can sell your furs where you want to. Why don't you sell 'em to McKenzie?"

"Can't. I already made my bargain."

Jim nodded. "I already made mine, too. And when I made it I wasn't going against old friends. If it comes to that now, I'm sorry. But I ain't going to change. See, Rich, there's something over and above who makes the money on this year's catch of buffalo robes. There's the Crow. They were in a bad way after Henry pulled out. The Blackfeet practically wiped out a whole village because the Crow had no powder and lead for their guns. They been trading with McKenzie for years now. He's here to stay. About the RMF—who knows?" Jim got up and pulled the scarlet blanket around him. "Make yourself comfortable, Rich." He went outside.

After the smoky warmth of the tipi the wind felt almost cold, and sharply clean. Roan Horse whickered and stamped at his picket. He was getting a little old now and Jim didn't run him quite so hard. He went over and rubbed his nose, and then went on to check the others, four of them, all prime buffalo runners, and Rich's Blackfoot horse, all tied close to the lodge for safety. The stars burned in the sky like the campfires of a vast army. It was very late and the camp was still.

Jim stood by the horses, feeling troubled.

Young Bear came soft-footed through the starshine. He stood beside Jim. "Talks-all-the-time has brought bad news."

"No," said Jim. Not unless I listen to him, he thought. Not unless I believe him. And who made Dave Richards the only man who knows the truth? About everything?

"He wants you to go back with him," Young Bear said, with the uncanny perception he had for Jim's moods.

"No," Jim said again, startled. Here was another one too smart for comfort, and the wrong guess had been too nearly right. But with Young Bear there was none of the feeling he had with Rich. Rich poked for the sake of poking, and it was hard to tell where friendship ended and malice began. Young Bear simply and honestly loved him as a brother.

"He told me there is going to be trouble," Jim said, "and perhaps I must fight against some white men who were my friends. Perhaps even against him."

"Well," said Young Bear cheerfully, "there's little trouble that you and I can't take care of together."

They stood for a moment longer, shoulder to shoulder in the still night. Jim smiled. "That's true, brother," he said. "Sleep well." He returned to the lodge.

Rich was snoring. Jim looked down at him and shook his head. Then he slid under the warm robes and took Cherry in his arms and she curled against him like a child, burying her head against his shoulder. Close by them in his nest of furs Little Jim made comfortable breathings and stirrings. "Truth!" Jim thought. "The truth is, these are mine."

He slept, holding Cherry close to him. But in spite of that his dreams were sad and wandering.

A year later there was a new fort on the Missouri. The RMF had moved in, almost within shouting distance of Fort Union. And in the Leaf Falling time the trouble came.

FIFTEEN

THE DUST CLOUD was long and bow-shaped, blown sideways by the wind.

"Broken Hand is not traveling alone," said Young Bear.

"No," said Jim. Broken Hand, otherwise Tom Fitzpatrick, was traveling anything but alone. Jim's eyes narrowed against the clear, glittering light through which the dust cloud moved. It was so far away that it hardly seemed to move at all, but Jim knew that it was moving, steadily, across the brown-dappled plain, riders slouched in their saddles, tireless, timeless, patient men all dust-colored on dust-colored horses, and pack animals with hung heads and busy hoofs, all dust-colored too except where the sweat had made dark cakings around the straps and cinches. About twenty men, Jim thought—no, more than that. Twenty-five, maybe, and about four times that many pack horses. Beyond them was a wall of mountains, the dark pines on their flanks looking at this distance like moss on old shattered boulders.

"They will reach the village in good time," said Young Bear.

Jim nodded. His face, always aquiline, had become sterner and more hawklike. His eyes, always proud, were assured now rather than defiant, and they were as fierce and wild as Young Bear's or any Indian's, but more slyly humorous. He thought of Tom Fitzpatrick. Fitz arrogant and ignoring him, Fitz curtly passing on Ashley's orders, Fitz clipping his hair with a bullet and then later on soaping him with charm as though he was too childminded to see through it. Jim smiled. Sitting his pony on the hilltop, with the wind blowing the feathers in his scalp lock, he whistled—an un-Indian trick that always startled Young Bear. Then he turned and rode whistling down the hill.

It was midafternoon when Muskrat came to Jim's lodge, bright-eyed and nigh to bursting with excitement.

"The trappers have camped," he said. "Talks-all-the-time is not with them, nor the Blanket Chief. But they have a big barrel of whisky and many horseloads of trade goods. Now Broken Hand is coming."

Jim was relieved that neither Rich nor Bridger was in the party. Apparently Rich had heeded his warning. He nodded to Young Bear. "It's time to go. Remind the others of what I told them. No killing." He turned to Muskrat. "You remember it too, younger brother."

"What if they shoot?" asked Muskrat.

"If you do as I've told you they will not be able to shoot. And throw away the whisky. My medicine tells me that this is poison to the Crow, and if they drink it their arms will become weak and their enemies will slay them and take away their women and children. Do you hear me?"

"I hear you, elder brother," Muskrat said sadly. "No killing, not even one small scalp, and do not drink the whisky." He made the polite greeting to his sister Cherry that was all etiquette allowed him and went out with Young Bear.

Cherry came and arranged the folds of Jim's blanket, his best one. He caught her hand and she looked at him proudly and smiled. Then she went back to her preparations for feeding a distinguished visitor. Little Jim had been sent to stay with Big Bowl and Captures-white-horses, where he spent half his time anyway, so that Jim's lodge had the quiet and dignity befitting his station.

He heard the stir and excitement outside, and the thumping of hoofs. Presently the flap was lifted and Fitz came in.

He was older than Jim remembered him, tougher, deeper lined around the mouth and eyes, and a good bit harder—not that Fitz had ever been soft, but ten years ago he could seek the distant mountain at least partly for the simple sake of finding it. Now the adventurer had become the man of business. It was a wild business in a wild land and a merchant had to be part Indian and part wildcat to conduct it. But there was a difference.

Fitz raised his hand and opened his mouth to speak, then paused and peered closer at Jim in the firelight. Jim said, "Hello, Fitz. Come on in."

Fitz let his hand fall. "No point wasting what little Crow I have on you." He smiled. "Hello, Jim. Rich told me he saw you last year."

Jim motioned to the place of honor on his left. "Sit down."

"Thanks—but later. I have business with the chief. I guess they didn't understand me—or I mistook the lodge they pointed out." He reached for the flap. "I'll see you—"

"Fitz," Jim said. "I am the chief here."

Fitz looked at him. "Where's Long Hair?"

"On Clark's Fork."

"Where's Arepoesh, then? Or Has-red-plume-on-the-side-of-his-head?"

"On Owl Creek and Wind River, or heading for there."

It was the time of year when the Crow band split into small groups and moved to their wintering grounds. Jim's village was a little one, mostly composed of his relatives, but such as it was it was his.

"You might as well sit down, Fitz," he said, playing the Indian and not smiling, though he wanted very much to smile.

Fitz sat down.

Cherry brought food. They ate, and Jim listened to the quiet beyond the skin walls. Fitz was thinking.

When he spoke he had put on his charm again, a little rusty and flawed, Jim thought, as though from disuse.

"You're a lucky man, Jim. You've done well." He looked around the lodge, admiring the wealth it reflected, and he looked at Cherry. "Very well."

"Thanks."

"Been keeping up with what's going on in the world?"

"Some of it," said Jim carelessly. "I know the General's in Congress now, and still backing Sublette. I know Bob Campbell came in with Sublette a while back and they've built a fort up on the Missouri, close by the Yellowstone. That's about all. Except I guess things are getting a little tight in the trade?"

Fitz shook his head. "Things have changed, Jim. When you and I were starving and freezing our way out here with Ashley nobody would buy the Rocky Mountains for a plug of tobacco. Now they're trampling each other down to get out here. Every season there's a whole fresh batch of 'em running up and down the rivers, building forts, killing out the beaver, and cutting in on our trade every way they can." Fitz was honestly bitter, honestly angry. "Maybe you wouldn't believe this, Jim, but beaver's getting scarce."

"I can believe it," Jim said. And for a moment he felt a kinship and sympathy with Fitz. "We broke the trail while they sat safe at home. Now when they see we've got a good thing they want to take it away from us." He added, with an abrupt quirk of logic, "There's getting to be too damned many white men out here." And he was thinking of Fitz's twenty-five or thirty trappers camped on his doorstep.

"That's what I came to talk about," Fitz said. "Maybe we didn't always see eye to eye, Jim, but we're both Ashley men. So are a lot of us in the Rocky Mountain Fur Company. Like Rich and Bridger, old friends. I know you're working for the AMF, but what I'm asking won't do them any harm—"

"Just what are you asking, Fitz?"

"Permission to conduct my fall hunt in Absaroka."

"Is that all?"

"Absolutely all," said Fitz, and sat waiting, candidly innocent of any knowledge of whisky barrels and many horse loads of goods for the Indian trade.

"I don't know," said Jim. "I'm trying to teach my Crow to trap more. If they spent their time trapping instead of going on war parties they'd be rich and comfortable, instead of getting themselves killed off." He was trying. He'd been trying for years. And as well try to teach so many eagles to scratch the ground like chickens. "I don't know if there'd be room for all of us." And he looked at Fitz, candidly unaware of certain instructions that had reached him from McKenzie. From far away he thought he heard a distant, confused shouting.

"Room!" said Fitz. "Crow country's big enough for half

the world to trap in. But if you tell me where you plan to hunt I'll guarantee to stay someplace else."

Jim thought, "I'll bet you will." Aloud he said, "I'll have to think it over."

"I could make it worth your while," Fitz said with a disarming smile, making the signs for Much and On-the-prairie. He glanced at Cherry. "I have a blanket beautiful enough for a chiefs wife. How long will it take you to think about it, Jim?"

With an Indian you called it presents. With a white man you called it a bribe. Jim wondered exactly where that left him. "Come back tomorrow, when the sun is there." He pointed to an hour before noon.

"Good." Fitz rose. He was still the tough, able, courageous, hawk-eyed mountain man that Jim had envied and admired but not liked ten years before. He did not have to envy him now. He still admired him. And he still did not like him.

The lack of love was mutual, he could tell from the overhearty quickness of Fitz's handshake. "Tomorrow," Fitz said, and left.

Jim turned. "Cherry," he said, "did you hear any firing of guns?"

"I did not."

Jim sighed. He sat still and waited, whistling softly, passing the time by calculating how long it would take an angry man to walk part way to the trapper's camp, a mile or so away, and then all the way back again. At intervals he heard the sounds of men coming quickly back into the village, singly or by twos and threes. The patch of light from the smoke hole moved as the sun got lower.

Fitz made it a little faster than Jim had figured, and he was not alone. A tall, black-haired, beak-nosed man with a commanding air and fire in his eye came shouldering through the entrance behind him.

Fitz stood with his feet spread wide and his fists clenched. He said, "God damn it, Jim!"

Jim got up. He looked at Fitz as though astonished. "What's happened?" Fitz was bareheaded and stripped to his shirt. "What is it?"

"What is it!" Fitz snarled. "What is it! Look, you—" He stopped and choked down something he had been about to say, and then started again. "You're chief here, I'm addressing you as chief. Your people have robbed my party of every horse, trap, gun, and personal possession they own, and I want them back. Some of your warriors stopped me and took my horse, my watch, even my hat and capote. And I want *them* back."

Jim made calming motions. "Sit down. Get your breath and your temper and then tell me what happened." He looked at the stranger, including him in the invitation. "I haven't had the pleasure—"

The stranger said, "I'm Stewart of Grandtully, and I'll not sit in the house of a scoundrel."

Jim had already guessed it. He had heard about Stewart at the fort, the dashing and adventurous British officer who wanted to learn all about life in the mountains. Stewart seemed to be respected and well-liked, but Jim had an idea that he and the Captain were not going to be good friends.

"A damned black scoundrel," Stewart added, and then Jim was certain of it.

"Now that wasn't very smart, was it?" Jim asked, smiling just a little. "Supposing I walked into Grandtully Castle and talked like that to you? Especially if I wanted something."

Fitz said, "I don't have to tell you what happened, Jim. You or the American Fur Company." He was so angry he was trembling. "Get rid of the competition and it don't matter how."

"You know Indians," Jim said. "Stewart here hasn't learned about 'em yet—"

"I've had a salutary lesson," Stewart snapped. "Beggars came into camp smiling and friendly and I thought nothing of it—"

"You thought?" asked Jim.

"He was in charge of the camp," Fitz said.

"Oh," said Jim. "I see."

Stewart turned even more crimson along the cheekbones. "I had understood the Crow were friendly and we had nothing to fear. I was not then acquainted with you, sir. When they started to plunder the camp they were so well situated that there was nothing I could do to stop them. They had us completely covered." He stepped up close to Jim and said in a low, hard voice, "I have a gray horse. I am very fond of that horse. I shall have him back, and I want no lies or excuses."

"Fitz," said Jim, looking at Stewart, "your friend may be famous for his good manners in Scotland, but they won't win him any prizes here." He turned again to Fitz. "As I started to say, you know Indians. Horses tempt them. Guns tempt them. All kinds of things tempt them. And you know how hard it is to control the young men. No chief can do it, not even Long Hair or Arepoesh."

He went to the entrance flap and held it for them. "I'll give you horses. Go to your camp, and I'll see what I can do about getting your belongings back."

Fitz seemed to have recovered his control, for his voice was as cold and steady as his eyes when he spoke.

"I seem to remember Rich saying something once about a sense of power. All right, Jim. Enjoy yourself. But this won't be forgotten."

He went out. Stewart did not. He faced Jim and said distinctly, "I will have my horse back, and be damned to you."

Jim laughed. "If he's not halfway to Wind River by now, you'll get him. In the meantime—"

He gestured, and Stewart stalked out. Jim followed him. Muskrat and two or three other young braves were lounging about nearby. Muskrat's face was solemn but his eyes sparkled with the sheer delight of doing what he had just helped to do. Mules, horses, guns, flints and lead and powder, cloth and knives and beads, tobacco and blankets, wealth in heaps and sweetened with the excitement of outwitting a potentially formidable victim—a day like this did not come often. Jim told him in Crow to bring horses for the honored guests, at the same time giving him a stern glare of warning. Muskrat went. Fitz and Stewart stood stiff as ramrods while they waited. Jim knew they were both busy trying to see some sign of the plunder in the village, but nothing had been brought here. Muskrat returned with two ponies, not the best, trailed by a gang of barking dogs. Without a word Fitz and Stewart mounted and rode away.

Jim went back inside and threw himself down on the buffalo robes. Muskrat came in and sat down, and in a few moments Young Bear joined them. Jim was still looking at the smoke hole and smiling, to himself.

Cherry spoke. "Broken Hand and the other white man were very angry."

"Very angry," Jim said.

"They will continue to be angry," said Cherry. "Perhaps formerly they were your friends, but now they will set ambushes for you."

She said it in a matter-of-fact way, quite without concern.

"They were never my friends," he told her. "Now they are enemies. But they have many things to do besides setting ambushes." Things like trying to carry on their business in spite of not being able to make a fall hunt this year, things like working hard for money. Things an Indian couldn't understand, any more than he could understand a man avenging an injury by writing to his Congressman, which Jim was sure that Fitz would do since the Congressman was General Ashley. The Congress, fortunately, was a long way off.

"Young Bear," he said. "Muskrat. This was well done today. Now we must give back part of what we took, enough guns and horses and powder to get them on their way. And the round silver thing that belongs to Broken Hand. And above all, the English captain's gray horse. Do you know the one I mean?"

"I know it," said Muskrat dolefully. "Elder brother—"

"No," said Jim.

"Well," said Muskrat, "it is nothing. I shall find another horse like him, when the pine leaves turn yellow."

Jim laughed. "I'll give you a horse like him," he said. He felt good. After Muskrat and Young Bear left he said aloud in English, "That's what's nice about this country. It's so big. If you look hard enough you can find a place in it where a damned black scoundrel can tell even a Stewart of Grandtully to go to hell."

Cherry did not understand the words, but she smiled.

Minus trade goods and whisky, greatly reduced in horses and other belongings but able to travel, Fitz and his party left before midday of the next day, headed out of Absaroka by the shortest road. Fitz was curt and cold, but Jim knew that he had been doing some thinking and had realized that all the Crow would be against him, not Jim's band alone, and that without Jim around he might be handled more roughly.

He had made his try at bucking McKenzie on Mc-Kenzie's own ground. He had been soundly trounced, and the best thing he could do now was to get out of opposition territory as quickly as possible.

Captain Stewart looked his gray horse all over for damage, then mounted and rode off. He did not say "Thank you."

Jim was relieved to see them go. Some of his young men had been thinking too, about the folly of returning good horses to men silly enough to lose them in the first place. Jim had had to call out his Big Dog soldiers to make sure none of them sneaked away to stage a second raid of their own.

That afternoon he sent the heralds around with word that their own camp was moving. That night the women packed, and at dawn they took down the lodges, lashed the poles, and loaded the travois. The village moved south into the Big Horn Basin.

They were calm, slow days. The village moved at the pace of the laden horses across a land of sky and mountain peaks, rivers and distance. Like a long, long snake it crawled, leather-colored against the leather-colored ground but set off from it by the splashes of crimson and yellow and blue and white that shone in the brilliant sun. Jim sent out scouts to watch for danger and settled into the creaking, dusty, peaceful rhythm. Cherry rode her white mare, heavy with embroidered trappings, and carried the Antelope's shield.

It was a good life. Jim hoped it would go on forever.

SIXTEEN

I T WAS SUMMER, and the Crow were gathered for war and hunting.

The heralds had finished going through the camp, calling the young men to rise and bathe and dress themselves for battle. They had finished their speeches extolling the bravery of the most distinguished warriors of the Crow nation, and the warriors had paraded before the people, making their boasts and their promises. Now the chief Arepoesh stood on a great pile of chips and offered his shield in augury.

"If it falls this way, we will go. If it falls that way, we will not go."

Four times he sang and made as if to toss the shield from him, while the watching crowd clapped their mouths and sang praise songs. The fourth time Arepoesh let go of the shield. It caught the air and flew a little way, then fell and rolled and wobbled to a stop, falling with the blazon up.

"I have said it," cried Arepoesh. "We will go. Already I see the enemy lying dead. Already I see them slain."

Some men hunting buffalo had cut the trail of a party of Blackfeet yesterday. The party was not large and Jim thought the fight would be an easy one. He was eager for it. The Blackfeet were mounted, which meant they were after hair, and that meant dead Crow sooner or later.

He rode out with Arepoesh and some thirty braves. Cherry and Little Jim, who was less Little Jim and more Black Panther every year, watched him go, their faces fierce with pride.

For half a day they traveled, in sullen heat that grew more and more intense while clouds boiled and blackened over the Big Horns. In early afternoon they found the enemy, fourteen Blackfeet dressed for war, riding in a long green hollow of the plain.

The two parties faced each other, in still air that glowed the color of brass. The feather pennons drooped on the lances. The sweated ponies dripped foam around the war bridles. Dry thunder rolled and cracked in the ledges of the mountains. Arepoesh looked at the Blackfeet. He was a great warrior, a great chief. He said, "Last year the enemy you see there killed my son. Since that day I have felt myself growing old. I do not wish to grow any older. Today I am going to die."

All alone he charged the Blackfoot line, stabbing savagely with his lance.

All alone he fell, with an arrow through him.

Jim charged, with the rest of the Crow, but there was no time for battle. The Blackfeet ran, taking their wounded.

They fled at the full stretch of their horses' speed, scream-ing triumphantly, and were lost in hissing veils of rain that rushed out from the mountain.

The Crow stood around Arepoesh on the ground. He looked up at them, thrust his shield toward Jim, tried once to speak, and died.

In beating rain, across dry channels leaping into flood, they took him home. Jim carried the shield, a sacred gift.

The Crow mourned.

They chopped off their fingers and gashed themselves with knives. They pierced their flesh with arrows. They cut off their hair. Even Long Hair allowed his medicine to be mutilated. The favorite war horse of Arepoesh was killed and others of his vast herd had their manes and tails shorn off. Bloody, gaunt, starved, and howling, the Absaroka paid respect to one of their most honored men.

They built the platform on a high place, the four-pole platform that gave man back at last to the sun and the four winds, and they laid Arepoesh on it, dressed in his war clothes, wrapped in his finest blanket and the softest of buf-falo robes. They planted a long pole with scalps on it to wave over him like a flag. And they left him, alone under the enormous sky.

But that was not the end of it. There was never an end.

The wife and family and relatives of Arepoesh loaded a fine horse with gifts and led it up to Jim. Cherry and Mus-krat were among the party, being clan connections of the dead chief. Both were ceremonially gashed, their faces painted with mourning paint. The widow of Arepoesh of-fered Jim a pipe.

He hesitated. If he took it it meant that he accepted two

things—the horse with its load of gifts, which he did not need, and the duty of leading a war party against the Blackfeet to avenge the death of Arepoesh, which he did not want.

These terrible whirlwinds of mourning were hard on the nerves. Perhaps that was why he had a feeling that if he took the pipe he would be unlucky.

But he looked at Cherry and knew that he had no choice.

Again the heralds went through the camp, and the Antelope with fifty warriors rode north into Blackfoot country.

Everything went wrong.

The weather turned bad. They could find no game. They shivered in cold rains and grew feeble with hunger, and there were no Blackfeet. The men began to talk seriously of turning back. The Antelope's medicine had become weak. The Ones-who-make-things-happen, whoever and wherever they might be, were angry for some reason. Even Young Bear advised Jim to go back. "This will not turn out well," he said. "If you return home, that will be well."

But Jim was mad. He had already come all this way. He could not go back to Cherry, to the whole waiting village, and say that he had failed. He was mad, and too white-man-ornery to quit.

The weather cleared. They killed a buffalo, gorged themselves and vomited, ate again and kept it down. They felt much better. And they found their Blackfeet.

It was a big party coming back from a raid on the Shoshoni, and Jim saw two scalps that had never grown on Indian heads, one reddish-brown, one sandy. Two more trappers had laid their bones beside the beaver streams. Now Jim was glad he had come. He laid his ambush well and caught the Blackfeet in a deep coulee, where less than half of them escaped. When it was over he had three men and himself slightly wounded, no one dead, and enough hair to wash the faces of the mourners clean.

"Who wishes to say now that the Antelope's medicine is weak?" he asked.

Triumphantly, they took the long trail home.

Some of the lodges were still burning when they came in sight of the camp. They saw the smoke long beforehand, a thin and dirty smudge across the sky. They rode like wild men, but there was not really any need to hurry.

Jim flung himself off his pony. It stayed with its head down and its legs spread, groaning. The lodge was still standing. Only a part of the cover had burned and the flap was still in place, moving idly with the wind. The air stunk of scorched leather and other more dreadful things. Jim moved toward the entrance. He seemed to move very slowly and there was a shimmering over his vision as of a heat haze. He heard sounds, people crying out, wailing, moaning, but they were a long way off. The flap made a rustling in the wind. He put out a hand and lifted it and looked in.

"The men were not in the village," someone was saying. "Long Hair called a buffalo hunt. The men were killing buffalo, that is how it was. That was when the Cheyennes attacked us."

Someone. Someone. Someone was talking.

"I saved the boy. He fought well. Even though young he fought well, like a Crow."

It was hard to see. Jim reached out. He felt someone grip his arm and then some of the darkness lifted and he saw that it was Big Bowl, his face grimed with smoke and blood and streaked with tears.

"The boy's mother," he said, "did not wish to be a captive. Although a woman, she fought bravely. Her I could not save."

"No," said Jim. There seemed to be nothing else to say.

He built the platform for her in the ruined lodge where she had died, and everything that was in it he left with her. He suffered his hair to be cut and watched stonily as Black Panther gashed himself with an arrow point, thrusting it deep in his flesh. He endured the waiting until all the people were finished with their burials, and he only spoke once. That was to Young Bear. "You said to me that if I returned home it would be well. Your medicine was stronger than mine."

Without the horses that the Cheyennes had run off, without the belongings that the Cheyennes had plundered, without all the women and children taken captive and without all those who remained behind in the death lodges, they moved the camp to a new place. And that year they held a Sun Dance.

Only a man who mourned very greatly and whose will was as strong as his wish for vengeance would pledge a Sun Dance in return for a vision. Muskrat had left behind in the death lodges not only his sister Cherry but his mother and father as well. Muskrat was the Whistler.

All the villages came in, to watch and share in the ceremony. The Antelope was part of it too. He was a Big Dog, and the Big Dogs were chosen to act as police. He was a distinguished warrior, and a relative of Muskrat, and there were duties and rituals for him to perform. He went through them in a kind of savage daze, desolate and full of hate, without a conscious thought in his head. The tide carried him, with singing and drumbeats, with the controlled frenzy of emotion that rose slowly toward explosion.

The massive detail attendant on the ritual had its own strange usefulness. It dragged out each separate action to its utmost stretch, so that the consummation was that much delayed, that much more anticipated. Muskrat, covered with white clay, his face painted with the tear streaks of the mourner, his body gaunt with fasting, danced on his knees in the preparatory lodge, blowing the sacred whistle made from the leg bone of an eagle, while the owner of the Sun Dance doll saw that all was done according to the vision handed down from the beginning, even to the stitching of the ceremonial kilt and moccasins. Muskrat, carrying the Sun Dance doll in its feathered hoop, led the procession to get poles for the Sun's lodge, which had to be cut by chosen persons in a certain way. Chosen hunters went to kill the buffalo for the bull hides that would bind the poles, and each bull must be dropped cleanly with one blow. Chosen persons cut the hides into strips, and every gesture was four times repeated and every song four times sung. The sacred lodge went up like something in a fever dream, endlessly promised, endlessly postponed.

Muskrat entered the Sun's lodge at last. The cedar post was set up according to the vision and the owner of the sacred doll hung the hoop on it so that Muskrat faced it, his head on a level with the doll's head with its tiny crown of feathers and its painted eyes. From now on his fast was absolute. The singing and the drumming began. Muskrat danced, all covered with white clay, wearing the ceremonial kilt and the necklace of skunk skin, the whistle between his lips. Staring at the doll he danced, without food or water in the summer heat.

Outside the lodge other men suffered, caught up in the passion of sorrow and vengeance, seeking their own visions. From the lodgepole tips long ropes of rawhide dangled, and the end of each rope was skewered into the flesh of a man who would hang there, dancing, until the skewers tore loose.

The Antelope watched. The lower part of the Sun's lodge was uncovered so that everyone could watch. The piping of the bone whistle sounded with every gasping breath as Muskrat danced. The singers sang and the drummers drummed. Close by the lodge a man walked dragging behind him five buffalo skulls tied with thongs to skewers through the flesh of his back. The dry white skulls went bouncing in the dust, clacking their horns together. The men danced at the ends of their ropes and the blood made bright patterns running down.

Into the parched blankness of Jim's mind came a memory. Several white men sat in a paneled room, drinking port. He himself, very small, crouched on a stair landing in the dark, watching and listening, while his father talked with fellow soldiers about the battle of Stony Point.

"War is good," Cirape told Old Man Coyote in the beginning of the world. "You have made a bad mistake. You have made all the people speak alike and understand each other. Hate they do not, fight they do not. Thus they are unhappy, they have nothing to do. If some spoke different languages it would be well. Then they could get angry, they could hate, they could be happy. Then they could have chiefs. Their warriors could have victory parades and flirt with the young women. At peace they are not content." And

First-Maker said to his younger brother; "Why, you are right. I did not think of that." And he made his people happy.

The Whistler and the bleeding men danced, all praying for a vision of dead Cheyennes.

Up in the north Blackfoot women were mourning their dead and someone was bringing a pipe and a horseload of gifts to a war chief, asking vengeance against the Crow.

To the southeast the Cheyenne women were dancing over Crow hair, but the Whistler would get his vision. Cheyennes would die in earnest. Then their women would weep and cry for vengeance. And more Crow would die, and again a pipe would be brought.

War in the white man's world was generally about something. Somebody won, somebody lost, something was decided and the war was over. Here war was its own cause and the idea of victory was unthinkable as a white man understood it. War was made because without it a man would have nothing to do.

Jim groaned. For all these days his mind had been like a thing asleep. Now it was waking, and it seemed that all the time it had been busy in its dark, secretive way, making decisions.

He knew that he would not lead any war party against the Cheyennes.

Rich was right after all. You could only be an Indian just so long, unless you were born to it. It wasn't the savagery or the bloodshed. A white man could shuck off his town-made civilization overnight, reverting to the primitive as though it was his natural element. It was the uselessness. If you had been born and raised outside the pattern, sooner or later you would find you could not fit into it any longer, because your habit of mind said that a pattern had to get you somewhere and this one didn't. It got you death, but the dying had no purpose. As well hate wind or lightning as the Cheyennes.

The man with the buffalo skulls came by. One of them had pulled out, leaving a torn place in his back. Blood ran down his left buttock and the back of his leg and dripped off his heel into the dust where the dry skulls rode. His face was ecstatic.

Jim turned and walked away from the Sun Dance lodge. He felt as though buffalo skulls were dragging at his heart. He loved these people. He did not want to go.

Toward the end of the Yellow Grass time Jim rode up to the fort, collected his pay from the American Fur Company, and took passage on a keelboat going down the river, back to the white man's world. He told his people that it was only for a short while, that he would come back, certainly, perhaps in the Snow Falling time, or no later than the time of Green Grass when the ponies grew fat. He tried to believe that this was true. But on the way down the river he got drunk and raged through the boat like a wild man, so that half the crew took to the water to escape him.

He was mourning Absaroka.

SEVENTEEN

S T. LOUIS HAD more streets now, more houses, more people, more business, more wharves and taverns and counting houses and brothels. To Jim's nose, after fourteen years of prairie and mountain, it smelled more. And it was noisier, with wheels and voices and the constant braying of mules.

There were other changes.

Strangers had the house at Beckwourth's Settlement. The old owner was gone, back to Virginia. An officious slave told Jim this and ordered him off the place, eyeing his Indian garb with righteous distrust. Jim was sorry, and at the same time relieved. It was hard for him to remember sometimes that Big Bowl was not his true father. And yet he would have liked to see Beckwourth, to say to him, "This is what I have become." Perhaps he would have been proud. Perhaps not. Perhaps in his father's eyes a Crow chief would not count very high. In any case, Jim was still grateful for the rifle.

Sam Carson was dead, so his opinion could not be had either.

Of the opinion of Jim's sisters there was no doubt. He had some little trouble finding them, and when he did they met him stiffly in their dowdy little parlor, in a narrow little house on a narrow street in the black quarter, looking at him as though he were some great gaudy disreputable bird of prey invading a hen roost. He hardly recognized either of them. He was not asked to sit down. He could see himself reflected all out of shape in the glass front of a cabinet—long hair, face weathered a deep bronze by a decade and a half of sun and wind, shirt of white buckskin, the last of all Cherry's handiwork, handsomely embroidered with dyed quills, the fine blue blanket edged with scarlet. Behind him the distorted reflection showed a dun-colored wall and a window hung with fine lace curtains that were worn and carefully mended, hand-me-downs from the parlor of some white lady. He began to smile.

"I guess I made a mistake to come here," he said.

The elder sister Mathilda said coldly, "You made a mistake to come back to this town at all."

"Oh?" said Jim. "Why?"

"Why?" said Lou, the younger one, her eyes glittering with indignation. "You think everybody here don't know what you've been up to, robbing white folks, threatening to kill them?" She gestured angrily at his clothing. "Suppose you think you can pass for an Indian now. Suppose you think everybody don't remember what color you are, and what trouble you got into here before. You're going to get yourself lynched, Jim Beckwourth."

Jim said slowly, "I don't reckon your mistresses would really hold that against you."

Mathilda's mouth pinched tight. "That's a terrible thing to say."

He guessed it was, but it was not said in anger. His sisters had a position in society, a very good one. They were of the aristocracy, almost as far above the black field hands as their employers. They were house servants, body servants. They were light-skinned and well-mannered, they were respectable, and they were not slaves. They were proud of themselves. Jim understood how they must feel about him, and he did not resent it. He pitied them, immensely. Suddenly he knew that for him everything, even the loss of Cherry, had been worth it. He knew what it was to live free. They never would. But that was not why he pitied them. It was because they would never feel the lack of it.

"Even when you were a little boy," Mathilda was saying, "you were a bad one. She spoiled you, Ma did, because you were a boy and you looked like *him*."

"I'll try not to shame you," Jim said. "Good-bye." He left them secure behind their lace curtains.

But now the city smelled hot and evil and the streets were like places of ambush.

Lynched. You'll get yourself lynched, Jim Beckwourth.

Let them try it. Let them see what happens when they put their hands on a Crow chief.

He went to the offices of the Western Division of the American Fur Company and asked to see Mr. Chouteau. When he came out again he found Dave Richards waiting for him.

"Don't look so surprised," Rich said.

"You have the damndest way of turning up."

"I ain't the only one knows you're here. You've got a mighty lot of people that don't like you, and some of 'em happen to be in town. They knew you were back as soon as you stepped onto the wharf." He looked Jim up and down. "You ain't exactly hard to notice."

Jim grinned. "How'd you know where to find me?"

"How do I know beaver'll come to bait? And anyways, where else is there for a trapper to go?"

Jim grunted. Things had changed, all right. The King of the Missouri, the mighty McKenzie, had got into trouble over a still he was running to get around the liquor law that everybody else was getting around. He was out. John Jacob Astor had sold his interests to Pratte and Chouteau. He was out. The Rocky Mountain Fur Company had foundered. It was out. Bill Sublette had capitulated to the enemy. So had Fitz and Bridger, who were now on the American Fur Company's payroll. And as Rich said, where else was a trapper going to go? North of the Platte, anyway. South of it, from the Arkansas to Santa Fe, it was St. Vrain and the Bents who were almighty. There were some small outfits still grimly hanging on in the Rockies, but Jim felt no desire to tie up with them. They were likely to die before you could turn in your catch, and then you had to let your furs go for whatever the company or some other competitor was minded to give you.

"How'd you make out?" Rich asked.

"If I go back to the Crow they'll be happy to go on paying me."

"But you ain't going back?"

"Not now, anyway. Not for a while."

Rich, with rare delicacy, let it rest at that.

"They don't need another booshway," Jim said, "but they'll be happy to have me on as an ordinary trapper. Usual deal, their outfit against my catch. But I can buy my own outfit. I don't know." His eyes roved restlessly along the muddy street where they stood. "Maybe I don't want to do anything right now. Maybe I just want to raise a little hell."

That's what all the trappers came to town for, to raise hell. And he had been longer in the wilds than any of them. He had it coming.

Rich said, "Before any of that gets started, Fitz wants to see you."

"Is he here?"

"Yeah. Fittin' out. He seemed real fired up about talking to you."

"All right," Jim said. "Let's go."

They walked side by side as they had walked here once

before. And Jim was glad of Rich.

They found Fitz buying mules. He took Rich and Jim aside where they could hear themselves talk over the hee-hawing and the clatter. Jim started to speak and Fitz stopped him.

"Give me my say, Jim. Don't get me riled before I start." He faced Jim squarely. "I was riled there on the Big Horn, and plenty. I wrote about it, to General Ashley and Milton Sublette, and word got spread around. But that's all. And if I've got a score to settle with a man I don't have to do it with a lynching party. I want that understood."

"Lynching party?"

"I understand there's one out looking for you."

Jim said, "Hell. I ain't overfond of you, Fitz, but I know that isn't your style."

"I ain't overfond of you, either," Fitz admitted. "But we shared a lot of campfires together and I like these polecats a lot less than I do you. Watch out for 'em."

Jim remembered Ginger Beard and Old Joe, and the friend on Tongue River. There had been others.

"Whisky traders."

"Lice," Fitz said. "Trouble was, you weren't really an Indian. If you were, they might have been sore but they wouldn't have taken it personal."

"I know," said Jim. "They're white folks."

Rich sighed. "I warned you, Jim. You didn't have to bust their kegs. Most of all you didn't have to talk about lifting hair. You'd be surprised at the kind of a reputation you've got."

Jim shrugged. He said to Fitz, "You still think you've got a score to settle with me?"

"You weren't square with me, Jim. I know what went on, even if nobody would admit it."

"You weren't square with me, either. What were you going to do with all that whisky and trade goods—swap 'em to the beaver for their skins?"

Fitz glowered at him. "I'd have done better if I'd tried it that way."

They both laughed.

"What the hell," Fitz said, "we're all working for the enemy now. I'm heading back out in three days. If you're still alive and tired of the city, I can always use a man like you to help kick the fat off the pork-eaters' bottoms."

He went back to his mules.

Jim said, "I meant to ask him what Captain Stewart did."

"He was mad," Rich said. "Real mad. He screamed like a wounded buffalo. A kind of an important man, a baronet, whatever that is, and not used to being rough-handled that way."

"Too bad about him."

"He ain't a bad sort at all. Real man, in spite of his ways. If you was two other people you'd get along fine."

They walked away from the mulepens. Carts and wagons creaked and jangled through the streets, their big wheels walloping the rutted mud into new and worse confusion. People trotted busily along or lounged idly in doorways. Now and again heads turned to watch the Crow chief go by. Jim felt cold between his shoulders.

Rich said, "I got an extra horse."

They walked a while.

"Don't suppose," Rich said, "you'd consider getting onto him and riding away?"

"No."

"A sensible man would call that being pretty smart. I suppose you'd call it running."

"I got a right to be here," Jim said.

Rich looked up into Jim's face. In Crow he said, "He is a Crazy Dog, he wants to die." In English he added, "Just plain crazy."

They walked. Dusk thickened in the alleys and around the clustered rooftops. The river showed a pale glimmer of yellow that faded into gray.

"It's the waiting I don't like," said Rich in a high, complaining voice. "Gets me all fidgety. Gives me the bloat and the heartburn. Let's make it easy for 'em to find you, and we can sit and get drunk a little while we wait."

They went into the quarter that was called Vide Poche, the Empty Pocket, because that was where the trappers went to empty theirs just as fast as they could, with friendly barkeeps and friendlier girls to help them do it. And it never occurred to Jim to tell Rich that he didn't have to get mixed up in this. He figured Rich knew that. He figured Rich had sought him out of his own free will. He figured to talk about it later sometime, if they both lived.

They went into a cramped little place with low ceilings and battered walls. There was a powerful smell of alcohol, sweat, dirty wool, and dirty leather. Jim coughed.

"Everybody says Indians smell so bad," he muttered. "Hell, the Crow take a bath every morning even when they have to break holes in the ice to do it. Wonder how long it's been since these boys washed?"

"Since the last time they fell in a creek," said Rich affably. "Just like it always was, remember?"

Jim laughed. The other seven or eight men in the place looked at them, especially at Jim in his Indian shirt and his fine blue blanket with the red edging, but nobody questioned him. The Vide Poche was used to 'breeds and all odd sorts of wild humanity. Rich got whisky from the bar. They sat down at one of the rough tables. They drank slowly. And they waited.

Men drifted in and out. Trappers in buckskins black with the grease and blood of many butcherings, the smoke of many campfires. Mule skinners and drovers from the Santa Fe trade, with a look of sun and dust about them and a special profanity all their own. There was a lot of talk. Taos, Bent's Fort, Bayou Salade, Fort Union, Fort Nonsense, who had been where, seen whom, done what. After a little while Jim became aware that one of the men sitting nearby was watching him with a heavy, fixed stare.

He was by himself. He looked as though he had been drinking for a year, and would be capable of drinking for another before he fell over. He was a powerful, thick-shouldered man with a crop of curly dark hair already gray-shot, though he was fairly young. He wore a filthy, beautifully made hunting shirt that had cost some squaw many hours of patient work. He watched Jim, and watched him, and Jim's belly tightened with the approach of trouble. The big man reminded him of a buffalo bull with his big hairy head sunk and snorting just before the charge.

Rich said, apropos of nothing in particular, "Jim, why do you reckon Astor sold out?"

"Maybe he got tired counting his money," Jim said, not caring.

Rich said darkly, "Astor's a smart man. And when a

smart man gets hold of everything he wants and then turns around and sells it, there's only one reason. He figures he's had the best of it."

The big man leaned over his table and pointed at Jim's shirt with the quill embroidery.

"Crow?"

Jim nodded.

"Crow!" He looked Jim in the eye. "You don't talk like an Indian."

"I was with them a long time." A lifetime, Jim thought. Time you don't measure in years. He stabbed his finger at the big man's breast. "What's that, Bannock?" The contemptuous way the other had said "Crow!" annoyed Jim, and he was being deliberately insulting. The Bannocks were considered not very much above the Diggers.

"Ute," the man said. He sneered. "Crow. Horse thieves."

Jim asked, "When did the Utes start going to church?"

"Church? You mistake me, brother. The Utes *are* horse thieves. The Crow just like to think they are."

"Is that right."

"How many horses do your piddling little Crow raids take? Maybe five or six. Maybe twenty. Maybe even a whole forty or fifty, if you're lucky." He breathed in Jim's face. "My Utes think they've had a bad day if they only lifted four hundred."

He let that sink in. Then he added, "Utes can't only out-steal the Crow, they can outfight 'em, too."

"Well, now," Jim said, "I can't remember any of 'em coming north to prove it."

A great wide smile spread over the big man's face. "Now you've done it, brother," he sighed. "It do beat hell how a man can't sit peaceful in a room drinking without some bastard comes along and starts a fight."

Beaming, he started to rise.

Rich said, "I'm sorry, stranger, but you'll have to wait your turn." He touched Jim's arm.

Ginger Beard stood in the doorway.

He looked at Jim, showing his big broken teeth. "There's the Crow," he said. Behind him the doorway was crowded with men. Jim recognized Old Joe with the cold hard eye, and a couple more he had had run-ins with, including Old Joe's friend from Tongue River. The rest of them he didn't know, but he was willing to bet that not one of them had ever been more than ten miles west of St. Louis. They looked as though they made their living in dark alleys, and went on lynching parties for pleasure. He counted nine men in all, and three of them had ropes. One of these laughed and said, "A real black crow!"

Rich said querulously, "Goddern it, Jim, why didn't you lift their hair and be done with it, 'stead of just talking? Won't you ever learn to either do a thing right or don't bring it up at all!"

The bartender leaned over the bar and spoke to Old Joe. "Go take your trouble someplace else. I don't want it in here."

Old Joe said quietly, "We got business with that black son-of-a-bitch, nobody else. But we got rope enough for anybody that asks for it."

The little mob moved into the room, looking ugly. Old Joe swept his cold fishy gaze around, from the bartender to the handful of trappers and drovers. In the uneasy silence Jim got out of his chair and stood beside it, letting the blanket drop from his shoulders.

"Anybody," said Old Joe.

The trappers and drovers sat quiet, not particularly afraid of the mob but not sure whether they wanted to fight right then, about something they had nothing to do with, and on the whole deciding they didn't. But the big drunken man finished getting up, with a lurch and a hop, and out of the corner of his eye Jim saw that he had a peg leg. He said to Old Joe in an aggrieved voice, "I tell you, brother, I don't like my plans upset. This fella here just started a private fight with me—"

"We'll take care of it for you," said Old Joe, and moved on.

Ginger Beard let go a yell. He capered in front of Jim. "Where are your warriors, Crow? Where are your goddam lousy thieving bucks? Who have you got to hide behind now?"

Jim threw his chair. It caught Ginger Beard on his hastily upflung hands and bore them back, smashing into his face. He went down howling. Jim sprang onto the table. He drew his scalping knife, gave the Crow war whoop, and launched himself straight at Old Joe.

And he could almost have laughed at the expression on Old Joe's face. He had expected Jim to run, or beg, or cry. They all had. It was funny, how astonished they were that he would fight. Lynchings were not supposed to go this way at all.

He bore Old Joe down but he did not get the knife into him. Old Joe had hold of his wrist, and while they were rolling and grunting on the floor the others were using their boots and their fists on Jim. They grabbed him and tried to drag him off, to pull him away into the street. Rich climbed onto the bar, carrying his rifle with the heavy barrel. Muttering and growling, he laid that long length of browned steel across everything he could reach, heads, faces, backs, arms. The bartender ran toward the door bawling for the watch. Somebody tripped him and kicked him under the chin to keep him quiet. Jim got his left hand free and pounded it into Old Joe's face but the others kept yanking and kicking at him and then he felt the rough rasp of hemp across the side of his neck. He went crazy. He surged up through them ripping and slashing, screaming like a panther, and they drew back, shocked.

Jim charged them.

Rich jumped down off the bar to back him up. The fight swirled around, confused, vicious, and quiet. The men were too full of killing to talk or shout. This was not the kind of fight a man joined into for pleasure, and the drovers and trappers went outside and watched through the window, all except the big man in the Ute shirt who stood where he had in the beginning, watching Jim. He was nodding his head and grinning fiercely. He began to unstrap his wooden leg. It was a good stout heavy one, and well-balanced. He took it off and held it in his hand.

"Hang on, Crow!" he shouted. "Here come the Utes!"

He gave a tremendous whoop and hopped powerfully into the fight, swinging the peg leg like a war club.

Jim, fighting in a blind fury, heard the head bones cracking and sensed that the tide had turned. He was aware now of men trying to get away. He saw them going toward the door and he pursued them. Rich was yelling at him, but he did not pay any attention. The big man roared and pounded the stragglers with his club. And then there was nobody left except the bartender on his hands and knees, shaking his head to clear it, and two men lying on the floor.

Jim turned to Rich. "What did you say?"

Rich wiped blood off his cheek with his sleeve. "Never mind. I was talking sense, and that's just a waste of time."

Jim cleaned his knife blade on the shirt of one of the men who lay on the floor. He sheathed it and went stiffly to pick up his blanket. His body ached. He had been cut twice, but not deeply. He threw the blanket around him and said to the big man, "Much obliged. I won't forget this."

The big man was strapping on his leg. "Mighty useful weapon," he said, "and I always got it with me. Whittled it myself. And I done the butchering on myself, too, when everybody else was scared to touch it." He seemed proud of that. Probably it was the first thing he told anyone he met that didn't know. "I had me a fight coming, remember? I take it back, Crow—there's one of you can fight as good as a Ute, anyway."

The bartender had made it to his feet and was lurching toward the door. Rich watched him sourly.

"He'll get the watch here pretty quick, and I'd just as soon not wait around for them." He reached out his foot and nudged the head of the man Jim had cleaned his knife on. It rolled soggily.

"There's a back way," said the big man, and stomped out behind the bar, into a dark and narrow alley full of evil smells.

Jim and Rich followed. They lost themselves in the night and the winding ways. Jim walked alone, though the others were close enough to touch. Their voices reached him like voices heard in still air across a valley. The rage had left him. He felt heavy and sick, and he felt unclean. Not dirty, but unclean, as the Bible used the word. His skin crawled and quivered at the remembered rasp of hemp.

He had thought he knew what hate was. He had prided himself on being a pretty good hater. Now he knew that before tonight he had hated like a child.

"You said you had an extra horse, Rich," he said. "I'd like to use him now."

"Might's well ride together," said the big man. "If you've got no objections."

"No objections," Jim said, "but I'm going now." He shivered with his need to get away out of this place. "Rich, I owe you for tonight."

"Oh, hell," Rich said, "I owe you, you owe me—I'm sick of this owing business. Let's just get ourselves clear of this stinking trap. Stable's that way."

Jim let himself be guided.

"Jim," said Rich, "this here's Pegleg Smith. He's been holding out with Walkara's bunch of Utes—Jim, you listening?"

"Mention horses," Pegleg said. "That ought to make a Crow prick up his ears."

"Horses, Jim. Not fifties, not hundreds. Thousands. You want to go back to trapping, or do you want to get rich on horses?"

But Jim had gone back into his private darkness. "White man's country," he said. "I hope to God they stay in it. I hope to God they let the rest of the land alone. Only good thing about white man's country is leaving it behind you."

Rich was suddenly in a shaking temper. "Will you quit

running down the white man! I'm white, ain't I? I had my neck stuck out right alongside of yours, didn't I? Pegleg too, didn't he?"

Jim stared at him, startled.

"It ain't all who's black and who's white," Rich snarled. "It's towns, and the way people have got to live in 'em. If you was white as the driven snow you couldn't live that way, no more'n I can."

Pegleg stood massively aside, waiting for them to settle things between them. Rich stamped his feet up and down in the mud.

"Fact is," he said, "if you wasn't too thickskulled to see it—fact is, Jim, that you and me, and Fitz, and Pegleg here—all of us—we ain't like anybody else at all, white, black, or red. We didn't have a place to fit us, so we went and made one. And if you—"

He stopped, run out of breath or words, or both. He looked around at the huddled buildings and spat.

"If you wasn't standing there blabbering like a god-damned idiot," he said, "we could be on our way back to it."

Jim's body relaxed. He began to smile. "I'm ready," he said.

They walked on toward the stable. Jim turned to Pegleg. "Was somebody talking about horses?"

"Um," said Pegleg. "Thought maybe you'd like to see how the Utes do it."

"Where?" asked Jim.

As casually as though it was right next door, Pegleg answered, "California."

EIGHTEEN

DAPPLED SUNLIGHT FELL through the vine leaves. It touched Amelita's high Indian cheekbones and made bright moving patches on her glossy hair.

"Are all Yankees so full of the wandering sickness?" she asked. "Don't you ever want to stop?"

"When we get old," Jim told her, in his just-adequate Spanish. "Don't you want to come with me and see what's on the other side of the mountains?"

"I do not!" she said, and laughed. "And I feel sorry for the woman who is ever foolish enough to say yes." She looked at him, up and down, from a little distance. "But not too sorry." She kissed him. "Good-bye, Yankee." She walked away from him, out into the clear sunlight and across the courtyard.

Jim watched appreciatively the free and graceful swing of her bare brown legs. Her skirt was short enough to show them halfway to the knee. The skirt itself was a poppy red, making a pretty splash of color against the baked hardpan of the ground and 'dobe walls with the whitewash crumbling off them. He watched her until she passed through a low doorway and was gone. Then he went down to the corrals, where Rich was waiting for him.

"Someday," he said, "I'm going to marry one of these girls and settle down."

"I'd thought of it myself," Rich said, "but I ain't sure how one of 'em would get along sharing the lodge with Grass."

Jim grinned and shook his head. "They're strong like the Indian women, and they've got the dignity, but they seem to be kind of lacking in patience. I'd hate to try lodgepoling one of 'em." He had never lodgepoled Cherry, but theirs had been an unusually good relationship.

"I would reckon," said Rich, "if you was to try it on Amelita, she'd have your gizzard out and thrown to the cat before you knew what happened."

He looked to see if the wranglers were ready to turn out their little *cavallada* of twenty-eight horses. Jim swung into the saddle of the claybank stallion he was riding, and all the *vaqueros* around the lower corral shouted and laughed at him. Jim rode Indian-style, or mountain-style, which was the same thing, with short stirrups. These *Californios* liked to ride standing on their toes with their legs at full stretch. They thought Jim was very amusing, even though he had shown them he could do one or two things they couldn't.

It worked both ways. "Come on," they shouted, waving coins in the air. "Once more, Yankee! Try once more."

"I'll be along in a minute, Rich," Jim said, and went over to the *vaqueros*. He made the stallion prance, and that made the half-broken colts in the corral shy stiff-legged and snorting from the fence. Some of the *vaqueros* were pure Indio, scattered out from the missions that had no further use for them after the Secularization. They were all superb horsemen. They were good-natured, proud, high-tempered, and tough as their own *reatas*.

One of them placed a coin with great care under each of Jim's knees, where they pressed against the saddle housing.

Jim asked, "Does anybody wish to bet that I don't lose

them both?"

They said he was insulting their mothers by implying that they had given birth to idiots. He had been here ten days and they knew him. Jim laughed and kicked the stallion into a gallop. The course was improvised. Over the tongues of three wagons parked beside a wall, thread a row of tall sycamores like a needle going through cloth, turn three times tightly around the well, and then back to the start at a dead run and bring the horse up rearing. Jim had lost both coins.

They were happy. They told him to go with God, and he thanked them and wished them well, and rode off after Rich. On the way he saw the *hacendado* Menendez coming from his house, a lean, straight-backed man walking like a king with a coiled whip in his hand and his huge spurs ringing. They exchanged courteous salutes at a distance. Jim reined up beside Rich at the head of the *cavallada*.

"I think these people are going to fight," he said.

Rich looked back at the sprawling, whitewashed buildings of the rancho as though he were thankful to see the last of them. "If they'd ever suspicioned for a minute what we were up to we'd have found out what they could do. I felt my hair turning white day by day."

Ostensibly they had been trading for horses, and if the *Californios* fought as hard as they bargained Jim thought that nobody could stand against them. He and Rich had been in California a month with their 'breed wranglers, traveling from the Santa Ana River up to San Luis Obispo and down again, and twenty-eight head was the best they had been able to do. They had lost money on the goods they brought in over the Spanish Trail from Santa Fe.

They expected to get it back.

The valley was wide under the peaceful sky. Low mountains closed it in on the west, and sometimes the wind that blew through the passes brought with it the smell of the sea. To the east the land lifted into rough hills cut with deep arroyos, and then into the foothills of a higher range with bare peaks of gray and sandy pink. Winter never troubled these inland valleys where the grapes and the olives grew. It was November and still warm. The sun had burned the grass to a rich dark gold, clumped with blackish-green live oaks. Beautiful country, Jim thought. A good place for a man to come to when he felt himself getting old. Right now, though, his eyes were less concerned with beauty than with horses.

Alta California was one vast range where the cattle and horses were so thick that in drought years thousands of them had to be slaughtered to save the grass. And from the Santa Ana River to San Luis Obispo and back, Jim and Rich knew exactly where the best horse herds were pastured, which ones were held in the open and which ones were corralled at night.

"I might," said Rich slowly, "feel a mite more guilty if these self-same *Californios* had been a mite more friendly when I was here before. As it stands, I got to admit that all I can think of is it serves 'em right."

The traders and the mountain men had a long, old score against the Spanish settlements. Jim had no personal grudge himself but he had heard enough stories from others, including even the almighty Bents. Individual Mexicans and Californians might be your faithful friends. They might love you, marry you, die for you. But the men who made the rules and signed the papers were a different matter. Bribery and extortion were a way of life. One time you might be given permission to trade or trap, the next time you got thrown into jail and all your possessions were confiscated. Sometimes you got shot. Imperial Spain had always claimed everything right up to the Arkansas and she tried her best to keep a stranglehold on it. Finally she strangled her own colonists into a revolution but it hadn't changed things too much for foreigners. A Yankee was still taking a risk, particularly since the *Texians* had tried the revolutionary shoe on the other foot and won their independence from Mexico, and the Mexicans didn't like it at all. California, being more remote, was less involved in these matters, but Jim knew what Rich meant. He would breathe easier when he saw Cajon Pass ahead of him.

He said cheerfully, "They've got so many horses here they throw 'em away when they get dirty. It won't hurt 'em to lose a few." He was feeling a pleasurable excitement that he had not felt since the last time his scouts came back and reported that they had found the enemy, and he began to plan the raid.

Rich said, "I hope Walkara don't mess things up again."

"He won't. He's smart, he won't make the same mistake twice." Jim laughed. "Besides, he got Pegleg so mad at him he wouldn't speak for three years, and he loves Pegleg better than he does his brothers. He won't do *that* again."

Once before, in the same guise of peaceful traders, they had come down the Spanish Trail to California—Jim and Rich and Pegleg, Walkara the Ute chief and two of his brothers, Arrapeen and Sanpitch. The third one, Tobiah, stayed with Walkara's braves in the outer canyons where they could wait unseen. Pegleg was thinking large thoughts. Jim had discovered that Walkara did not at all feel that he had had a poor day when he ran off four hundred head, or even one hundred. But Pegleg was thinking in thousands, and not just any horses, but the best. This was going to be a real expedition, carefully planned. Everything went well until the Hawk of the Mountains got impatient with the slowness of the white man's methods and whistled his Utes down out of the hills for a raid of his own.

He got a little over two hundred head. A hard-riding group of *Californios* got some of those back. The expedition went up in a cloud of dust, and Pegleg, Jim, and Rich went flying out through the Tehachapis to save their necks. When they got back to Walkara's windy roost on the Spanish Fork, Pegleg packed up his squaws and moved out. Walkara was brokenhearted. But it was three years before he saw Pegleg again.

Jim and Rich trailed with Pegleg for lack of anything more pressing to do. They wintered at Santa Fe and then worked the southwestern country which was Pegleg's old stamping ground. They didn't do well. They moved north again, into the valley of the Green and on, ranging the familiar mountains and trapping the familiar streams, but it was not the same. Beaver was scarce. The mountain passes and the camping places in the "holes" were full of strangers, and many of the old acquaintances were gone, killed and scalped, frozen, starved, drowned, gone under.

Even the old enemies were gone. Smallpox had swept the lodges of the Blackfeet. Many of the young men lay dead, with no one to bury them, and the war parties no longer harried far and wide as they had used to. And farther down the Big River, the Arikara towns were also desolate.

Jim felt a strong yearning to go home. Several times he saddled his horse, and once he actually rode for half a day toward the Wind River range and the passes he had first seen so many years ago. He never made it. Something in him had been broken and was not yet healed. The time for going home would come, he knew that, and he knew that he would recognize it when it came. This was not it.

He returned to Rich and Pegleg and plunged into the icy streams again, setting his traps and noticing in a vague sort of way that when Rich came out of the water after hours of work he had trouble walking, as though his joints had stiffened.

The summer rendezvous were still wild, loud, and drunken, but they were like something hanging on after the need for them was over. There were new trading posts everywhere now, in business all the year round. And all of a sudden Jim found that he and Rich and Fitzpatrick and Bridger, who was now known as Old Gabe, were of a different generation, and there was a whole new young breed to sit at their feet and listen to how it was in the old days before the Platte trail was a beaten highway.

There was something else different from those old rendezvous, when Jim had envied Fitz and Bridger their fame. He was famous himself now. Beckwourth, they would say, and look at him, the milky greenhorns. The name had stories to go with it, and Jim heard them, though not often to his face. Beckwourth the runaway slave who had tried to murder his master. Beckwourth the renegade, who set his Indians onto white traders. Beckwourth the horse thief, who put Fitzpatrick and Stewart helpless on the prairie and then stole their watches too. Beckwourth who had a hundred scalps in his tipi and over half of them white, and there's plenty of men in St. Louis can swear to it because they saw them.

Jim was furious at first. Then he took a contemptuous revenge by frightening the greenhorns out of their skins, acting as wild and savage as they thought he ought to. Rich sweat blood and got him out of there as soon as he could.

The third winter was a hard one and the spring hunt failed. And there was still a market for horses. So once more they rode down to the valley by the Spanish Fork. This time Pegleg laid down the law to his brother the Hawk of the Mountains. Jim and Rich would go ahead to California and spy out the land. Pegleg would go east to see to the marketing end of it—he had cracked a town official over the head with his wooden leg on that last ill-fated visit and thought it wiser to remain out of sight—and Walkara would gather his band of outlaw Utes. At an appointed time they would rendezvous in Cajon Pass.

This, now, was the time.

Jim and Rich, with the *cavallada,* moved at the steady Spanish lope that shook the dusty miles behind them, stopping only long enough to change horses. At sunset the pass was before them. The horses began to labor on the steady grade. Darkness caught them, but the pass was broad and the trail well-worn, and they kept going. When they reached the crest they stopped to let the horses blow. The wind was strong up here, a desert wind smelling of sand and dryness. The stars were very bright, and it was cold.

Jim heard the sound of a pony's hoofs clicking up the

trail on the other side.

The horseman came in sight, riding with the limber slouch of the Indian, and Jim recognized Walkara's brother Arrapeen. "We're here," he said. "All's well."

Arrapeen turned his head and whistled. His profile against the starlight reminded Jim of a hunting owl. They were all handsome men, these brothers, with narrow heads and finely cut faces. Walkara had more wives than he could keep track of, and he was as much of a dandy as he was a warrior. He came up the pass a moment later with Sanpitch and Tobiah, and Pegleg Smith.

The Hawk of the Mountains was impatient again. "My men are ready. I am ready. Tell us, Antelope, where the horses are."

"Hold on," Pegleg said. "Our friends have had a hard ride. They look downright lathered." He unhooked a leather bottle slung from his saddle horn and took a long swig himself, then handed it to Jim. "I got everything settled eastward. Bent's Fort, top price for prime stock, and nobody cares where we get 'em. How did you make out?"

Jim told him. When he was finished Walkara said, "Good. I will take the northernmost herd and come through the Tehachapis."

They planned how it would be done, standing in the starlight at the top of the pass with the desert wind blowing the long hair of the Ute chiefs, and Jim felt alive and good. They would separate into small bands that could stay hidden and move fast, and they would funnel their herds all into Cajon Pass, except Walkara who would join them somewhere out in the Mojave.

"When you start moving," Jim said, "don't stop." He

was talking to Rich and Pegleg, because they would go together. "Because if you do I'll be over the mountain and gone. This child don't intend to linger."

"When?" said Walkara.

They discussed how long it would take to get their men into position and let their horses rest.

"Two days from now," they said, "after the sun is down."

NINETEEN

T HEY LAY IN the brush on top of a hill, waiting for sundown.

The horses were hidden in a deep arroyo behind them. In front was the long, long slope of dark gold that went rolling away to the floor of the valley. There were horses grazing on that slope, or standing comfortably head to tail, brushing the flies from each other and thinking of warm sun and the dry sweetness of grass. Far away the whitewashed buildings of Menendez' rancho caught the light. It was infinitely quiet. Jim felt as peaceful as the drowsy horses.

From time to time a mounted *vaquero* moved across the landscape. There was some action at the corrals. Probably they were busy with the endless and pleasurable work of breaking colts. Dust rose in the air like smoke and drifted slowly away. Jim wondered what Amelita was doing. Cooking frijoles, probably, bending over the fire in her poppy-red skirt, stirring the big iron kettle with a big iron spoon while the heat made her cheeks glisten.

Rich and Pegleg slept. Ten of Walkara's Utes were

passing the time in the arroyo. Birds called and whistled. High up in the blue sky broad-winged buzzards circled, silently, patiently, riding the wind. The sun dropped toward the hills on the other side of the valley. They became one-dimensional, shapes cut out of paper, purple and blue. The sun burned fiercely on them and then was gone. The valley filled with blueness. Lights pricked out among the buildings of the rancho, and a change came in the air, a cool breath chilling the sweat of the day's warmth.

Rich and Pegleg woke and sat up. They ate jerky and cold tortillas, and drank from a leather bottle. The last glow faded from the land. They slid down into the arroyo and led their horses out over rottonstone that turned under their feet. Then they mounted and rode.

The Utes strung themselves out like shadows, riding fast and without sound except for soft chirring noises they used to start the scattered horses moving. Jim, Rich, and Pegleg rode straight for the rancho. They hid in a clump of live oaks, giving the Utes time to finish their sweep and get the herd bunched up and going. In the windows of the rancho some of the lights went out, and then more. They were an early-rising, early-sleeping folk except when there was a fandango. When the time seemed right Jim said, "Let's go."

They burst out of the live oaks running, heading for the corral where the best of the saddle stock was kept.

The dogs began to bark. Jim bent low over his horse's neck, urging him on. The rush of air whipped the mane across his face. He reined up beside the corral and began to drop the bars of the gate. The penned-up horses squealed and blew, shying this way and that with their necks over each other's rumps. The dogs were screaming now in their rage. Candles were being lighted in the buildings. Men came running out with their shirttails flapping. They shouted to one another, flourishing pistols. Rich put a shot carefully into the 'dobe over the heads of the ones he could see the best. They took cover, and Jim charged into the corral. He yelled like a Crow and beat the horses with his hat. They broke out through the gate in a solid stream with Rich and Pegleg hazing them on each side and Jim behind them howling. Pegleg and Rich gave the war cry too and the Utes out on the slope joined in. It sounded as though Walkara's whole band was there. Jim fired his rifle in the air. A few pistol shots followed them but the stampeding horses were quickly out of range.

The valley lay open and quiet before them. All along the slope more horses were running, in twos and threes and bunches, driven on by the Ute riders. They came pouring together like a gathering of rivulets in flood-time until there was a river of horses rushing down the valley, swallowing up and carrying with it the forty or so that Jim and the others were driving. They fell out to the side and rested a minute, watching the dust and the tossing heads go by.

Rich looked back at the rancho. "How long?"

"They'll round up horses," Pegleg said. "They always got more. Give 'em a half, three-quarters of an hour."

Jim said, "I worry about them, but I'm worried more about the ones lower down."

From then on they hung beside the leaders, keeping the herd pointed. The horses could not keep up that pace forever. They slowed to a steady lope and the dark land rolled by. The stars swung overhead, very slowly, and the air was chill. Jim shivered, more with pleasure than with cold. The strong-driving body of the horse was pleasant between his knees, and the clean warm smell of the herd was pleasant too, the smell of victory. He was suddenly keenly lonesome for Young Bear and Muskrat.

Ahead in the night there were cries and a drumming thunder.

Jim stood up in his stirrups. Then he heard Pegleg bawling, "Turn them! Turn them!" The noise came closer, the sound of an avalanche rolling down a mountain. Jim saw Rich beside him. They yelled and beat the leaders' faces with their hats, shouldered them with their mounts. They turned. A solid mass of horses came bolting out of the dark at breakneck speed and shot across what had been their front. Utes hung on the flanks of the herd, screeching. Pegleg roared at them. One of them paused and flung an arm toward the backtrail. *"Californios!"* he yelled, and raced. on. Pegleg shouted in Ute, in Spanish, in profane English. The herd moved faster, following the one that was now ahead of it. Jim and Rich let the Utes handle it and dropped back to join Pegleg in the dust of the drag.

They ran under black mountains. And now out on the broad plain there were pinpricks of light. Scattered ranchos, a distant pueblo, were aroused and angry. Boots were thumping the hard-packed, wind-eroded streets of the pueblo, the huge Spanish rowels dragging and clinking with their own harsh music. Men were shouting, boys were running four horses, and pistols, smooth-bores, anything that would shoot were being snatched up and loaded. From the low doorways and deep small windows with the iron grilles women and large-eyed children were watching, and the thin-bellied dogs were everywhere, yapping. Jim thought of the *vaqueros* who had played the coin game with him and won, and he multiplied those hard hands and faces by the scattered lights. It had been easier to raid horses from the Blackfeet and Cheyennes. If they pressed you, you killed them. This was different. The Utes did not make war on white men. Certainly he and Rich and Pegleg would not do so.

"If we can't outrun 'em," Pegleg said, "shoot their horses. They're harmless on foot."

"What do we do until daylight?" Rich asked cynically. "I'm a middling good shot but only when I can see."

"Godamighty," said Jim. "Look there."

There were horses, hundreds of horses, racing across the dark plain. Jim had been staring at them for a long time without seeing them, and then all at once he had sensed movement, a fluid streaming of the darkness in many places, and he knew what it was. There must have been seven or eight herds of varying sizes, coming from different directions but all heading toward the same place, the place where their own wild torrent of horseflesh was heading, Cajon Pass. Pegleg let his breath out in an exultant howl. He cursed and pounded his wooden leg and laughed. "This is a horse raid!" he said. "This is some!"

A lot more quietly Rich said, "Horses." He rode coughing in the dust a little way. "There's our answer. Horses."

The herds rushed nearer, converging, their tossing fronts showing dark and tumultuous out of the paler dust clouds they carried with them. The cries of the Ute riders sounded, shrill and sharp.

There were other sounds. The voices of white men, and shots banging, not far away.

"Horses," Rich said. "We can spare a few to hide behind."

Jim fired his rifle, high. Rich fired his, and then Pegleg. The authoritative voices of those long mountain rifles would give the *Californios* something to think about for a minute or two. The three of them made for the nearest of the converging herds. A man rode to meet them. From his voice and the way he rode Jim recognized Sanpitch. Pegleg told him in rapid Ute what they wanted. Sanpitch objected, and Jim said, "We can lose a few horses now and get through the pass, or we can lose a lot more later. Look at them, Sanpitch. There are more than we can drive."

Sanpitch was an intelligent Indian. He gave in. But Jim knew that he would about as soon have given up his right arm as part of the herd he had taken.

They caught up with the leaders and turned them, heading them toward the trail where the voices and the shots came from. Presently they saw the riders, a long dark blot moving fast, picked out with starshine on metal. The Utes had been working hard to cut the herd. Jim and Sanpitch and the others dropped back and let the point of the herd go by itself. The mass of horses separated. What had been the swing became the new point and the bulk of the herd tore off toward the pass. The detached point went careering into the bunched up riders, scattered them, tossed them, absorbed them, and carried them away.

Jim said, "We ain't got it licked yet."

"Let's be happy with right now," Pegleg said, and made his horse jump.

The river of horses flowed into the pass. It streamed upward along the winding grade, wild eyes and shaking manes, straining shoulders and flying legs, slowed by the ascent and constricted by its own numbers but pushed on by the howling Utes and the pressure of those that came behind. The head of the river snaked up over the crest and plunged downward, gained speed again, and went bursting out into the desert with a roar and a squeal and a great fragrance of trampled sage.

The weaker ones were falling out. They let them go. The more there were for the Spaniards to round up the slower the chase would be. They kept pushing the herd but not so hard. Dawn came gray and cool over the infinite desolation of the Mojave, and then as the sun rose the grayness and the coolness slid away in the hollows of the sand. A marching line of mountains, naked as gnawed bones, turned a faded pink streaked with white as though by the droppings of gigantic birds. Sand and sage became a monotony painful to the eye, except for those places in the distance where alkali flats glittered with a searing whiteness. Almost at once it was hot. But not so hot as in summer, when animals dropped in their tracks even sooner than men.

Pegleg stood on top of a dune and watched the horses go by. "How many do you make 'em?"

Jim said, "Call it two thousand."

"Two thousand!" Pegleg cried. "Hell, man, there's three thousand right in front of your eyes and more coming. Call it four, anyway. Call it five!"

Jim didn't argue. He didn't care. It was a lot of horses. He thought it was probably the biggest lot of horses that had ever been lifted in one raid. He was satisfied. His chief worry now was hanging onto them.

After a while a dust devil came chasing them on a long

slant from the north. It was Walkara, bringing in a small bunch of only sixty head. But Jim knew that herd and how much it was worth, and how very well it was guarded. He said gravely to Walkara, "The Hawk of the Mountains is a great lifter of horses."

Walkara smiled, a proud, handsome man in the bitter sunlight. "The Antelope too is great," he said generously. "Before he raided like a Crow. Now he raids like a Ute." He rode up along the vast herd to talk to his brothers.

The sun rose higher. The dry wind sucked the moisture out of skin and flesh, scarified the mouth and tongue. The horses were tired. They lagged with their heads hanging. And Rich pointed back through the shimmering white glare to where another dust devil was moving, still far off but coming swiftly, from the direction of the pass.

Walkara and his brothers joined the white men at the tail of the herd, looking back. Walkara echoed Jim's earlier thought. "If they were Shoshoni it would be easy."

"Pity they ain't," Pegleg said, "but they ain't."

"Well," said Walkara, "there's another way." He nodded at Sanpitch and laughed. "My brother is sad that he had to part with many of his horses."

Rich looked at Sanpitch and then at the herd. "You wouldn't say," he asked, "that your brother is maybe just a little mite greedy?"

Sanpitch said, "It may be true that I have enough horses. But what shall I do for saddles?"

They rode a little farther. Then Sanpitch and his brothers dismounted with twenty picked men. "The herd will have to run now," Walkara said. "They're tired but it won't kill them." He looked at the white men. "This has to be done on foot."

Pegleg shook his head. "I'll stay with my horse."

"What does the Antelope say?"

Jim looped up his reins and turned his horse into the herd. He didn't want to, but he couldn't let these Utes go back to the mountains with a story of how the Antelope had ridden away like a squaw. He didn't have Pegleg's excuse. Rich followed him, and for once he did not swear or complain about Jim's foolishness. He simply wore an expression of resigned disgust.

Pegleg and the Utes forced the herd into a sullen, heavy run. They all seemed to go away quite rapidly. The desert opened up wide around the dismounted men. Heat burned up through the soles of Jim's Spanish boots and he felt shrunken to the size of a child. Very bitterly he regretted his horse.

The dust cloud raced toward them. Walkara smiled. "We have time for a drink," he said.

In this blistering desolation there was water, if you knew where to find it. It came up out of an ancient well with a broken coping, and it was cool, and bitter with alkali. The riders had been here, stopping one by one as they passed. The horses would not drink until they reached the river. Around the well there were the remains of ancient walls and a scattering of natural rock heaped in tumbled piles and carved to queer shapes by wind and chafing sand. The men drank and then found places in the rocks and lay close in them, waiting.

The *Californios* came.

It was a large party, perhaps sixty men. They had ridden hard for a long way and they were white with dust like millers. Peering at them through a chink in the rocks, Jim hoped that Sanpitch and Walkara knew what they were doing. These were angry men. Jim did not blame them. He had had horses run off himself. He had no wish to kill any of them. He had no wish to let any of them kill him, either. For the first time he was sorry he had got into the whole business.

Sanpitch waited until all the Spaniards were standing around the well, unsuspecting and concerned with water. Then he screamed the war cry. The other Utes took it up. There was a tremendous volley of shots from behind the rocks, all high, but the Spaniards would not realize that until later. They dived for cover behind the walls. The horses bolted. Lean half-naked shapes ran among them, grabbing trailing reins, swinging up to ride clinging flat to the horses' sides. Jim fired and reloaded and fired again as fast as he could. The rifles behind the rocks were keeping the Spaniards pinned. There was a constant wolfish howling.

Walkara came past, leading horses. Rich rose and scuttled to him. Jim ran after. Now that the rifle fire had slackened, the Spaniards began to shoot over their walls. Jim's hat spun off and he fell flat, knocked down by a stunning blow on the head. He struggled to get up and felt someone pulling at him. It was Rich. He staggered to his feet, saw a horse in front of him and climbed onto it, more by instinct than reason, with Rich hauling and swearing at him. By the time his sight cleared, he and Rich and all the Utes and all the Spaniards' horses were going full tilt away from the well.

"They'll have a long walk home," Walkara shouted, and the Utes all laughed. Sanpitch was astride a fine black stallion with saddle trappings all trimmed in silver. He was yelling as he rode, for sheer pleasure.

Jim lifted his hand and felt the place where the ball had grazed him.

"Leave it alone," Rich said. "I'll fix it when we get to the river." He looked hard at Jim. "And this one you owe me for!"

Jim began to laugh. They had all done a mighty thing, and they were safe now, and still alive, heading for the Colorado with a fortune in horses and nothing to bar the way. What was one small headache?

He rode up beside Sanpitch and raced him, yelling.

TWENTY

THEY WERE AT Bent's Fort on the Arkansas. They were rich. They were full-fed and getting drunk.

"What'll you do with your money?" Jim asked.

"Spend it," Pegleg said. "What else is it good for?"

William Bent laughed, "God help Taos!" He was a lean, wiry man with a predatory nose and a sharp, bright, intelligent eye. He and his older brother Charles had been beaten out of the fur trade in the north, but they had not suffered by it. They were kings in this great adobe castle that looked south across the river into Mexico. With their partner Ceran St. Vrain they had made the Santa Fe trade and they still controlled it. Charles was married to a Spanish lady and spent much time in Santa Fe now. William's wife was a Cheyenne, the beautiful Owl Woman, and this was his domain, a vast spaciousness of sky and sun and desert rivers, winter northers and summer storms, and a wide,

wide tawny plain where the Cheyenne bands came riding down to trade and you could see the dust of their coming a hundred miles away. Jim liked William Bent.

"I think," said Rich slowly, and stopped. He was far gone, in a gentle meditative way. He stared for a while at some pleasant vision. Then he said, "I think I'll buy me a rancho."

"Where?" Jim asked.

" 'Round Taos. Somewhere. Settle down. Run some stock."

"Settle!" Bent said. "Kiowa, Comanche, Apache, and Ute, they'll settle you. They'll run your stock."

"Um," said Rich, nodding. "But them beaver streams are cold. Wasn't ever anybody up to beaver like I was, and I never minded getting froze, but I mind now. 'Specially when beaver's scarcer than redheaded Indians, and don't bring hardly a plug of tobacco when you get it."

It was early afternoon and the light that came in from the courtyard was bright enough in spite of the lean-to roof that shaded the room. There was no particular reason why Jim should pick that moment to see in that inflowing light that Rich was gray as a badger and that his face was no longer young.

"Fur trade's coming on bad times," Bent said. "Some are still making out, and I guess some always will, but it's not what it was." There was a certain note of satisfaction in his voice when he added, "The boys were so busy cutting each others' throats they never once realized they were cutting their own."

"See?" Rich said. "I got to buy me that rancho." He stared out the window and then said in that same slow, mild voice, "Those two are still standing there watching." He was not quite as far gone as he seemed. "There was four. Other two went away 'bout the time I really began to drink."

Jim had noticed that too, but he hadn't said anything. The Cheyenne warriors stood where they had stood for almost two hours, on the opposite side of the courtyard against the wall, tall, slender men with their blankets folded close around them and eagle feathers drooping from their hair. There were nearly always Cheyennes around Bent's Fort, friends or relatives, and often a village was camped in the Big Timbers farther downriver, where there was wood and grass. There was one camped there now, and Jim was figuring time and distance.

Bent said, "It isn't so many years since you were running off their horses and killing their young men. Indians have long memories."

"They paid me back," Jim said softly, and got up.

"Where are you going?"

Jim made the sign for Talk and started toward the door. Rich's voice stopped him.

"Will you wait till I sober up?"

"No."

"I'll try and buy your scalp back," Rich said dreamily.

Pegleg said, "He's too drunk, and I ain't drunk enough. Wait a little till I work up some fight."

"There won't be any fight," Bent said curtly. "I'll do the talking, Jim."

Jim nodded. "They'll come asking for the Crow, and you'll refuse to give him up."

"Naturally. You're safe here."

Jim looked through the doorway at the enormously thick high walls, with towers at two of the corners where men could sweep all the approaches with rifle fire, and he laughed. "Sure. Only I ain't fixing to settle here permanent. What'll you do, send a hundred of your men with me when I leave?" He gestured at the warriors. "All they have to do is wait, and in the meantime two things happen. They get a grievance against you for protecting an enemy. That's what started the whole Arikara war, remember—when some trappers wouldn't give up a couple of Sioux they had with them. And—"

"My Cheyennes—" said Bent.

"Your Cheyennes will think I'm scared of them," Jim said, "and they'll rub me out the way they would a dog, the very first time they catch me in the open."

"He thinks like an Indian," Rich muttered. "Rather get killed than let somebody think he's scared. Can't argue with him. Tried."

Jim looked at Bent. "You know I'm right."

"In theory, yes. But in practice—"

"Kiowa, Comanche, 'Pache, 'Rapaho," said Jim. "I wouldn't try it. These are Cheyennes. They're like the Crow. They're men."

Bent shrugged. "It's your scalp."

"Try to buy it back," Rich murmured again. Jim went over and dropped the little poke of gold coins that was his share of the horses into Rich's hunting shirt.

"Don't waste it on hair," he said. "Buy cattle." He turned to Bent. The whisky was burning in him and he felt reckless. "Tell you what, I'll make a bet with you. If I don't come back, I lose. If I do, you take me on. Rich can have his rancho, but I ain't ready to settle yet."

"If you come back," Bent said, "I wouldn't think of losing you."

They shook hands and Jim went out and walked across the wide courtyard to the tall Cheyennes who waited there.

In sign language he said, "I am the Crow."

They answered, "We know."

"I am going to your camp. I wish to speak to your warriors."

Their eyes glittered darkly in the sunlight. "They know you. They are coming now."

"I will meet them," Jim said. He turned away, leaving them to follow if they would. He felt the way he had felt the day he fought the Blackfeet with Rainbow and his Shoshoni, when his medicine was strong and he knew it, and knew that he could not fail. He mounted and rode out of the great gate, onto the scorched plain above the river bed. He rode toward the Big Timbers with the two Cheyenne braves behind him. He knew that every man in the fort was up on the wall to watch him. He did not once look back.

He saw a dust cloud coming toward him. He rode to meet it. There were twenty-three warriors painted for war, carrying their round shields with the covers off so that the blazons shone. Several of them wore bonnets of eagle feathers. When they saw him approaching they looked at each other in surprise and pulled up their horses, waiting. Jim rode up to them and stopped. The two Cheyennes who had come with him spoke to the party, but he paid no attention to them. He sat as tall and impassive as the warriors. The wind ruffled their white plumes and shook the pennons on the lances. He looked them one by one in the face, and he had an Indian's eye and an Indian's memory.

"Cheyennes!" he said. "I am the Crow. I am the Antelope, the Bloody Arm, the Enemy of Horses. You know me. Many times we have met." He spoke aloud in Crow, but his hands spoke the universal language of the Plains. "You!" he pointed to a warrior. "On the Medicine River we fought."

The warrior said, "I am the Bob-tailed Horse. I remember."

"Did I fight strongly that day, like a man? Or did I run away?"

"You fought strongly. You captured a gun."

Jim turned to another. "You came to run off Crow horses. With eight warriors you came. Three of these warriors did not leave Absaroka. Silent they remained. Crow horses you did not get."

"I am Leg-in-the-water. That was the first time as leader that I signaled a loss. I remember."

"Did I fight strongly, or did I run away?"

"You fought strongly, you did not run."

"Cheyennes! I am here. I do not run. Formerly I was your enemy. Now I am your enemy no longer, though your warriors have made my lodge empty and my hearth cold, so that I may no longer live in Absaroka. Kill me if you wish, run from you I will not. If you do not kill me, then I will be as your brother and the brother of the Little White Man. I will bring the goods of the Little White Man to your villages to trade, and I will not cheat you. Cheyennes! I have said."

He waited. The wind blew over the plain where the stiff yucca stood, and the prickly pear. The Cheyennes sat like statues on their horses, considering.

Leg-in-the-water said, "The Crow is a brave man. I will not kill him."

The white plumes nodded, the wind-blown pennons shook.

"He speaks like a warrior. Let him live."

Bronze faces in the hard sunlight, men giving judgment.

"Had he run away I would have killed him. But he did not run."

The Bob-tailed Horse spoke to Jim. "Crow! The Cheyennes have said. They are men, they do not break their word. From this time we are no longer enemies."

Jim answered, "It is well."

They rode back together to the fort, remembering old battles and comparing their coups.

The next day Rich and Pegleg rode south over the mountains to Taos and Jim did not see Rich again for a long while. Messages came up with the wagon trains from Santa Fe and Jim got them, sometimes at the fort, more often in some far-flung village of the Cheyennes.

Rich had bought a small ranch. He had some horses and some cattle, chiefly draught oxen for the trade. He had trouble with Indians, but he could still shoot plumb center and they did not push him too hard. He was more worried about the Mexicans. They seemed to like foreigners less and less. After the *Texians* tried their march on Santa Fe the citizens threw Charles Bent into the *cárcel* for nothing, and for a while it looked like war. Between one thing and another he slept with one eye open and his rifle loaded, but it was better than setting traps for beaver that didn't come. He was taking good care of Jim's investment and in a little while it would pay off. Meantime, the fandangos in Taos were *some* for getting the stiffness out of a man's bones!

Jim was always glad to hear these things. He was not tempted to go and share them. He was living Indian again and he was happy. In a way it was better than going home. The Cheyennes accepted him and even honored him. He danced with them, hunted with them, joined the Dog Soldiers society and fought with them, but he did not have any family or clan ties with the endless responsibilities that went with them. He came to the Cheyennes as a trader from their brother, William Bent, the Little White Man, and that was his position with them. He could have the best of both worlds.

This relationship, which did not involve his emotions too deeply, made it easier for him to do something he could not have done with the Crow, and that was sell whisky. The Cheyennes had had it for a long time and there was nothing he could do to change this. He sold it more or less without compunction, only insisting that the women should trade their robes first for the things they needed, so that only a portion of the village wealth was squandered.

There were times when he thought of marrying again. The Cheyenne women were beautiful and renowned for their chastity. He would have liked to have a lodge of his own once more. Only he kept remembering Cherry and what had happened to her, and thinking how easily it could happen again. The war went on, as it always had and always would. Crow, Arapaho, Comanche—there were enemies on all sides. He did not take another wife.

Word came to him from Absaroka, the first direct contact he had had with his people since he left. Bridger brought it to him. Old Gabe, the Blanket Chief, was a power among the Crow, not as Jim had been but as a white man they liked and respected. One day he came into the village where Jim was staying, and after the greetings were over he said, "I have a message for you, Jim. From Young Bear."

"How is he?" Jim asked, a great pang of homesickness running through him.

"Fine. He's a good man, respected in council. He says to tell you that they know you're with the Cheyennes now."

"What do they think about that—the Crow?"

"They're pleased. They think the Antelope is doing a smart thing, spying out their enemy. They think that when you've counted their warriors, mapped their trails, and tallied up their horses, you'll come back and show them how to rub out the whole Cheyenne nation."

Jim considered that. "What does Young Bear think?"

Bridger looked at him with those blue eyes that seemed to have gotten lighter and sharper with the years until they pierced like spearpoints.

"Young Bear says the Antelope must go where his medicine tells him. Every year he builds a small sweat lodge for you and prays to the Ones-who-make-things-happen. I guess he figures you'll come back when your medicine says it's time. He says to tell you Big Bowl and Captures-white-horses are well but getting old, and your son is a man now. He's taken the war trail twice against the Dakota."

He let Jim consider that too, for a while, in silence. Then he said, "The Dakota are moving west, Jim. Really moving, the whole nation. They're driving the Crow back into the Big Horn Basin."

"I know," Jim said bitterly. "I do some trading with the

southern bands. They've bragged to me about it. But they say the white men are driving them, moving all the time from the east. They say all the land treaties and the promises ain't worth the price of a dead horse."

"It's true," said Bridger.

"Does Young Bear think if I was there we could keep the Dakota out?"

"I think he reckons it might help."

Jim shook his head. "We both know better than that. The Crow are a small nation. The Dakota are like the leaves on the trees. We couldn't stop them no matter who was leading."

"It's the buffalo they want. Where the white man comes everything else goes. Not men like us, Jim, we live with the country like the Indians. I mean the kind that build houses and tear up the ground and chop the forests down, and make a damned cow pasture where there used to be game. You can't blame the Dakota. They got to have meat."

"You know what?" Jim said. "Right from the beginning, with Lewis and Clark, people that came west of the Mississippi made a bad mistake. We made it. We had to brag how good we were, breaking that trail along the Platte, and pretty soon every jackass with a mule and a dozen traps was heading out to take the beaver away from us. Nobody should have told anybody where they went or how. Then only the people that had a right to go could have gone."

Bridger sighed, a tall, big-shouldered, broad-jawed man staring into a fire and feeling a faint breath blowing from the east, a breath with a bad smell in it, the smell of towns. "They're talking Oregon now. They're even talking California. There's already been two things go over the

Rockies I never thought to see, and that's wagons and women—white women. Well, the country's still mighty wide. I reckon it'll take some time to fill it, more time than you and I have got."

He stayed a few days, then shook Jim's hand and rode west.

A few months later Rich came in. He had a thin small poke of coins for Jim, his share of the profits from the ranch.

"It ain't much," Rich said cheerfully, "but even poor bull's better'n nothing." He ate fat cow at Jim's fire and sniffed the air, the Indian smell of smoke and leather. "I reckon to go on up to the Snake and see how Grass and the girls are doing."

He looked well. He seemed to have got over his rheumatism, not having to wade all the time in ice water. He was full of talk about Mexico and the settlements, the pretty girls and the Taos whisky. Pegleg had torn the town up so bad that his friend had had to drag him away and lock him up for a while. There were hints of trouble flying through the air all the time, but it didn't pay to listen to them. If a man minded his business and kept his powder dry he could make out nearly anywhere.

"When are you coming down?" he asked. "I'd like you to see the place. 'Sides, I figure you're young yet, with a lot of hard work left in you."

"Sometime," Jim said carelessly. "Give Grass my regards, and I'll ride a piece with you on your way."

He rode with him. They came out on the low bluffs above the Platte and saw a long, long string of wagons moving on the flat land below, beside the shallow river.

They stopped and sat their horses and looked and did not say anything for a long while.

The wagons crawled steadily forward, the teams leaning patiently into their collars. They were very big wagons, with tilts of canvas to cover them. There were men with them, and women, and young ones. There were loose horses and cattle and a mighty amount of dust. And out of the wide still river bottom where once there had been countless buffalo, there rose now a creaking and a clattering and a bawling and the shrill thin sound of human voices.

"I'll be goddamned," Rich said softly at last. And again, "I will be goddamned!" He struck his hand on the saddle horn. "There's the end of us, Jim. The good people are coming, the women and the preachers, the ones that shut the windows and lock the doors." He stared down, hating them. "Look at 'em, Jim—with their petticoats and corsets, and pots and pans, and plowshares and washtubs, and all that goes with 'em. You know how I feel? I feel like a Blackfoot wanting hair."

Jim said, "They ain't about to settle here. They're only passing through, to Oregon."

"Jim," said Rich, "that's just how it happens with the smallpox. One case, passing through."

Jim was silent. There was something about the slow, remorseless pace of the wagon train that appalled him. It was like the creeping of time, that could not be stopped nor turned.

TWENTY-ONE

MOVERS, THEY WERE called. They came from everywhere, the failures, the shiftless, the impoverished, the impractical, people who had nothing where they were and who hoped for better things beyond the mountains. Year by year they came in their increasing hundreds until the valley of the Platte was filled all summer long with an endless procession of wagons. Where there had been the lines of buffalo trails and the Pawnee Trace there was now a great churned and rutted track running like a raw scar clear across the country, from the jumping-off places in Missouri to the Pacific Ocean.

There were other signs to show where the movers had passed. They ate up the grass and stripped the groves of cottonwood trees. They slaughtered and drove away the game. They left behind them a three-thousand-mile-long scattering of garbage and broken wheels, worn-out animals, cast-off clothing and discarded junk, and their own dead.

Watching them, Jim was moved to a bitter kind of laughter. He had worked so hard to open that road.

There began to be trouble. The Indians whose lands were being invaded and defaced became resentful, and then alarmed. Jim wanted no part of that trouble. Fitz and Clyman and others of the mountain men had laid by their traps and hired on as guides for the wagon trains. Jim would have nothing to do with them.

"First place," he said once to Fitz, "they'd never hire me." He had ridden into camp one evening to sit by the fire and talk. The wagons were drawn up in a circle and the people were getting their suppers, looking weary and dragged-out. Children squalled and mothers yelled at them. The men sat with the lumpishness of exhaustion. "They think they've got it hard," Fitz said, and laughed. "If we'd had all these wagons and supplies when we came this way, and our wives and families with us, we'd have thought we were living like kings. And you know another funny thing about 'em, Jim? They've never been here before, but they're pretty sure they know more about it than I do, and they're mighty sure they understand Indians better than I do. They get uneasy and suspicious when I talk to Indians—they figure that a man who can get along with savages has just got to have something the matter with him. These are good Christian folk, Jim. I hear a lot about the children of Satan and the disgustingness of marrying squaws."

"You're welcome to 'em," Jim said. "Anyway, the kind of stories I've heard told about me, I'd never last out to Independence Rock with a crew like this. They'd shoot me down the first time they saw six Indians coming, figuring the old renegade had already sold their scalps for a dollar apiece."

Jim left the Platte, and the Cheyennes, before any of the spilled blood could splash onto him.

He went south over Raton Pass to Taos and spent some time with Rich, helping to build another room on the tiny adobe hut that passed for a ranch house and planting cactus fences for the corrals. It was beautiful country, high and clean, with mountains jagging the blue sky. Taos itself was a nice town, sun-bitten and wind-worn like all these Mexican towns in this dry blazing country. He liked it, and there was a girl there, another Amelita with high cheekbones and lithe brown legs. He began to think, just a little in odd moments, about settling on his share of the ranch.

Then in 1846 the long-smouldering trouble that had begun over Texas burst into a full-fledged war, and everything went to hell in a whirlwind.

In the villages of the Comanche, the Kiowa, the Apache, and the Ute, the young men danced and painted themselves for war. The whites were busy fighting each other, and while their backs were turned and their hands occupied it was time for the Indian to strike. Mexican and American both were intruders in this land that did not belong to either of them. Now was the time to sweep them out.

They almost did it.

Jim and Rich wound up, when the war was over, without a head of stock to divide between them, and they were luckier than many of the rancheros south of the Arkansas. They were still alive. And the end of the war did not stop the raiding. Every season the tribes grew more angry at the increasing influx of whites. The Comanche robbed and murdered wherever they could, and even the Little White Man's Cheyennes had been pushed almost beyond restraint. It was not then a peaceful nor a prosperous country.

On top of that, Taos had lost its charm for Jim. He and Rich were there with the volunteers who put down the uprising. They saw Charles Bent lying dead on his own hearth, scalped Pueblo-fashion with a bowstring, and the streets of the town never looked so pretty afterward, even when the flayed and mutilated bodies of the other American residents had been taken away and the bloodstains faded by the sun to a dull unnoticeable brown.

After the uprising they carried dispatches for the Army between Santa Fe and Fort Leavenworth, a long, hard ride each way with Apache and Comanche out for their hair and Rich grumbling, growling, and cursing at every step. In the midst of all this it seemed completely unimportant that Jim's girl became violently Mexican and refused to have anything more to do with him.

"I think," said Rich, when it was all over, "I've seen enough of this country. I want to look at some other rocks and sky for a spell."

"California's American now," Jim said. "It ought to be safe to go back there."

Rich nodded. "I'm going to find me a vine and a fig tree, like it says in Scriptures, and just set. I'll set in the shade when it's hot, and I'll set in the sun when it's cool, and other than that I ain't going to move."

"Leave some room," Jim said, "for me."

He had money waiting for him at Bent's Fort and they went to collect it. William Bent looked twenty years older, and he no longer laughed. Charles was dead and so was Owl Woman. The Santa Fe trade was dying. The trading posts along the Arkansas were shut, and there was talk of the Army buying this mud-walled castle as a fort from which to subdue the Indians. Jim walked across the huge courtyard in a high hot blaze of sun, but it seemed to him that the shadows hung very heavy under the porches, and the wind had a hollow sound where it blew. The many men who had been here were gone, the trappers and traders and clerks and hunters. In the empty rooms there was a stillness and a cold peace. Jim was glad to draw his money and go.

He and Rich rode north to the Platte by easy stages. The

Cheyennes were in an ugly frame of mind. Talking to them, Jim began to understand that what was making them ugly was fear, even though they did not realize this themselves. Control of their lives and affairs was being taken out of their hands. Strangers were coming in and changing everything and never asking them if they minded. There were soldiers, and threats, and promises, and all the time the buffalo grew scarcer and more and more strangers came and were furious if the Indians objected. Word had come to the Cheyennes that Broken Hand was on his way to Bent's Fort to be their agent, and this was good, they trusted Broken Hand, and he would carry their words to the chiefs of the white men. But they remembered a day when they had not needed Broken Hand or anyone else to plead for them, when no army of soldiers threatened their villages, when the buffalo were plenty and no white teamsters shot their people along the Platte.

"Fitz had better do a good job," Rich said. "The 'Rapaho are mad too, and the Sioux got *their* backs up—I don't know, Jim. I don't know how it'll all end."

"It won't end," Jim said. "It'll go on for a long time, getting worse." He added viciously, "Why did you reckon I said California?"

"Oh," said Rich, "I knew that. If you was Indian you'd stay and fight the white man. But you ain't. And if you was white you'd stay and fight the Indian, but you ain't." He paused, frowning. "No, that's not right, either. I'm white, but I don't figure to fight for something I don't want, which isn't white nor Indian, but *towns*. You know, Jim, I'll bet if Indians all clumped together in a mess as big as St. Louis I wouldn't like them one bit better than I do white town-folks. Seems to me people are only good in small bunches. So I don't have a side to fight on either. Why did you reckon I said I'd go to California?"

They followed the emigrant road, up to Black's Fork of the Green where Old Gabe had built a fort and trading post with the veteran Louis Vasquez. Old Gabe was doing well, selling horses and supplies and blacksmithing to the movers, who were pretty well out of everything by the time they got that far.

"I could see it coming," Bridger said, meaning the migration and the changing times. "And a man can't make do with trapping alone any more." He looked across his beautiful valley, at the mountains. "I can tell you, though, I wasn't cut out to keep store." He laughed, shaking his head, and his eyes were bright and restless.

There were several lodges of Shoshoni camped at the fort. Rich was able to get word of Grass and his daughters. They were far up along the Snake, too far for a visit unless Rich wintered over. The season was getting late and the Sierra passes would be blocked with snow.

"Do whatever you want," Jim said. "It's all right with me. California won't run away." The boiling troubles in the eastern plains seemed very distant here. He would not have minded roaming over the old country again.

"No," said Rich, "I got my mouth made up for that vine and fig tree, and I never saw any of either growing in a winter camp on the Snake. Grass can wait another season." He sent a message and a bolt of red cloth.

They passed westward over the mountains, avoiding the new Mormon settlements where they did not take kindly to strangers, and avoiding the Utes, who did not always take kindly to white men these days. Not all their chiefs had Walkara's feeling about them. Jim wondered how long Walkara himself would keep it now that he had a white invasion on his own doorstep. The Mormons were not like Pegleg Smith. They were stayers. They would rip up the sod and fence in the pastures and build towns. The Hawk of the Mountains might see the day when he was as frightened as the Sioux and the Cheyennes, not of death but of destruction.

Over a high and difficult pass in the Sierra Nevadas they came again to California.

There were not immediately any vines and fig trees. Rich said that a man would be foolish to pick the first place he saw and sit down there, no matter how pretty it was. A man ought to look around. Jim agreed, knowing what Rich's real trouble was. Now that he was here he wanted to put off settling just a little longer. Jim felt that way himself, he wasn't sure why, except that there was a strange finality about coming up hard against the Pacific Ocean. All their lives they had fought to go west and farther west, and now they had run out of westing. The mountains were no longer before them. They were at their backs.

So they looked, and while they were looking gold was discovered on Sutter's Creek.

TWENTY-TWO

J IM LAID DOWN the pokes of gold dust one by one, stacking them. They made little fat slapping sounds, very pleasing to the ear.

"Behold!" said Jim. "Thou settest a table for me in the presence of my enemies."

"If they ain't our enemies," Rich said, "they ought to be, the prices we charge 'em." He patted the stack of greasy leather pokes. "Mighty pretty. I don't know how long this'll last, but it sure beats trapping for beaver."

"This" was keeping store, and Jim remembered what Bridger had said about that. He agreed with him. Only the money came in so fast and so easy you couldn't turn it down, so you kept staying with it a while longer.

When the first wave of the flood came pouring into the diggings around Sonora, he and Rich started with a tent and two muleloads of supplies, pants and shirts, picks and shovels, thick-soled boots. Now they had a building and a full-fledged business. Jim knew he ought to be content. He was past fifty, and if he was ever going to lay up enough of this world's wealth to do him any good it had better be attended to now. The trouble was that he did not feel any different physically from the way he had always felt, and not very different mentally in the fundamental ways that mattered. So he was no more content with being penned up and quiet than he had been at twenty.

"Yeah," he said carelessly. "It sure does." He swept the pokes together into a sack and tucked the sack into its hiding place between the wall studs at the end of the counter, where it would take several determined men a long while to find it. It was dark outside. The front window was covered with calico curtains, which had been made for it by the only women in town, who lived all together in a big house down the street and were not very good at sewing. There was a candle burning, only one because candles were scarce, and by the light of it Rich watched Jim and the way he moved and handled things. From time to time Rich drank from a bottle he took from under the counter and then replaced.

"I was thinking, though," Jim said, "we ain't doing so good we couldn't do better."

"Uh huh," said Rich.

Jim walked around the storeroom, slapping and shaking the piles of clothing into order on the tables, shoving the hardware back with a clang where it had been disarranged, kicking some loose boots together on the floor.

"When are you leaving?" Rich asked.

"Who said anything about leaving?"

"Well," said Rich, "I'll tell you. I've known you for just about thirty years, and being a real shrewd individual, I've got so's I can recognize certain signs. Like when it gets to be spring and you start kicking the boots. Slapping the pants around and cussing the shirts is kind of a beginning twinge, you might say, and when you kick the boots, that's it."

Jim laughed. "All right, I was thinking of taking another look at some of that high country. Stands to reason the gold has got to wash down from someplace, and it might be—"

"If you find any," Rich said, "bring me back a bucket or so, but just spare me the buffalo chips."

"I don't believe it's been thirty years," Jim said.

"Sure it has. Count it."

"No," said Jim firmly, "I couldn't have stood you that long." A minute later he said, "Why don't you come with me? The weather's good."

"And I feel good," Rich said, "so why should I crank my bones all up again sitting in a cold river shaking gravel?"

The rheumatism came back on him pretty hard by spells in the rainy season. "I'll stay and keep the store." He drank again. "You 'bout ready? This bottle's running dry."

"I'm ready," Jim said, and blew out the candle. They locked up and walked along the straggling dusty street to the saloon. Rich spent most of his off time here, yarning with the miners about the old days, old Indian fights and buffalo hunts, the big horse raid, how things used to be. He drank quite a lot these days. Jim could never stay very long in the saloon. He was a great yarner himself. He could sit for hours beside a campfire and talk, lying mountain-style when he ran out of truth, so that the tales got steadily taller as the night got later, but this was different. Somehow the four walls and a roof choked off his wind and he could find no inspiration in the attitude of the miners. Either they listened with frank, tolerant disbelief, or they stared with the solemn reverence they might have given to a man who walked in and said he was one of Noah's authentic crew on the Ark. This did not seem to bother Rich. Jim thought he was telling the stories to himself more than to anyone else, just getting gently drunk and remembering. It made Jim feel sour and old.

The world had moved fast, he knew that. Since the spring of '49 it had moved so fast that a man had to run hard to keep up with it. Spanish California was already mostly a memory. Settlers were pouring across the plains in vast numbers, bringing the cholera with them to wipe out whole villages of Cheyennes and Kiowas and line the Oregon Trail with their own graves. William Bent had destroyed his mud castle on the Arkansas, burying half his life in the rubble, but new forts were building along the rivers and beside the emigrant road, and blue-coated soldiers rode the old trails with men like Bridger to guide them. Still and all, it was only a few years. A man wasn't a curiosity just because he happened to span them.

Or perhaps it was not so much time as it was distance. These miners were town men. They were noisy and rough and dirty like town men, they worked like town men, they robbed and brawled and murdered like town men. The mountain men had gone, soft-footed and quiet as wolves, running in small packs and leaving little sign of their passing. The miners came like bullocks in great herds, roaring and bellowing, tearing and trampling and fouling the streams. Maybe, Jim thought, it was simply that he and they were of different breeds and that was why there was a gap between them. Certainly there were men much older than himself swinging pick and shovel after gold, and these too had the same way of looking at him as though he belonged to a different century.

Whatever it was, Jim could only put up with it so long and then he would have to get up and go.

This night he got his supplies together, ready to load on the pack mule. He slept a while, in the bachelor loft over the store where he and Rich nested. He heard Rich come bumbling up the stairs and fall into bed, and that was the end of his sleeping. Long before daylight he was on his way out of the spraddle of tents and shacks that was so rapidly becoming a town, heading toward the Sierra Nevadas.

He did not expect to find any great riches. He was making money the best way there was to make it in the gold fields, and he thought probably all the big strikes had been made in these parts anyway. Prospecting was simply an excuse to get out and travel, and if it paid off in the shape of a nice little pocket of dust, which it sometimes did, so much the better.

He traveled north and east, not hurrying, taking a sort of mute animal joy from the clean wind and the quiet. Some days later he fell in with some Spanish-speaking Indians he knew and camped with them for several weeks, moving from place to place. They were prospecting too. Many of the California Indians were good miners. Jim had several working for him on shares in the diggings, and others came with gold dust to the store, either to buy or to ask Jim to pack in supplies to their remote camps. He got along with them, as usual, better than he did with most of the whites, and the Indios got along with him much better than they did with the general run of *Americanos.* For this reason a lot of people assumed that Jim was a half-breed, and he did not argue about it.

Perhaps he should have, because some of the Indians were good at other things than mining.

Jim looked long and hard at the horse that a smooth-faced young man named Bartolomeo was riding. "It seems to me," Jim said, "that I have seen that horse before. It seems to me that that was once the horse of Señor Wallace, who owns a ranch over Stockton way."

"It is possible," Bartolomeo answered, with a shrug and a smile. "The ways of horses are well-known. When they escape from a pasture they run far. Who can say how far this horse may have wandered?"

"See that he does not wander back," Jim said, "when you are riding him. The *Americanos* are very angry against persons who find lost horses in a certain way. They have things called Vigilance Committees, because at one time a man's horse could become lost from the hitching post in front of his own house if he did not stand by with a gun to guard it. I would not like to see my friend Bartolomeo hanging like a ripe fruit from a tree."

Bartolomeo smiled again, very widely. "This horse is happy now. He will not run away."

"Bartolomeo," Jim said, "I hope you will never be tempted to make my horses happy."

Bartolomeo went into a great whoop of laughter. He told the other Indians and they laughed too. "The Vigilance Committees are white men. If we let ourselves be caught by them we deserve to hang. But you—" Bartolomeo shook his head, making circular motions with his finger around the crown, "We are civilized, Christian Indians. We do not wish to be scalped by a wild Indio of the plains."

"And don't you forget it," Jim said, making the scalp-yell so that all the horses jumped.

It was on this trip, scrambling over cruel ridges covered with snow and ice, that Jim saw what appeared to be a notch in the mountains far to the southward.

He asked the Indians about it. They said they did not know, and he thought they were probably telling the truth. Their people had no desire to go east of the Sierras. There was nothing out there but alkali deserts, thirst, and the wild Indios with the scalping knives. Jim left them and went by himself to investigate.

It was a long way, and several times he thought he must have been mistaken, for the shapes of the mountains changed as he came near them. It was virgin country that he traveled through, aromatic with pine forests and cool with the breath of the snow fields. When he came upon the valley at last he was almost as surprised as though he had not been looking for it.

It was a beautiful valley, broad and rich and green as the valleys of Absaroka, with deer feeding on the flats and towering snow peaks above, and a clear bright river flowing through it. Jim sat on his horse and looked at it for a long time. Then he rode slowly down into it.

He kept on riding, following the stream.

Rich was sitting in the sun in front of the store when Jim got back.

"Find any gold?" he asked.

"No," said Jim. He busied himself hitching the horse and the pack mule. "Found something better."

Rich looked at him, not knowing just how to take that.

"A pass," Jim said. "Must be close to two thousand feet lower than any of the others. The Feather River goes through it. It wouldn't take much work to make a wagon road. It'd be the quickest and easiest way there is through the mountains."

"You don't say." Rich sat up straight, thinking of all the possibilities this discovery opened up.

"Found something else, too," Jim said.

"Oh? What's that?"

Jim said, "My settling place."

TWENTY-THREE

J IM WAS OUT with some of the Indian *vaqueros* rounding up a bunch of colts for the breaking when Bartolomeo came galloping to find him.

"Rich is waiting for you," he said. "He has a stranger with him."

"A stranger?"

Bartolomeo shrugged. "He has not been here before, anyway, and I do not know him from Marysville."

Jim left the colts to Bartolomeo and the *vaqueros* and rode back across the valley. Beckwourth Valley it was now, officially, signed and deeded. A wagon road led through it from Beckwourth Pass and on to Marysville and the American Valley. Jim rode like a *hacendado* over his broad lands, coming finally to the road and following it by the pastures and corrals to the settlement.

There was the trading post he had built, and a wide campground where the wagon trains could stop, and a long rambling structure that was partly home and partly hotel and tavern. There was nothing between here and Salt Lake, and the emigrants who had suffered through the killing heat and thirst of the long desert march were thankful to stop for a while. There were twenty-two wagons parked in the grounds, their bleached and cracking flanks still white with alkali dust. A little tributary ran close by, slipping noisily over flat stones. Children played in the water and a long line of weary-looking women with straggling hair and sun-blistered faces knelt at the stream's edge washing clothes. Other women were at the trading post, buying flour and coffee, sugar and potatoes and greens and fresh meat, the first they had seen in weeks. At this time of day the men were either busy with repairs or hanging around the corrals looking mournfully at their worn-out and alkali-poisoned stock and figuring on some horse-dealing. Later, when the sun went down, they would do some hard-earned drinking. Jim regarded these people with a sort of cynical compassion. They and their kind had destroyed much that he loved, and they were destroying more every year. He could not stop them, but he could make them pay. On the other hand they were human beings, pretty wretched at this point in their journey and with more hardship than they knew still ahead of them. So he did not make them pay more than was fair. And more often than he would admit, when they could not pay at all, he gave. No one went hungry in Beckwourth Valley, or went out of it destitute.

Rich's trap was at the hitching rack, the ewe-necked brown mare standing hip-sprung and drowsy in the shade of the trees. Rich had found that driving was easier on his bones. He hardly ever rode now. Jim left his fine bay gelding to talk things over with the mare and walked up to the house. He still moved with the same lithe ease. His back was still straight and his belly flat, and his hair was as black as ever. Only the lines of his face were cut deeper and the angled bones were sharper at cheek and jaw. His eyes had not changed at all. He was a landowner now, a houseowner. He had settled down. But his eyes were not those of a domesticated animal. Even when he was most content they still had the restless brilliance that belongs to wild things.

He was not content now, and he was not feeling peaceful. He crossed the porch and went inside, and in the dimmer light his eyes glittered, black and fierce.

This was his own room here, shut off from the tavern part, private. Rich was sitting by the window. Serafina had brought him whisky and tobacco and was making sure he was comfortable. Serafina was Bartolomeo's sister, a widow and far too pretty to be going to waste in rusty black. Jim liked her in red, or yellow, sun-colors to go with her warm brown skin. Today it was yellow. She smiled at Jim and said in Spanish, "You need not look so like a wolf. You'll frighten this nice young sheep."

The nice young sheep had been sitting in a cowhide chair. He got up when Jim came in. He had light hair and an eager, pleasant face that probably looked younger than it was because of its smoothness and the extremely round blue eyes. He was dressed like a man who had not been in the country long. He stood hesitantly, looking at Jim, and Rich said, "Jim, this here's Tom Bonner. He's come all the way from Sonora to see you."

"What for?" Jim asked, and looked narrowly at Rich, seeing on his face the same half-laughing, half-malicious slyness that had been there when he told the story of Jim's Cheyenne captivity to the Crow.

"Mr. Beckwourth," said Bonner. "Mr. Richards has explained to me why you don't care much for outsiders, but I—"

"Depends on which way they come," Jim said. "If they come across the desert from the east I don't figure they're going to make me any trouble. If they come from the other direction I figure they are. I came here in the spring of '52. I found the pass, I found the valley, and whatever there is here I built it. It's only the fall of '54 now, and they're already trying to get it away from me. I won't sell and I won't portion and that's the end of it."

Rich said, "You all finished, Jim? No, I'm sorry I asked that. Forget it. Just shut up and give the man a chance to say his say."

Jim turned on Bonner. "All right, say it."

"I want to write a book about you."

Jim stared at him. Then he looked at Rich. Rich grinned and sipped his whisky, watching Jim's face.

Jim turned back to Bonner. "Why?"

"I've heard a lot about you," Bonner said.

"I'll bet you have."

"Both good and bad," Bonner said, "but I don't care much what people say, I like to see for myself. Anyway, the important thing is what you saw of this country and the Indians and all before it changed. You know Kit Carson?"

"Sure," said Jim. "Know him well."

"Books about Carson are being read by everybody in the east, he's famous, and most of the books are lies but nobody cares about that. Your book would be the truth—"

Rich laughed, insultingly.

"Why me?" Jim asked. "Why not Rich? He was a mountain man before I was. He's gone as far and done as much."

"No, sir," Rich said. "I don't like people. I went to the mountains to get away from 'em. I don't want 'em pawing and chawing over every little thing I've done, believing the lies and sneering at the true things, and looking down their nose at me because I married a squaw and bred up half-breed kids, and didn't go to church every Sunday. The hell with 'em."

"It's you I'm interested in, Mr. Beckwourth," said

Bonner.

Jim looked hard at him and asked again, "Why?"

"Maybe it's because of the stories I've heard. A man doesn't get talked about either for good or bad unless he's led a pretty interesting life. Anyway, as I said—Bridger, Fitzpatrick, Carson, you—there aren't too many of you left, and I think you're worth writing about. I think you did great things, and people ought to know about them."

He added candidly, "There's also a chance for both of us to make some money. I don't know about you, but I could use it. I'm a journalist, which is not the highest-paid profession in the world."

"When you're telling your story, Jim," Rich said, "leave me out of it."

"Have I said I was going to tell it?"

"Now, Jim, just listen to what I'm saying. First place, like I just told you, my doings are private—'cept the ones I choose to tell about myself when I get liquored up and most of those never happened anyway. Second place, I'm damned if I want to sit and read how you saved my life ninety-seven times 'stead of just once, and how—"

Jim laughed "That's one thing you'll never have to worry about doing."

"All right," said Rich with dignity. "But I could always get somebody to read it to me. And who's going to read it to you?"

"Serafina," Jim said, and then shook his head. "No, she only reads Spanish, and not much of that." He looked at Bonner and then walked out on the porch and stood there thinking. He began to get very excited. Carson, Fitzpatrick, Bridger—they were all famous now, already in their lifetimes becoming as legendary as the heroes of folk tales. But who knew about Jim Beckwourth? His friends, his enemies, and the purveyors of prairie gossip, that was all. Yet he was as good a mountain man as any. He had not sinned more greatly than most. There was no reason why he should be forgotten, or remembered only, like the dark-skinned Edward Rose, for his villainies, whether he had committed them or not.

"Bonner!" he shouted. "Tom Bonner, come out here."

Bonner came. Jim walked with him away from the house, out of earshot. He stood with him under the trees.

"Some people think I'm an Indian 'breed," Jim said. "Maybe you heard that. I'm not. I'm black. Does that make any difference to you?"

"On the contrary," Bonner said. "I think it does you more credit than if you were white. It was that much harder for you to break free." He looked around almost sadly at the beautiful valley and the line of wagon tilts partially visible beyond the trading post. "That's what I want to get into the book, the wonder of what I was born too late to see. Real freedom, before there were settlers and soldiers and all the regulations and troubles that go with them. I suppose there wasn't any way to stop them coming, and I suppose in the long run its a good thing, the railroads are coming through and the country will be civilized and prosperous and that's the way it ought to be—at least so they tell me. But I envy you, Mr. Beckwourth. I envy you with all my heart."

There was a silence, while the wind blew gently through the trees.

"I'll tell you my story," Jim said, "on one condition."

"What's that?"

"My color's not to be mentioned."

Bonner looked at him surprised.

"The people that read the book won't know me," Jim said. "Maybe if you don't tell them I'm the wrong color and slave-born, they'll take me just for what I did and for what kind of a man I am. I don't care what they think of me," he added, knowing that he did care and being angry with himself that it was so. "I don't care if they think I'm the worst villain that ever lived, so long as they've got an honest reason for it."

"People are always ready and willing to believe the worst about anybody," Bonner said.

"Yes," said Jim, "but if it's about a white man there's always some that at least give him the benefit of the doubt. A black man is different. They've cut a pattern for him and made him fit it, and as long as he does he's a fine fellow and they'll be friends with him. The minute he steps outside that pattern they're through with him. He's branded himself. He's a bad one. They don't have any doubt about him, no doubt at all." Jim grinned, rather ferociously. "On top of that I'm a squaw man. I live with Indians. The whites don't care for that. They figure if I'm with Indians I have to be against whites. That's one reason they want me out of Beckwourth Valley. They look at all this land and they think it ought to belong to someone worthwhile, like themselves. No, they don't think much of me at all."

He took a deep breath and glared around at the green meadows, the pine-clad slopes, and the towering peaks with their eternal snowcaps. "We'll write a book, Mr. Bonner. When do you want to start?"

"What's the matter," asked Bonner, "with right now?"

All that fall and winter, between the things that had to be done on the ranch and around the trading post, Jim talked and Bonner listened, writing endless notes, while Serafina kept the glasses filled and the tobacco close at hand, and set the pine logs crackling like musket fire in the grate. Jim told the truth plain sometimes, and sometimes he trimmed it up just a little so it would look better. Sometimes he lied mountain-style, which meant that where he had run ten miles to save his scalp he now ran a hundred, and where he had fought forty Blackfeet he now fought a thousand, and this was natural lying. But other times he lied out of bitterness and frustration, out of pride or shame or sheer sadness of heart, telling things the way they ought to have been rather than as they actually were. When the telling was all done Bonner said, "It's a great story, Jim, but I have a funny feeling. I think the best parts of it are the ones you didn't tell."

"Well, it isn't finished yet," Jim said, with his arm around Serafina. "Maybe we can write Volume Two in another twenty years or so."

"I'll come around," said Bonner.

Later Jim said to Rich, "Young Tom's a smart boy, and knows all about books and writing, but he don't know anything about the mountains."

"Oh well," said Rich, "he ain't likely to make any more mistakes than you told lies, so it ought to about even out."

It was a cold March night, with rain rattling on the windows and a booming wind. Rich sat looking into the fire for a long time without speaking, so that Jim knew he had something on his mind. Finally he said, "You been sitting with your bowstring pulled for an hour. Will you let that arrow fly?"

Rich leaned back in his chair and sighed. "Might's well, though it ain't going to hit anything and well I know it. I hear talk in Marysville." Rich had sold the store in Sonora and moved there, and that was technically where he lived, though he spent a great deal of time in the valley. He refused to accept Jim's invitation to stay there permanently, and Jim, respecting his desire for independence, only asked him once.

"What are they talking about in Marysville?" Jim was somewhat sour about his neighbors on more counts than one. When he opened up the wagon road through Beckwourth Pass they had seen the advantages the town would gain from it and they were more than willing to promise money to pay for the necessary work. Jim wound up putting more than sixteen hundred of his own dollars into the road, and the promises were all he had ever gotten back.

"They're talking horse thieves," Rich said.

"Is that anything new?"

"No," said Rich. "And yes."

"They hung up some horse thieves just this January. Ain't they satisfied?"

"Seems like people are still losing stock. They're talking Indian now."

"The ones they hung were white."

"They figure the ones they're looking for now are red. Has Bartolomeo been behaving himself?"

"Sure he has. First place, he's my friend. Second place, he knows better. He knows I'd kill him."

"What about all the rest of 'em, Jim? Can you trust 'em all?"

Jim got up. "What you're saying is, I ought to get rid of them. Fire the ones that work for me and tell the others not to come back."

"Hotbed is the word they're fondest of in Marysville. Next to kennel. Look at it from the outside, though, if you can. This is a big valley. All kinds of people drift through it to your trading post and you don't turn anybody away. You've got a lot of Indians here and you ran a lot of stock. You've got a highroad out to the desert and points east, and it's no secret that you and I helped run a lot of California horses east once before. If you ain't in the horse-stealing business now they figure you ought to be."

"Let them," said Jim, "figure whatever damn way they please."

He would not discuss it any more. But the next day he talked hard to Bartolomeo and then spent almost a week with him talking to other Indians, resident or encamped, and combing the valley for any piece of horseflesh that didn't belong there. He didn't find any, and the Indians he talked to seemed to be telling the truth. They were Christian Indians, barring the ones that had backslid. Even so Jim gave them a big talk about his medicine and how strong it was and how it could smell out evildoers no matter where they were. He built a small sweat lodge in the Crow fashion and smoked it, and made paint for his face and sang the songs, praying to his medicine. He promised it that he would put up a scalp pole for the hair of horse stealers. The Indians were impressed in spite of their Christianity. They believed Jim, if they didn't believe in his medicine. The day after the ceremony Bartolomeo told him that four of the men had left, going away quietly in the night.

Jim was relieved. He was not in the least concerned whether the local ranchers lost their horses or not. He was only concerned about the Vigilance Committees and keeping his neck and his valley out of their hands.

Whether the men who had left so abruptly were the culprits or not, the horse-stealings abated and things quieted down. In spite of that Jim was not easy in his mind. He wished he could be as sure of his medicine as he had said he was. He rode the valley, and he felt as he had felt once before long years ago, when the life and the people he loved were still his and there was no reason to think of their going and yet they had seemed to slip away out of his grasp.

Secretly, all by himself, he went away up the valley and built another sweat lodge and blackened it with charcoal. He blackened his face, the color of victory, and he offered the smoke of tobacco and fragrant pine leaves to the Four Quarters, to the earth and the sky, to the Ones-who-make-things-happen. "Year after year may I remain here. Whoever comes against me, may he not succeed."

He washed his face and rode away, still unsatisfied and sorry he had done it, because it made him all the more clearly remember Absaroka.

Throughout the next three years the pressures grew stronger. More and more people were settling in California. More and more people wanted land, and Jim was sitting on miles of the best land there was. Big ranchers wanted the whole valley. Small ranchers wanted part of it. And Rich told Jim repeatedly that he should sell.

"If you don't, I'm warning you, they'll find a way to make you. This country's getting respectable, and crowded. Might's well face it, Jim, you and I aren't the kind they want for their big landowners." He stopped, looking at Jim. "All right, I know, it's yours, every damn blade of grass and drop of water, and you ain't going to part with one of 'em. Then you better get rid of some of the people you got here. Like Bartolomeo. They never could catch him, but they were pretty sure of him around Stockton way, and the Marysville people know that. All they have to do is find one single horse on your land that don't belong here."

"Look," said Jim. "If I was to throw every Indian out of the valley including Serafina, would that make them feel different about me? Would they take me to their bosom? Would they invite me to their houses and let me dance with their daughters? Would they even just let me alone? The hell they would. You said it yourself. You and me, we're not the kind of men they want at the head of their community."

Rich sighed. "I guess there ain't any use denying that, Jim. And it don't seem fair, considering if it hadn't been for men like us they wouldn't be here."

"They may find some way to take my valley," Jim said, "but I'm damned if I'll give it to them."

In the end he was never sure just how it did happen.

Rich came pounding on the door one summer midnight. He had ridden all the way from Marysville at a pace that left his horse in a white lather, and he was barely able to stand with the stiffness in his joints.

"Vigilance Committee," he said. "I'm ahead of 'em but I don't know how far."

Serafina stood with her eyes wide and stricken, watching Jim dress.

"Why?" asked Jim, bitterly, furiously, not pausing in his dressing.

"They say you're working with horse thieves, or at least helping them. They say somebody ran a bunch of stolen stock out through Beckwourth Pass a week ago. They got some of 'em back, and they're all primed for you. Now maybe they're lying. I don't know. I don't think it matters."

"If there were thieves," Serafina said, "Bartolomeo was not among them."

"I know that," Jim said. He didn't. He didn't know anything at this moment. "Go and warn him." He put his arm around her once and let her go, and she ran away out of the room.

Rich said, "Jim—"

Jim stood facing him. Rich looked at him briefly and then turned toward the table, reaching for the bottle that was there. "I'd ride with you, but I can't. Not this time." He changed the bottle from one hand to the other and put it down again unopened.

Jim said, "I owe you for this one."

"Oh, Christ," said Rich furiously. "That again. Go on, get the hell out of here."

Jim hesitated. Then in a low voice he said, "Thanks, Rich." He went out.

Rich did not turn around.

There was half a moon, enough to show Jim the road. The snow fields glimmered high against the night. The meadows were a faint silver, with the dark pine slopes above. He rode fast. He did not feel afraid. He was astonished that he was not even angry. He felt alone. He felt old. And he did not know where he was going.

He went out of Beckwourth Valley into the pass, heading east. Now the white man's world was all around him. He could not think of any place where he might escape it.

SNOW FALLING

TWENTY-FOUR

THERE WAS A cold, fine, drifting rain. It hid the mountains and moved in clouds of soft gray across the high plains. It made the clothing sodden and chilled the flesh, and it lay on the faces of the men like an icy sweat. They had been riding into it ever since they left Fort C. F. Smith at dawn and they were getting tired of it. Jim turned in the saddle, wincing at the stiffness the rain had wakened in his bones. He looked back at Lieutenant Mays and the two troopers. No more than boys, these three, and Jim smiled. Pushing hard against seventy and creaking with rheumatism, he could still outride them.

"Step along," he called cheerfully. "Step along!"

Lieutenant Mays said, "We can't push these horses, Beckwourth. We've got a long way to go." He was a clean-cut youngster, fair-haired and sunburned, fresh out of West Point, knowing nothing of the strange wild land he had been sent to tame. Lamb to the slaughter, Jim thought, and was sorry for him. If he lived long enough he might make an officer, but so many of them didn't. So many of them mistook wisdom for cowardice and experience for partiality, and they went prancing off to destruction with the smart-ass cockiness of babies who, knowing nothing, are sure of everything. Dispatches were full of their names and the graveyards were full of their bodies.

"That's the trouble with the Army, Lieutenant," Jim said. "That's why you're always two jumps behind."

"I've heard that," Mays said, "till I'm sick of it."

"It's true. Big long-legged horses, all size and no bottom, and all that equipment loaded on. You ought to get Indian ponies and ride light."

He kicked his own pony into a lope, setting his teeth hard against the pain. Mays, exasperated, looked at his retreating back and then snapped an order at the troopers. They all quickened their pace. Jim didn't care whether they kept up with him or not. He didn't need them and he had not wanted them. For once he did not have to take their orders. This was his mission. His alone. For once, at this long, long last, the white man needed him.

Jim was going back to the Crow.

All day long he rode across the cold gray plain. He forgot the young lieutenant and the troopers lagging tired at his heels. He was in a hurry. It was not a conscious thing and he was only half aware of it himself. When the rain stopped and the clouds broke in the west he saw that it was sunset and he was angry, because it meant he had to stop.

In the evening light the country revealed itself to him with the loveliness of familiarity. He checked his horse on the crest of a swelling ridge and looked around. "Over there," he said, pointing. "A good place there is to camp."

He saw Mays and the troopers staring at him. It was a moment before he realized that he had spoken in Crow.

When they came to the camping place he was hardly able to dismount. He stood beside his horse for some time, clinging to the saddle, before he could trust himself to walk. Mays asked him if he needed help. Jim thanked him and said no. He felt better when the troopers got a fire going and he could sit and get warm. He noticed that Mays was studying him intently and he asked why.

"You were pretty sick down at Phil Kearny, Beckwourth. I was just wondering—"

"That was almost a month ago," Jim said irritably.

"But—"

"It's only the rheumatism. Old trappers get it, Lieutenant. I had a friend—" He paused. The flames curled and whispered, blowing in the October wind. "He's gone under now," Jim said. "Back in '63. He suffered from it something terrible, but I never thought I'd get it. It took me after I went back to trapping again, and I was well past sixty. Those beaver streams are cold, boy."

He had a bottle in his pocket. He poured some of the whisky into the steaming coffee one of the troopers handed him, and drank it slowly. It tasted good. He did not want any food, only the hot liquid.

"Better than towns, though. I had enough of towns. I practically founded Auraria when they made the gold strike there. Kept a store for old Louis Vasquez, managed a farm for him, even bought property of my own. Pretty soon it was a big town and they were calling it Denver, and I had to move on where there was more room." He laughed. "I got my aches and pains for nothing. Trapping hadn't got any better since the last time I tried it."

"You've scouted for the Army a long time now," Mays said. "You don't think much of it, do you?"

"There's good men in the Army," Jim said. "Carrington's

a good man, I wish there were more like him. He'll fight Indians but he doesn't hate 'em. He tries to be fair. When you get men like Harney and Chivington—" Jim spat. "I'd rather work with Blackfeet. They're more decent."

Bristling just a little, Mays said, "I understood you were Colonel Chivington's guide to Black Kettle's village."

"They said they'd hang me for a renegade if I didn't. The Cheyennes were my friends and they knew that. They knew they were always camped around the farm in Denver." Jim smiled, a vicious smile. "It was terrible cold on the way, though, and I got so stiff I couldn't ride. Somebody else had to do the guiding after all. And I saved who I could when the killing started. I saved young Charlie Bent, Owl Woman's son. I wish I could have saved more. That day I was ashamed of my white blood."

He turned suddenly on Mays, so fiercely that the young man was startled. "You learn one thing, boy, before you go leading men to wipe out Indian villages. You learn to tell hostiles from the peaceable ones, and if they ain't hostiles you let 'em alone. That's one of the main reasons you've got this war on your hands. Old Black Kettle was a good man. He did everything he could to make peace, and what happened to him and his people? The Indians figure it's no use to talk peace with the white man."

"The Indians," said Mays, "have been known to break treaties themselves."

Jim shook his head with the weariness of long frustration. "We've been shouting ourselves hoarse for years, me and Fitz and Old Gabe and the others that know, and nobody listens. Sure they break treaties. Comanche, Kiowa, Apache, you can't trust most of 'em out of sight of your lodge, though I've had some friends among them. The Sioux and the Cheyennes, they're different, only you don't understand. First place, they don't hold property like the white man and they don't even know what you're talking about. Second place, there isn't any one chief that speaks even for all his own band, let alone the whole nation. I am a Crow chief. I could sign a treaty, and keep it, but that wouldn't bind anybody else. If some of White Bull's young men took the war road I wouldn't be responsible, but your soldiers would come and kill me anyway."

"It seems a pretty silly way to run things," Mays said. "They ought to have better organization."

"You better be thankful they don't. If they'd formed this Confederacy twenty years ago and hung to it, you wouldn't be building forts in Absaroka."

"We'll beat them," said Mays, "Confederacy or not."

Jim smiled. He said sadly, "No you won't. Hunger will beat them. I said that years ago in my book. When the buffalo goes the Indian is finished. He has to make peace. He has to come begging for the white man's beef."

Mays knocked out his pipe with an angry gesture. "Beckwourth, I'm beginning to wonder just what you're going to say to your Crow."

"Makes you uncomfortable, don't it?" Jim said. "Here I am, with all your lives riding on my shoulders." He laughed. "You don't like it at all, do you?" He was happy. He wished that Rich was here, to see what a real sense of power looked like. "Don't worry, boy. I'm going to tell them the truth, just like I always did."

He rolled up in his blanket with his feet to the fire. Even so the cold crept back into him. He was very tired. He drifted into a state that was half sleep, half stupor, and he dreamed of old things. They were good dreams, and the happiness and pride stayed with him. After all these years his people still wanted him. They stood on the edge of a precipice, and he was the only one they trusted to tell them what to do.

The next afternoon under a great blue blaze of sky, a horseman came toward them from the direction of Clark's Fork, where they were going. Jim recognized him a long way off and rode to meet him.

It was Bridger, and Bridger was glad to see him. "I didn't know if Carrington would have sense enough to send you." He nodded toward the north. "They're waiting for you. The head chiefs of the whole nation are there, and Young Bear, and your son. They say the Antelope will speak to them with a straight tongue." He held out his hand. "Good luck."

Jim said, "You've always been a good friend to me." He had worked out of Fort Bridger a good deal these past years, since he left his valley. It was because of Bridger's message that he was here now. "You never cared what I was, outside of a man." He shook Bridger's hand. "I will speak to them," he said, "with a straight tongue."

He smiled at Bridger and rode on, gaunt and old, with indomitable eyes. Bridger went on his way toward the fort, and he too was gaunt and old and made of iron. Mays and the troopers watched them, feeling a little scornful in their neat uniforms and polished gear and their round-cheeked youth, but they were a little awed too, as though they might be sensing that these two old men were the relics of giants.

That night Jim had to be lifted from his horse. Mays was worried. He wanted to turn back, but Jim sat cheerful and straight by the fire, drinking his coffee well laced. "I'll get there all right," he said. "Never you fear."

The days were bright and crisp. The wind was piercing clean, and the mountains towered. The plains stretched wide. Jim pushed his tough little pony, dropping the long miles behind. The big cavalry horses wore down, and Mays said finally, "We've got to rest."

Jim nodded. "You stay in camp tomorrow. I'll go on alone."

"Oh, no," said Mays. "We—"

"You stay," Jim said. "The village is less than half a day's ride and I'm going in alone. Do what I tell you, boy, or this whole trip will be for nothing. I'll send a messenger, and for God's sake don't shoot him."

Mays did not like it, but he stayed. He had had his orders, which were that he was to be guided by what Beckwourth said.

Jim was on his way before daylight.

The distance was a little greater than he had said, and it was midafternoon before he saw the yellow-banded lodges of his people, scattered out on a grassy plain beside the river. He would have liked to stand a while, seeing, remembering, but one of the young boys tending the horse herd saw him and went galloping hell-bent into the village. The people began to gather in the open places. Jim lifted his head and straightened his shoulders. He rode into the village, making his tired pony prance.

The chiefs stood together. There were none that he recognized, though he might have known them as young warriors. He had seen Arepoesh die. Long Hair and Has-red-plume-on-the-side-of-his-head were laid on the four-poled platform long ago. A tall old man stepped forward and held out his hands. "Already I am well again," he said. It was a moment before Jim realized that this was Young Bear. "Always," he said, "when you go away, may you return with your face blackened." They held each other's arms.

There were many people gathered close around, staring at Jim in wonder, whispering. He had been gone for thirty years, but they had not forgotten him. Memory ran long with them, like their rivers, and the little children barely free of the cradle boards knew the Antelope, the Bloody Arm, the Enemy of Horses.

Jim greeted the chiefs.

When he was through a warrior approached him. He was a man of forty or so, dressed handsomely, and Jim knew him because his own face and Cherry's were mirrored there together. "You are Black Panther," he said, and the warrior nodded. "That is so. For many years I was without a father. Now my father has returned."

"Every year," said Young Bear, "I have built a sweat lodge."

"I have gone where my medicine told me," Jim said. "Sometimes it has been well. Sometimes it has not been well." He looked from one to the other. "Now it is well."

He turned to the people. "Crow!" he said to them in a strong voice. "For many years I have been away from you. I have been with the white men in their camps. Very much I have seen, very much I have learned. Now I have returned to you. Now I will go in and speak with your chiefs."

"Year after year," they said, "may you continue to see the long rains. Wherever you go, may you find fat buffalo." They were a troubled people, seeing the break and fall of things.

Jim entered the lodge of White Bull. He sat in the place of honor, and the fire was warm and bright.

"The Blanket Chief has spoken to us," White Bull said. "He talks peace. He is a good man. But we are tired and confused. We no longer see clearly as we used to. The Dakota and the Cheyennes already have taken much of our land. Now the blue-coat soldiers come and build their forts in Absaroka. Always we have been at peace with the white man. The Antelope knows this, it was so in his time, and when the young men took horses from white trappers the Antelope was angry and punished them. Now we do not know. Why do the soldiers build forts in Absaroka?"

"Because," said Jim, "white men have found gold in a certain place. The forts are to protect the road to it. The blue-coats have made a talk with the chiefs at Laramie."

White Bull said bitterly, "We have heard of that."

"The forts we do not like," Young Bear said. "The soldiers we do not like. Now, elder brother, things are very different. Those who formerly were our friends have become our enemies, and those who formerly were our enemies wish to become our friends. The chiefs of the Dakota send us the pipe. They have made peace between themselves, they share their lodges, and also among them now are other old enemies, Comanche, Kiowa, Arapaho, Apache. They wish us to join them, taking the war road against the whites. They say that we can drive them forever from our lands."

"They are fools," said Jim. "They are brave men. They will kill many soldiers, but in the end they will die. They do not know what they are fighting."

One of the war chiefs said, "I see only a few soldiers, hiding afraid behind their walls."

Jim held up his hand, showing the tip of his little finger. "What do you see there? A little thing, if you cut it off you will surely destroy it. But as for me, I will not know that it is gone."

He looked around the lodge at the grave brown faces of the chiefs.

"You wished me to return to your council. You said that the Antelope had spoken always with a straight tongue. You said that the Antelope was a Crow and that he would know best what his people should do, because of the many years he has spent with the white men. Now I will tell you what is best for the Crow.

"Against the Dakota and the Cheyennes you could not stand, although you fought strongly. They were too many, you said. They were like the leaves of the trees, you said. You could not kill enough of them. How will you stand against the whites, who are more numerous than the flakes of snow that come in winter? Only the first handful of those snowflakes have you seen. But they will bury your lodges."

He paused, so that they should have time to think and understand.

"Not because I love the white men do I say this." Although, he thought, I can't deny my blood, even if they deny it. I can't be like young Charlie Bent, who perhaps I should not have saved at Sand Creek. "Not because I love the white men, but because I love the Crow, I tell you to remain at peace."

He made the sign that he was finished.

The chiefs talked. Jim sat looking at Young Bear and remembering.

White Bull said at last, "As the Antelope says, we will do. We will remain at peace."

"It is well," Jim said. Still he looked at Young Bear. "You do not think it is well?"

Young Bear did not answer, but Jim knew what was in his mind.

"That time is gone," he said. "Not only for the Crow. For everyone. You and I were fortunate. We were young in a good day."

White Bull said, "If the Antelope were to remain now with his people, it would be well."

Jim nodded. "I will remain."

He arranged for Mays to be brought to the village on the following day. Then he went with Young Bear to his lodge. There was warmth and food and much talk, a constant coming and going of old friends, a streaming of people he did not know, Black Panther's children, clan connections, the children of friends. Faces blurred and ran together in the firelight. Voices were strident, painful to the ear, and then they receded, and there was a feeling of joy and peace, and a pleasant darkness.

"He is sleeping," Black Panther said.

Young Bear shook his head. "Perhaps. Stay by him."

In the middle of the night Black Panther woke his uncle. "He is awake. He is talking, but he speaks to ghosts. He asks my mother to make him moccasins for the war trail. To Muskrat he speaks of warriors to lead against the Dakota when green grass comes." Muskrat had been dead for twenty years.

The two men listened, heavyhearted and afraid, until finally the Antelope slept again.

Lieutenant Mays came into the village late the next day. He stayed, not because he wanted to but because he felt that he must. He waited four days, and on the last one Jim knew him and told him that the word he would take back to Carrington was peace. After that Mays was awakened by the sound of wailing.

The Crow began their mourning. It was a great mourning, and Mays was frightened by the violence of it. He saw Jim's body laid out, dressed in the buckskins of a chief, wrapped in fine blankets of scarlet and blue, with the bow and the battle-ax he had once used placed ready to his hand. Then they brought buffalo robes for the final wrapping, and they brought the shield that Arepoesh had given him and laid it on his breast with the blazon covered. All the time the crying and the wailing kept up, and the people fasted and gashed themselves, and the Antelope's son and brother built the four-pole platform on a high hill, barren of trees, where a man might look every way and see the wide land of Absaroka. Mays looked at the blood and the mourning paint, the shorn hair and torn clothing, and thought that it was all hideously savage, and at the same time he was sure that no nation of people in the world would ever mourn him at all.

He stayed to the end. The Crow hardly noticed that he was there. They laid the Antelope on a travois and took the long slow way to the hilltop. It was almost sunset when they reached it and lifted him onto the platform, with the wind sweeping shrilly across the land and the tops of the mountains turning red. Black Panther set the long pole, bracing it with rocks on that hard hill, so that the scalps at the end of it stood high, hanging like a banner above the covered shield on the Antelope's breast.

That was the last that the white man's world ever saw of Jim, when Lieutenant Mays looked back from the foot of the hill at the banner of scalps blowing in the gathering dark.

Center Point Publishing
600 Brooks Road ● PO Box 1
Thorndike ME 04986-0001 USA

(207) 568-3717

US & Canada:
1 800 929-9108